MW01029324

# Death by Opera

By Erica Miner

Twilight Times Books
Kingsport Tennessee

**Death by Opera**

*This is a work of fiction. All concepts, characters and events portrayed in this book are used fictitiously and any resemblance to real people or events is purely coincidental.*



Paladin Timeless Books, an imprint of
Twilight Times Books
P O Box 3340
Kingsport TN 37664
http://twilighttimesbooks.com/

First Edition, May 2018

ISBN: 978-1-60619-130-9

Library of Congress Control Number: 2018940490

Cover art © 2018 by Tamian Wood

Printed in the United States of America.

# Foreword

Reading *Death by Opera,* I am reminded of the opportunity I had showing Erica Miner around the Santa Fe Opera so that she would have a complete sense of the wonderful atmosphere of the place (the only opera company in the world with its own swimming pool).

Erica and I have worked together as colleagues, she in the orchestra pit as violinist, and I onstage singing in the operas, at both the New York City Opera and the Metropolitan Opera in New York. Erica's firsthand knowledge of operatic repertoire, violin parts, and further, her dramatic understanding of the operatic works, gives special insights to the particular productions that are the setting for this mystery. But even more, one gets a sense of the valued, ultra-important contribution of a top-notch violinist to the job of concertmaster in a major opera company.

The operas in this story are not ordinary, when one starts out with Alban Berg's *Lulu,* traversing Gounod's *Roméo et Juliette,* then Donizetti's *Lucia di Lammermoor,* and finally *Salome* by the great Richard Strauss. There is plenty of death and mayhem in all of these operas, even without this added mystery, and they all have been in the repertoire of the Santa Fe Opera.

This is a wonderful read, but Erica also brings so much more to the story than merely solving the crimes. She really shows the inner workings of the theatre and the relationships between individuals functioning in their many varied jobs at this unique major opera festival; and she paints a portrait of the atmosphere of the company against the matchless background of majestic mountains, compelling history and intriguing spirituality than can only be found in New Mexico's "Land of Enchantment."

*Baritone David Holloway, who himself was an apprentice singer at the Santa Fe Opera in the late 1960s, has over a fifty-year connection with the company. Having served as Director of the Santa Fe Opera Apprentice Program from 2005 to 2017, he now has been named its*

*Director Emeritus. David has sung with the Metropolitan Opera, as well as all of the major opera companies in the U.S., and for ten years was leading baritone with the Deutsche Oper Am Rhein, Düsseldorf/Duisburg Germany.*

## Acknowledgements

*Many thanks to my colleagues from the opera world who helped me create this book:*

**David Holloway**, baritone *extraordinaire* and Director Emeritus of Santa Fe Opera's Apprentice Program, for providing me an entrée to the behind-the-scenes world of The Santa Fe Opera

**Arthur Makar**, for his all-important inspiration and belief in this project

**Elaine Bloom**, who encouraged me to send Julia and Larry on their next adventure

Baritone **Richard Stilwell**, for sharing his many authentic, captivating Santa Fe Opera stories

Tenor **George Shirley**, for providing wonderful accounts of his Santa Fe Opera experiences

Mezzo-soprano **Jennifer Larmore**, whose insights on *Lulu* were hugely helpful

Mezzo-soprano **Michelle DeYoung**, for her astute perceptions on Bartók's *Bluebeard's Castle*

Santa Fe Opera Costume Director **Missy West**, for a memorable insider's view of her department

Santa Fe Opera Wig and Makeup Director **David Zimmerman**, for his valued information

**Rob Dean** of Patina Gallery in Santa Fe, for his keen interest in this project

Santa Fe Opera music director **Harry Bicket**, for graciously spending time with me

Santa Fe Opera flutist **Peter Ader**, for his insights into the workings of the Opera orchestra

**Phaedra Haywood** of the Santa Fe New Mexican, for providing facts about the New Mexico prison system

**Maggie Sophia Allen**, my granddaughter, for sharing her keen sense of plot and detail

**Sonette Bales**, for her lively descriptions of Santa Fe Opera and for her passion for this story

**Marghreta Cordero**, for providing intriguing background about La Posada de Santa Fe

Writing colleague **Erica Hidvegi**, for her insights into the Hungarian psyche

**Lida Quillen**, my publisher, whose continued belief and faith in me is so very much appreciated

And finally, the late **Craig A. Smith**, a writer and journalist of great talent and integrity who was always there for me when questions arose in my journey with this story, whom I hold in the highest regard, and to whose memory this book is respectfully and admiringly dedicated.

## Characters

Julia Kogan, young violinist from New York's Metropolitan Opera
Larry Somers, NYPD detective; Julia's significant other
Stewart Blatchley, Santa Fe Opera Music Director
Alan Reynolds, Santa Fe Opera General Director
Katie Ma, violinist, Julia's colleague from the Met Opera
Matt Kim, assistant concertmaster of the Santa Fe Opera Orchestra
Stella Peregrine, Santa Fe Police Department detective
Constantin Grabowski, detective, Stella's partner
Marin Crane, mezzo-soprano, Julia's friend from the Met
Emilia Tosti, Italian soprano diva
Goran Řezníček, baritone, Emilia's leading man
Salman Kipinsky, stage director for *Lulu*
Deborah Alley, Emilia's understudy
Steve Cañon, head stagehand
Magda Kertész, Santa Fe Opera costume director
Sandor Kertész, tenor, Magda's brother
Daniel Henderson, Santa Fe Opera wig and makeup director
Rob Cheever, Santa Fe Opera apprentice program director
Sam Chapman, fight director
Andrew Stillman, opera impresario
Adam Conrad, *comprimario* tenor in *Lucia*
Nick Pleasance, Chief Medical Investigator for the SFPD

*"Our day of dependence, our long apprenticeship to the learning of other lands*
*draws to a close. Events arise that must be sung."*
*~ Ralph Waldo Emerson*

*"Opera, an exotic and traditional entertainment.'*
*~ Samuel Johnson*

*"Those of us whom God has willed to sing and dance and play will perform on the street corner if there are no more theaters."*
*~ John Crosby*

*"For every person on an opera stage, there are at least three people backstage."*
*~ Seattle Opera*

*"Touch the country [of New Mexico] and you will never be the same again."*
*~ D. H. Lawrence*

*"In a murderous time/the heart breaks and breaks/and lives by breaking."*
*~ Stanley Kunitz*

*Hamlet:*
Swear by my sword
Never to speak of this that you have heard.

*Ghost:*
[Beneath] Swear by his sword.

*Horatio:*
O day and night, but this is wondrous strange!

*Hamlet:*
And therefore as a stranger give it welcome.
There are more things in heaven and earth, Horatio,
Than are dreamt of in your philosophy.
~ Shakespeare, *Hamlet,* Act V Scene I

*Badate! Questo è luogo di lacrime*
Beware! This is a place for tears!
~ Puccini, *Tosca, Act 2*

*And the Devil taking him up into a high mountain showed unto him all the kingdoms of the world in a moment of time…*

*And the Devil said unto him, "All this power will I give thee, and the glory of them;*

*for that is delivered unto me: and to whomsoever I will give it.*

*"If thou wilt worship me, all shall be thine."*

*And Jesus answered and said unto him, "Get thee behind me, Satan."*

## Prologue

AT THE BASE OF THE SANGRE DE CRISTO MOUNTAINS OF SANTA FE IN THE summer of 1610, on the site of an ancient Pueblo Indian ruin called *a place of shell beads near the water*, Governor Don Pedro de Peralta and his band of kinsmen assembled the plan for a city that was to be called, *La Villa Real de la Santa Fe de San Francisco de Asís*—The Royal City of the Holy Faith of Saint Francis of Assisi.

This night, hundreds of years later, the high desert terrain of the mountains resembled a moonscape: dark, unforgiving, barren and desolate.

Silent, a shadowy figure broke from the stillness, dragging a shovel. Next to a scrubby chaparral, the figure dug a deep hole, heaving aside the dry desert dirt; then walked away, leaving the hollow void gleaming in the eerie light of a moon that loomed exceedingly large; one that Millennials know as a Super Moon.

## Chapter 1

*Mia Tosca idolatrata, Ogni cosa in te mi piace*
You are my idol Tosca, All things in you delight me
~ Puccini, *Tosca,* Act 1

BEAMS OF EARLY SUMMER SUNLIGHT SPILLED OVER THE WHITE DUVET tucked around Julia Kogan's bare feet as she kept her nose buried in the Santa Fe Opera brochure that had occupied her thoughts for days. Her emotions fluctuated between wild excitement and utter panic. Tomorrow she would be heading for New Mexico's "Land of Enchantment" to begin a stint as the concertmaster of the opera's orchestra, starting right off with *Lulu,* one of the most difficult operas in the repertoire.

That was the exciting part. But she wasn't at all sure she was ready for the pressure of performing, not only in a whole new milieu, but under the vigilant eye of one of the opera world's most demanding conductors, who recently had been elevated from the position of chief conductor to the more prestigious post of actual music director, the company's first in its history.

At the moment, however, she tried to focus on the more beguiling aspects of her prospective new environment.

"What's a 'high desert?'" she asked Larry.

Julia's boyfriend, Larry Somers, buried in the blankets beside her, stirred, blinking. "It's the opposite of 'low desert,' I guess. Why?" He reached over and gently stroked the smoothness of her calf.

Julia read aloud from the brochure for his benefit. "'The Santa Fe Opera shines in the high desert, mystical and magical, taking you to a timeless place where the experience is unlike any other.' Huh. You know what this makes me feel like? A New Yorker."

She stretched out her hand for her latte cup, Dean and DeLuca emblazoned in a small, tasteful white font on the black porcelain, and took a sip. The familiar, blissful taste always gave her spirits a lift. She had heard the coffee in Santa Fe was outstanding, but somehow she doubted it would compare with the flavor of the blends made with New York's unique-tasting water.

Outside the window of her fourth-floor walk-up on the Upper West Side of Manhattan, traffic sounds made a dissonant music that she rarely heard consciously. She tried to imagine creating music in the silence of a southwestern desert surrounded by mountains.

"You are a New Yorker. We both are." Larry sat up a little, appropriated the cup, took a sip, and handed it back, frowning. He preferred less sugar than she did.

"Do you think it means 'high altitude' desert?" She didn't wait for a reply this time. "How close is Santa Fe to the Los Alamos National Laboratory?"

"Not that close." Larry yawned and ran a hand through his thick hair, the sunlight playing over a rugged body somehow stark against the soft duvet. "Why?"

"You know I'm chemically sensitive. If there's still any fallout around—"

"That's why I didn't schedule a stopover in the test flats."

"But do you think it gets in the air? Maybe comes down as rain?" She knew she was being overly finicky. She also knew Larry could handle it. "I just want you to take my sensitivities seriously."

"I do." He peered at her, doubtfully. "What's happening here, Julia? You're the one who wanted to go to Santa Fe. Are you having second thoughts?"

"They wear cowboy boots to the opera there, Larry."

"Sure they do. It's the southwest. The opera campus used to be a dude ranch. Anyway, it's too late. You've signed the contract."

"I suppose you're right." She knew he was. Her anxiety had little to do with cowboy boots and everything to do with her apprehension over fulfilling the new conductor's exacting demands.

"Of course I am. It'll be a great experience for you."

"And for you." Julia smiled.

"Me? That's a different story. Somebody once said opera can be deadly for non-opera people."

Julia felt uneasy at the reminder. "I'm sure that was a joke."

"And remember the cougar who ran off in terror after someone started singing opera to it?"

"That was in L.A. Nothing is real there."

"You see? Compared with New York and L.A., Santa Fe will be relatively stress-free for you. Plus, it's hot and dry during the day, brisk in the evenings."

They both hated how humid New York summers could be. "What's not to like about that?" Larry said. "And all that history. Now there's something I can relate to. It's the second oldest city in the U.S."

"Where the Spaniards tried to crush the spirits of one hundred thousand Pueblo Indians. I've done my research, too," Julia said, starting to feel excited once again by the prospect of exploring new, exotic places. "Though the altitude is seven thousand feet. If I screw up because I get short of breath—"

"Let me stop you right there." He covered her concerned pout with an affectionate, if not entirely passionate, kiss. "You'll be fine. We'll be fine."

"Right. It can't be worse than opening night at the Met."

Both excitement and trepidation dissipated in a wave of melancholy as the memory of the previous year's tragic events overcame Julia. On the night of her debut performance in her first season as a fledgling twenty-two-year-old violinist at New York's venerable Metropolitan Opera, her mentor, conductor Abel Trudeau, had been shot and killed on the podium, before her eyes.

Abel had been like a father to her and trying to do her job without his benevolent caring and guidance had been a constant struggle. Worse, in the course of an investigation that she had gotten herself involved in she became caught up in an ominous web of jealousies and rivalries she never knew could exist in an opera house. Yet, despite the hazards and impediments, Julia had completed the rest of the Met season with her self-respect and her life intact.

Larry, almost twenty years older than Julia, had been the NYPD detective assigned to the murder case. The unlikely pair had become friendly as a result of their working together toward the goal of exonerating Sidney Richter, Julia's closest colleague at the Met, framed for Abel's murder. Larry had started out concerned for Julia's safety and welfare but had come to care for her in other ways. Now they were an item, spending more nights together than not.

Once the investigation had been completed, and Sidney cleared of all charges, Julia had felt free to soar to the heights of musical accomplishment of which Abel thought her capable. She had performed at such an exceptional level that she caught the attention of Stewart Blatchley, the Australian conductor of the Santa Fe Opera, who had offered her the position of concertmaster for the company's summer season. It was not unusual for Met Orchestra members to spend their summers performing at Santa Fe Opera, when the Met was on hiatus, and she jumped at the opportunity.

"Besides," Larry said, "How often does a twenty-three-year-old get a chance to be concertmaster of a major opera company?"

"Abel always told me I would be a concertmaster someday. But what if now is just too soon?"

"If Abel were here, he'd say you were more than ready. And he would be incredibly proud of you. So would Sid."

Julia's eyes misted over at the thought of Sidney, who had recently collapsed and died under mysterious circumstances in front of a restaurant in lower Manhattan. "I miss Sid. Nothing is the same without him."

"I totally agree." Larry attempted a cheerful smile. "But think of all the challenges ahead of you. Once you start playing that violin of yours in Santa Fe, they won't know what hit them."

"I hope you're right."

"Believe it. Plus, I get to tag along for the most erotic and murderous season in years. *Lulu, Salome, Lucia*—"

"Sex and violence, right up your alley. You're so predictable." Julia gave Larry a playful nudge. "But you're right. All that gore in *Salome.* St. John's severed head. It could hardly be bloodier."

"Do you think that's why John Crosby programmed a Richard Strauss opera every season?" Larry said. "Because he liked violence?"

"No, I think it was because Strauss was one of Crosby's great passions. He programmed plenty of other Strauss operas, not only the violent ones. I can't wait to play more of them."

Both Julia and Larry held huge amounts of respect for John Crosby, who had founded the Santa Fe Opera in 1957. Against all odds, Crosby had taken a leap of faith in establishing an opera company in the middle of the desert, framed by New Mexico's mesas and mountains. Civic pride skyrocketed in Santa Fe as a result of Crosby's creation of what was named the "Salzburg of the Southwest."

Though he had passed away in 2002, Crosby's belief in his "temple of music" continued to be justified. After sixty-plus years, the company's reputation was at an all-time high. And Julia felt privileged to have been tapped for such a major role in it. But at the moment, doubtful feelings swept aside her self-gratified ones, especially when it came to the music of Richard Strauss.

"The Nazis liked Strauss, too. What if there are some neo-Nazis lurking about Santa Fe?" Julia's thoughts turned back to a more immediate fear. "Or worse, what if Blatchley hates my playing?"

"Julia, get a hold of yourself. Do you want to go to Santa Fe or not?"

She flipped to a page showing a stunning photo of Santa Fe Opera's John Crosby Theatre against the backdrop of a New Mexico sunset, and suddenly remembered how thrilled she was at the prospect of her new adventure. "Of course I do, silly. Who wouldn't want to play opera in this amazing atmosphere? Especially *Lulu* and *Salome,* two of the most challenging operas out there."

"And both very sexy, especially *Salome.*"

"I can't argue with that. That opera was banned in Vienna and London as obscene, and after just one performance at the Met for the same reason. Critics called the story repugnant. Just the sort of thing that would inspire you."

"A banned composer. I like it," Larry said. "Who wouldn't be psyched to see the *Dance of the Seven Veils*? Though I suppose it depends who's doing it." He smirked. "Can you imagine the Austrian premiere with Puccini, Mahler, Schoenberg, and Berg in the audience? That must have been something."

Julia knew Larry had been enlightening himself about opera since the two of them had first started working together—and sleeping together. She was pleasantly surprised at the level of sophistication of his newfound knowledge. But she didn't want to admit it.

"Some musicologists have called *Lucia* a more violent, updated Scottish *Roméo*," Julia said. "Maybe that's why they're doing *Lucia, Lulu* and *Roméo et Juliette* in the same season."

"*Lucia*, an updated *Roméo*?" Larry shrugged. "I don't think so."

"Since when are you such an opera expert?"

"You wouldn't want it any other way, would you?"

"No." Julia secretly felt proud of him. "I wouldn't."

Larry reached under his pillow and pulled out a rectangular plastic box. "I got you something. A gift to commemorate you embarking on an important new chapter in your career."

Julia eyed the box, intrigued. "But I didn't get you anything."

"No worries. Just open it."

She placed the brochure on the night table, slid the cardboard sleeve off the box and gasped. "A Fitbit! You sly animal, you knew I've been wanting one. And purple, my favorite color."

"Try it on."

Larry aided Julia in her struggle to remove the wrappings and tape that sadistic designers always included in their packaging, lifted out the device and helped clasp it around her wrist.

"I figured you're going to be doing a lot of walking up and down hills and around the Santa Fe campus," he said. "This will motivate you. Plus, if someone calls you out for looking at it during boring rehearsals, you can always say you're checking your step count. Or tracking your sleep." He grinned. "This latest model even has a flashlight. Perfect for snooping around backstage in the dark." Larry demonstrated the button that controlled the flashlight mechanism.

Julia was uncomfortable, remembering the trouble she'd gotten into for nosing around hidden stairways and hallways at the Met during the murder investigation. "There'll be no snooping. But thank you. I love it."

Flushing with pleasure, Julia admired the gleaming chrome case and streamlined display and imagined herself showing off the spiffy piece of technology to her new orchestra colleagues. She kissed him on the cheek.

"I'm just sorry it doesn't match your locket," Larry said. "It didn't come in gold tone."

Up until recently, Julia usually wore the silver letter 'J' pendant she had gotten years before for her sixteenth birthday. But growing up, she always had admired the delicate, half-heart shaped gold locket her mother's sister, Zsófia, wore, and often fantasized about what had happened to the other half. When Zsófia had passed away a few months ago, her daughter, Julia's cousin, knowing how much Julia had coveted the piece, had gifted it to Julia. Now she wore it constantly, replacing her previous pendant.

Julia instinctively reached for the locket, now nestled at her throat. "That's okay. Chrome goes with everything." She hesitated. "By the way, I hope you don't mind if I cut my hair for the summer. I'm tired of blow drying it to get it straight." She knew how much Larry loved her long, flowing dark hair.

Larry studied Julia's face for a moment. Then he drew her close. "I do mind, but who am I to argue with a strong-willed woman?"

"I didn't know you thought of me that way."

"Are you kidding? Strong-willed, Jewish, beautiful and smart. Taking you on has been my most challenging project." He ran his fingers through her hair. "Can you at least keep it chin length?"

"I'll consider it. Now let me up," she said. "I have to practice those fiendish solos from *Lulu*. Otherwise I'll self-destruct, just like her character does. After she destroys every poor slob unfortunate enough to fall under her spell."

He pulled her back onto the bed. "I had a different kind of practicing in mind."

"For an opera buff, you can be absurdly unoriginal," she said.

"That's what you love about me," he said, wrapping his arms around her.

## Chapter 2

O *welche Lust! In freier Luft den Atem leicht zu heben*!
O what joy in the open air to breathe with ease!
~ Beethoven, *Fidelio,* Act 1

THE VIEW, AS JULIA AND LARRY DROVE FROM ALBUQUERQUE AIRPORT toward Santa Fe, was more glorious than they had anticipated. Mountain ranges on all sides filled their eyes and captured their imagination: Sangre de Cristo Mountains to the east, Jemez Mountains to the west. The fragrance of piñon trees, made pungent by the summer rain, infused their senses.

Forgotten were the usual hassle with the flight attendants over carrying her violin onto the plane (Julia had guarded it with her accustomed diligence and stood firm when the attendant had tried to have it checked into the hold), Julia's initial spaciness from the extreme change in altitude from sea level to thousands of feet above, and her unrelenting anxiety over the anticipated stresses of her new job.

Her attention was focused on the natural wonders surrounding her, eyes glued out her window as Larry drove.

"It's as magical as everyone says, isn't it?"

"More," he said.

"And it has such an air of mystery about it." A sliver of lightning tore through the sky, followed by a clap of thunder. "Wow," Julia said. "Spectacular."

"I thought you were afraid of thunderstorms, Julia."

"According to Marin, people view the ones here as natural wonders rather than scary. I'm trying to think of them that way."

"I wonder if Marin is here yet," Larry said.

Marin Crane was one of Julia's singer friends from the Met. She and Julia had first encountered each other at the cafeteria on Pit Level after Julia had played a rehearsal of Offenbach's *The Tales of Hoffmann* in which Marin sang the role of Hoffmann's sidekick, Nicklausse. Julia was so impressed with the way Marin tackled the vocal and dramatic subtleties of the character that when she spied Marin waiting in line at the café cashier she overcame her innate shyness and complimented the singer. Marin, who was not yet feeling comfortable in the role, was gratified and thanked Julia. They sat down over coffee, and a friendship began.

"I would hope so. Marin told me singers need even more time to acclimate to the thin mountain atmosphere," Julia said. "Can you believe she's singing the role of Countess Geschwitz in *Lulu*?"

"Why wouldn't she be?"

"Because Nicklausse is sweet and sincere, and Geschwitz is the female lover of, well, the Devil."

Larry smiled. "Maybe she really gets off on it."

"You're incorrigible."

"I thought you knew that about me by now."

"I do. But it never ceases to amaze me…Oh, there's our turnoff." She spied the main building of the Pueblo Inn on the left and was taken aback at the starkness of the landscaping surrounding it. "Wow, there's absolutely nothing around here."

"New Mexico is all about wide-open spaces. And it's our home away from home from now through August. Get used to it."

Larry pulled into the parking lot, parked the car, hauled their carry-ons from the trunk and began to wheel them across the pavement. Julia followed him, holding tight to her violin case, gazing in awe at the Spanish Pueblo Revival-style buildings that clustered together in this alien new environment. The structures looked to her like contemporary versions of photos she'd seen of ancient Anasazi cliff dwellings. The ones making up the Pueblo Inn were low-slung, square and rectangular-shaped adobe-pink boxes. The roofs were flat, and strange-looking wooden posts protruded from the walls. Attached to the main building was a turret-like structure made of light-colored brick.

As Julia stood in front of the entrance to take in the view of the scrubby native vegetation and the mysterious Sangre de Cristo Mountains in the distance, a female concierge came up to introduce herself. She led Julia and Larry through a leafy garden and across a courtyard dominated by a large, chunky fountain, describing the hotel's architecture as they passed by each building.

"The design shows the influence of New Mexico's indigenous Puebloan Ancient Ones, but also that of Colonial Spain," the concierge said. "The presence of the Ancient Ancestors is very keenly felt."

"What was that tower attached to the main building?" Julia asked.

"That's our *Kiva.* It represents Anasazi religious practices but also symbolizes the watchtowers that were found all across the Southwest. We also have a Southwestern style wedding chapel—in case you're interested," the concierge added, smiling. "You'll find it off the Enchanted Courtyard, the one we just passed through."

Larry leaned over to whisper in Julia's ear. "Is everything enchanted and haunted in this place?"

"Do you suppose we'll have a ghost in our room?" Julia whispered back, somewhat anxiously.

"Maybe you should request one."

"Very funny."

Marin also had filled in Julia about the local ghost lore. Evidently Santa Fe was considered one of the most haunted places in the U.S. That made Julia significantly more uneasy than the thought of electrical storms.

Their room was decorated in typical Southwestern style. A heavy, wooden king-sized four-poster bed draped with thick homespun curtains and festooned with a colorful Navajo wool coverlet and matching throw pillows dominated the space. Above the bed, two sepia-toned Native American photo portraits looked off into the distance. Completing the effect were immense rough wood exposed ceiling beams, which Julia in her research had found out were called *Vigas.*

"The bed's got curtains. How cool," Julia said, after the concierge had left.

"Good. We can take cover behind them when the ghost comes by tonight."

Hiding her unease, Julia chose to ignore him and peeked into the bathroom, where she spied a traditional pueblo ladder serving as a towel holder.

"Oh, look, *Latillas*. I saw them in the brochure," she said. "Puebloan mud houses had no doors, so they entered them with ladders opening onto the roofs. They used them to climb from one level of a building to another. That design is what eventually developed into the pueblo style, using the more long-lasting brown-earth adobe, which the Spanish learned to use from the Moors."

"Aren't you the historian?" Larry said, opening up his carry-on to start putting things away.

"I probably should have been researching less and practicing more. I'm getting *Lulu* anxiety."

"Maybe our ghost can help you."

"Your jokes are beginning to get tarnished, Larry," Julia said. "Like a silver Navajo necklace that's been exposed to a southwestern storm."

Julia opened the window and gazed out at the light rain that had begun to fall. She had envisioned a Santa Fe out of the past: dust-covered roads, cowboys and Indians on horseback. She never expected to be surrounded by mountains enveloped in mist, inhaling the scent of piñons in the rain-soaked air. She sighed with contentment.

*It really is a "Land of Enchantment."*

ꟹ

At night the room was quiet, perhaps too quiet. Despite the bed's relative comfort, with its hefty curtains blocking out any ambient light, Julia felt restless. She generally was a light sleeper, but somehow this was different. She wasn't sure if it was the time change, the altitude, or nervousness over starting her new position, but something just didn't feel right.

She lay listening to the rain and glanced over at the LED clock on the night table.

*Four a.m., too early to even think about rising and practicing. I'll have to practice in my head.*

Her photographic memory conjured images of one of the more difficult solo violin passages from *Lulu*: cascades of sixteenth notes in quick succession, climbing and falling, from bottom to top of the staff and beyond. She tried to hear the music in her head, but it was much too complicated. Not exactly easy listening.

Sighing, she turned over and, as she tried to go back to sleep, felt a sensation, as if someone had plopped down next to her on the bed. Larry was in his usual position, which never changed during the night.

Again, she felt the imprint of a body on the mattress, but this time it moved closer.

*Don't open your eyes, don't open your eyes.*

Was it the ghost of one of the Native Americans pictured on the wall, come down to avenge his ill-treatment at the hands of Spaniards or Americans, angry that the population of Native Americans in the region had dwindled to a mere two-and-a-half percent? A wounded soldier from the Mexican-American War? A Spanish missionary killed in the bloody battles with the Comanche, or a Pueblo Indian rebel? Julia had a hard time reconciling any of these. Her Russian-Hungarian-German-Jewish ancestors came to America in the 1920s and never went beyond New York, though it occurred to her that Spanish Jewry had made their mark as merchants and artists in Santa Fe. Still…

*You're crazy, Julia. Let it go.*

She would have had to see the ghost to believe in its presence, so Julia fought off her curiosity and followed her gut feeling, i.e. to keep her eyes tightly shut and not to tell Larry about it.

*It must be the altitude that's making me spacey. Now I understand what "high desert" means.*

That morning, she rose before Larry and went to the front desk to request a room change. Larry was wise enough not to ask any questions.

## Chapter 3

*Un nobile esempio è il vostro...al cielo attingete dell'arte il magistero che la fede ravviva!*

Yours is a noble example...you draw from heaven the mastery of art to revive the faith of men!

~ Puccini, *Tosca,* Act 1

Julia tried not to think about her supernatural experience of the night before as she and Larry drove north on Highway 285 toward the opera campus. Her heart was racing. She imagined some of her palpitations might have stemmed from her adjusting to the altitude, but more likely they were a result of her nervous yet eager anticipation of the days ahead: meeting the Opera's general director, the conductor and her new colleagues; and most importantly, proving her mettle.

"I can't wait to see the campus," Julia said. "When it was just starting out, they called it 'One of the most beloved venues in the country…A miracle in the desert…A shining white cloud in the red hills.' All the major media have gone ape over it."

Larry, eyes trained on the road ahead, raised his eyebrows. "Oh? With a sky as flawless as this one, I'd be surprised to see even one shining white cloud."

"Just wait a minute or two. The sky here tends to change without warning."

They turned on Opera Drive, passed by the OPERA TRAFFIC KEEP RIGHT sign, and wound along the 1.6 miles toward the campus. Julia looked out across the Tesuque Valley, surrounded by the Jemez and Sangre de Cristo Mountains. The horizon seemed to go on forever.

"What a magical setting. No wonder people keep coming back to work here year after year."

Larry pulled up to the curb in front of the entrance to the box office. "I'll drop you here and meet up with you later."

"Must you? I'd rather not face this alone."

"Nonsense, it's not the Spanish Inquisition. Go forth and impress people. It's your show."

"Okay. Don't forget the water bottle. It's so dry here."

"Your servant, Diva."

Julia reluctantly climbed out of the passenger seat and closed the car door. As Larry pulled away, she shrugged off her nerves and made her way along a path lined with adobe-pink pavers toward the entry portal where she stared up at the open-air theatre, its gold-toned letters spelling out "THE CROSBY THEATRE." With its soaring roof and ship-like baffles, the building evoked pleasant memories of the set of Wagner's *Flying Dutchman*—an opera that had fired up her imagination when she had played it at the Met the previous season—combined with some of Frank Gehry's designs for the Bilbao Art Gallery in Spain and the Walt Disney Concert Hall in Los Angeles.

She approached the campus and stopped at the gate, where a security guard manned his station.

"May I help you?"

"Yes, please. I'm Julia Kogan, here to see General Director Alan Reynolds. He's expecting me."

"Of course. I'll buzz him."

"Thank you. Oh, and my colleague is parking the car. Could you allow him in when he gets here? His name is Larry Somers."

As the guard wrote down Larry's name on his clipboard, Julia gazed admiringly at her surroundings. The plaque honoring John O'Hea Crosby and his parents Laurence Alden and Aileen O'Hea Crosby was impressive, but what struck her most of all was the newness of everything, especially when compared to the Met. There the stage door area dated back to the mid 1960s and, as far as Julia knew, had not been renovated, at least extensively, since then.

But this theatre, the third such structure since the company was established in 1957, had opened in 1998 and was meant to show that the company was all about the twenty-first century.

A tall, lanky man, his sand-colored hair peppered with grey, approached her. "Julia, Alan Reynolds. Welcome to Santa Fe."

Julia shook his extended hand. "Thank you, I'm honored to be here."

"The honor is ours. Your reputation precedes you," he said. "Stewart is anxious to meet you."

Flustered at the thought of meeting the music director, Julia hid her disquiet with a smile and followed Alan inside the gate.

"You have such a beautiful environment. I can even hear the birds chirping," she said.

Alan laughed. "They sing more sweetly here. I think the music inspires them."

"And the Crosby Theatre façade is exquisite. I can't wait to see the interior."

"We're quite proud of our theatre. Fodor's named it the second best outdoor venue in the U.S. If I'm allowed to boast, that is."

Julia was surprised at how affable and unpretentious he was, and how comfortable he made her feel; a huge contrast to her nemesis at the Met, General Manager Patricia Wells, whose overt lack of respect for the musicians and disdainful attitude had made Julia's life miserable. Julia sensed she was going to have an astonishing experience at Santa Fe Opera.

At first Julia tried not to reveal how impressed she was at the wonders Alan was showing her, but soon she gave in and murmured appropriate sounds of appreciation. He guided her past the box office and adjoining Opera Shop, down to the central plaza and the theatre exterior. She pointed, awed, at several enormous white structures off to each side that looked like twist-up ice cream pops.

"What are those huge, gauzy things?"

"They're baffles for keeping out the wind and rain," Alan said. "Mostly for the benefit of the orchestra. To prevent your instruments from being harmed during our heavy storms."

Julia had never heard such a concern expressed for the orchestra at the Met. "Amazing."

"Wait till you see the interior. It's magnificent," Alan continued. "It's actually our third theatre, constructed between the 1997 and

1998 seasons, which replaced the second one that was built after the fire—"

"The one in 1967? Did they ever find out what—or who—started it?"

"No..."

"Julia, there you are." Julia heard a familiar voice behind her and turned to see Larry approaching. "Wow, that security guard—I haven't witnessed an interrogation like that since my latest one at the NYPD."

Julia turned, glanced approvingly at Larry's water bottle, and drew him toward her and Alan. "Alan Reynolds, Larry Somers. Larry is a detective with the NYPD," Julia said.

Alan and Larry shook hands. "I'm just Julia's chauffeur," Larry said with a wry grin.

"You were saying, Alan—about the fire," Julia said.

"Ah, yes, the fire...it remains a mystery." Alan paused, frowning slightly. "Shall we go inside?"

Julia and Larry followed Alan through the entrance. Julia gasped at her first sight of the theatre, open at the sides and at the rear. Its sweeping stage, clerestory window adjoining the two roofs, and mountain views from every vantage point, left her wide-eyed.

Her reaction brought a smile to Alan's lips. "The clerestory window allows natural light to come in. Like in a church nave."

"It's all so new," Julia said. "So...modern."

"We've always had a modern spirit," Alan said. "That's our hallmark, and it's unique here. We've charted new territory in American musical life."

"I see the roof is curved," Larry said. "Is that for acoustics?"

Alan nodded. "Yes, for reflecting the sound from stage to audience. But also, its size and curvature make it capable of collecting rainwater for use in maintaining the infrastructure and landscaping. The water goes directly into tanks below the theatre," Alan said. "John Crosby knew well the importance of having water sources in this desert climate. He did everything he could to make sure his operation was as green as possible, even back then."

"I can appreciate that." Larry gulped from his water bottle.

"Some local ranchers swore that the rainouts in the early performances were responsible for ending a sixteen-year drought," Alan said. "They became big fans."

"Is it true that, when he wasn't conducting or studying a score he was directing traffic?" Larry asked.

"Or fixing the coffee machine. Though tending the gardens was his greatest pleasure. Most days he'd be out there in his Bermuda shorts and straw hat, clipping away, or watering the birch trees." Alan watched as Julia glanced down into the pit. "It's not as large as the one at the Met. But it was recently refurbished. I think you'll find it reasonably comfortable."

"I'm sure I will. I've seen much smaller ones." Julia smiled, remembering her very first union gigs in her Juilliard days, playing in postage stamp-sized Broadway pits. She gestured toward the stage, where stagehands were assembling a set. "Is that for *Lulu*?"

"Yes, how did you know?"

"I kind of guessed. One of my friends from the Met is singing Countess Geschwitz."

Alan nodded. "Ah, yes, Marin Crane. She'll be at rehearsal tomorrow.".

"She's told me a lot about playing that character. So many different aspects you can delve into, she says, characters who share a world of destruction, who are all doomed." Julia suppressed a shiver of dread. She thought the story creepy and disturbing, but she also didn't want to come across as unduly affected by it. "I imagine it will be just as challenging to adjust to the difficulties of playing a twelve-tone violin part with no home key as it is for the singers to adjust their ears to such a raw musical style."

"Sounds like you've analyzed the score already."

"She always does." Larry squeezed Julia's shoulder. "She believes in being a hundred-twenty percent prepared."

"Maestro will be happy to hear that," Alan said. "I'm sure you're familiar with the stage manager's desk backstage, Julia, which is similar to the Met. Perhaps you'd like to see the dressing rooms and shops instead? You could even sing a few notes on stage."

Julia's skeptical expression told Alan she wasn't eager to accept his offer.

"She has a pretty voice, but a small one," Larry winked. "And shy about revealing it."

"That is a pity," Alan said, as he led Julia and Larry through a door adjacent to the stage.

Julia leaned over and whispered to Larry. "I can't believe we're getting a personal tour of the backstage."

"Perks of being a concertmaster," he whispered back. "Enjoy it while you can."

## Chapter 4

*Ma dee luminoso...tal astro qual sole brillare. Per voi ciascuno dovrà palpitare*
But your luminous beauty should shine here...like the sun. For you, every heart here should beat faster
~ Verdi, *Rigoletto,* Act 1

"SOME AREAS HADN'T BEEN MODERNIZED SINCE THE YEAR AFTER THE FIRE. The backstage spaces recently underwent a thirty-five million dollar overhaul, increasing them by more than ten thousand square feet, making it safer for workers. Their safety is our top priority," Alan told Julia and Larry as they followed him to the backstage wings. "Even with all these improvements, we still manage to keep our budget balanced. As a member of one of the world's biggest opera companies, I'm sure you can appreciate how expensive it is to produce opera."

"Absolutely." Julia hid her feelings of discomfort. Having already witnessed a contract negotiation in her first season at the Met, she had learned that the huge operational costs of running an opera house were a perennial sticking point with management.

Alan led the way down a stairway, stopping by a room labeled "Chorus Dressing Room." Julia peeked in to see a generous-sized space crammed with costumes and wigs, hats and shoes, neatly organized on shelves labeled with opera titles. A large, cylindrical canister holding an impressive cache of swords fitted with red leather straps caught Julia's eye. "Are these for *Roméo et Juliette*?"

"Yes. And for *Lucia,*" Alan said.

"I've never seen so many shoes and boots," Julia said.

"Our costume and wardrobe people have their hands full. Shall we have a look at their shop?"

He pointed Julia and Larry toward a high-ceilinged, well-lit space at the end of the hall. To Julia's awestruck eyes, it seemed to rival Grand Central Station in size and breadth.

"Previously it was a dark and cramped space with a few tiny windows and no air-conditioning," Alan said as they entered the shop. "Now it's been expanded by five thousand square feet."

Larry looked around at dozens of costume worker-bee teams, cutting, stitching and draping, and grinned. "That must put these people in a better mood to work."

Alan laughed. "Undoubtedly. We have twice as many fitting rooms now, plus an entire room just for threads, zippers and other sewing necessities, which they all have access to. We call it 'the vault.'"

Julia gaped in wonder at endless racks of vibrant-colored costumes, stacked bins of accessories, and enormous worktables too numerous to count. Perched on each table was a heavy, industrial-sized hand iron with a long, thick cord attached to it at one end and to the ceiling at the other to keep it from falling off. A number of other tables held gleaming electric sewing machines, which seamstresses kept humming.

Julia's wide gaze led her to the far end of the expanse, where she spied a door with a lit sign above it marked, "Emergency exit only. Alarmed."

"Where does that door lead?" she asked Alan.

"If you look out that window, you can see that door goes outside to Stieren Hall, the orchestra rehearsal space. But no one accesses it from here. The costume workers don't really like people to use that door because traffic coming through here disrupts their work."

"Is that why it's alarmed?"

"Actually, it's not. We've just marked it that way to discourage people from using it. It is an exit technically, because it pushes out and has a bar. But when this room is full of people—about seventy, all told—there is so much 'stuff' everywhere, it's better if 'outsiders' don't use it as a through passage."

"Where does it lead, aside from Stieren Hall?" asked Larry.

"From the exterior, you can walk all the way around to the backstage and eventually the cantina. You can also access a staircase that goes all the way up to the roof."

"Really?"

"It's another way to get there other than through the theatre. In the theatre, if you look up to where all the lighting equipment is, you can see the access to the roof, just as you can in any theatre, although in our case, we also have birds up there." He chuckled softly.

Julia spied rows of mannequins, some dressed in Empire-era gowns, placed around the room. Then she turned her gaze toward a sea of tables heaped with bolts of cloth separated by dark and light shades and texture, and countless bins of fabric pieces in all sizes, colors and thicknesses. Slews of assistants expertly sorted, measured and cut them.

Julia felt a momentary twinge of nostalgia as she pictured her Aunt Zsófia, her mother's sister, peddling away at the ancient Singer sewing machine she had brought from her native Hungary.

"Wow, this is a lot for one wardrobe person to handle," she said to Alan. "Or is it 'costume person?'"

"Costume director. Wardrobe is costume maintenance and running of the shows. Costume is building and altering costumes for the shows," Alan said. "And it is a lot of work. But our costume director, Magda Kertész, is exceptional, very organized. She knows every inch of fabric, every detail of each costume. We have massive machines for washing and for dyeing as well."

Julia gaped at a row of huge steel drums that were hard at work churning and agitating. An immense cylindrical kettle sported a sign reading, "FLAMMABLE, KEEP FIRE AWAY." She was beginning to get a keen sense of the dangers inherent in running an opera's inner workings.

Walking over to some mannequins lined up side by side, Julia admired one draped in a slinky sequined 1920s-era black dress. "I wonder if they'd let me wear something like that in the pit."

Alan laughed. "It's one of the *Lulu* costumes. I'm sure we can arrange for you to borrow it."

"Oh, I was joking. But I do have a fascination for costumes."

"Then let me introduce you to Magda." He gestured toward a petite, ebony-haired woman who was draping fabric on another mannequin. She looked to be in her late sixties, perhaps older, and, despite her diminutive stature, projected a steely strength, both physical and mental.

Alan drew Julia closer to the woman. "Magda, this is Julia Kogan, our new orchestra concertmaster, from the Metropolitan Opera. And her companion, Larry Somers."

Magda, Julia, and Larry shook hands.

Alan turned to Julia. "Magda actually came to us from the Met, too."

"Many years ago, before you were born, Júlia my dear. And you may borrow whatever you like. We have a very liberal policy, especially for someone with such a lovely figure as yours."

"Thank you," Julia said, blushing. "I just love your accent. Hungarian?"

"*Igen*. Yes. *Te magyar vagy*? You are Hungarian also?"

"*Nem*. No, my mother Olga came from Hungary, but she died soon after I was born. My mother's sister, my Aunt Zsófia, taught me just a few words. *Csak egy kicsit beszélek magyarul*."

"That is more than a few words. Your accent, very nice."

"*Köszönöm*. Thank you. But I have to work at it. I have no one to speak it with."

"You can speak with me any time you like. And with my brother, Sandor, too. He is tenor. He sings role of Alwa in *Lulu*. You have met him?"

"No, I haven't started rehearsing yet," said Julia.

Magda smiled. "You must introduce yourself, *Igen*?"

"*Igen*." Julia returned Magda's smile. "Do you work closely with the wig and makeup person?"

"Yes, and scenic shop. We all work as unit. I dress singers. Wig director Daniel coordinates makeup with costumes, and property shop provides safe background and props."

"No wonder it takes so much money to produce opera," Larry said.

"And more hours than you can imagine." Magda eyed Julia's gold locket, which gleamed under the costume shop's fluorescent lights. "That is beautiful piece."

"*Köszönöm.* It belonged to Aunt Zsófia. Her daughter, my cousin, gave it to me when Zsófia died recently."

"Very classic Hungarian design. I have seen similar ones in old city of Budapest."

"Really? It's a vintage piece, supposedly one-of-a-kind. Zsófia told me the other half of the heart had been in the family, but it was lost."

Magda examined the locket more closely. "I have seen necklace that looks exactly like other half of yours, at Radiance Gallery near Santa Fe Plaza."

"Here in Santa Fe?" Julia was astonished. "That would be amazing. My aunt's husband was Mexican and came out here after she died. If the other half actually did end up here, that could explain why."

"You must go to gallery to see if piece is other half of yours, yes?"

"Absolutely. Where is it located?"

"West Palace Avenue. All pieces are unique, handmade, from international artists. Silver cigarette box Karl Larsson created as gift for John Crosby was exhibited there."

Julia was impressed. "That sounds wonderful. I definitely will pay a visit there. *Köszönöm.*"

"*Szívesen.* Regretfully I must get back to work now. Much to do before opera opening. But come back and see me."

"I will. Goodbye, Magda."

"*Viszontlátásra,* Júlia."

Magda went back to her draping. Julia felt a *frisson* of nostalgia to hear Magda pronounce her name as her Aunt Zsófia always had done, with the Hungarian-accented "ú."

"That's so cool. The other half of your locket in a gallery here in Santa Fe," Larry said.

"If it really is the other half," Julia said.

"We'll just have to find out, won't we?"

"You were quite a hit with Magda, Julia," Alan said. "Not many people here speak Hungarian."

"I only speak a little, just what my aunt taught me," Julia said. "And my father was Russian, so he didn't speak Hungarian. But he was my first violin teacher."

"Is your father still alive?"

"No. He was killed in…" She hesitated. It wasn't something she liked to think about. "…An accident. When I was ten."

"I'm so sorry," said Alan.

Larry changed the subject. "This girl loves languages," he said to Alan. "She studies all the librettos at the Met."

"Very unusual for an orchestra player. Stewart will be happy to hear that," Alan said. "Well! Shall we proceed to his dressing room?"

Julia did her best to hide her trepidation. Touring the opera house was a nice perk, but sooner or later she knew she would have to face her intimidating new boss.

"Lead on," she said.

# Chapter 5

*Regardez donc cette petite...Je suis là...voilà!*
Just look at that young girl...Here I am, at your service!
~ Bizet, *Carmen,* Act 1

JULIA TRIED TO TAKE A FEW DEEP BREATHS TO QUELL HER NERVES AS SHE, Alan and Larry hovered outside a door posted with an elegantly engraved sign reading: "Music Director, Maestro Blatchley."

The intimidating phrase made all of Julia's insecurities converge at once: her doubts as to her readiness to tackle such an important position as a newcomer in a company that was so well established, and her lack of experience in such a milieu. The vague inadequacies she had felt up to this point became all too real. Suddenly she felt completely deficient in the face of her new boss, worried that she wouldn't be able to live up to his standards.

The blood was coursing through her veins, pounding in her eardrums. Part of her wanted to cut and run, to get on the next plane back to New York.

But she knew that somehow she had to conceal her apprehensions from Blatchley; somehow she had to come across as being confident and adept.

Alan rapped lightly on the conductor's dressing room door.

"Come," called a voice from inside.

Alan opened the door and ushered in Julia and Larry. At the piano, a chestnut-haired, impeccably dressed man was practicing a passage from the score of *Lulu,* perched on the music holder in front of him. He stopped playing and turned.

"Alan! I'm glad you're finally here. I have a coaching with Emilia in..." He glanced at his diamond-studded Rolex. "Ten minutes."

"Sorry, Stewart, I'd forgotten. I would have brought these illustrious people to you sooner."

"*C'est pas grave.*" Stewart rose and appraised Julia with an exacting eye. "You must be Julia."

Julia, surprised to hear Stewart's accent was decidedly British and not Australian, eyed his flawlessly tailored suit. She felt self-conscious, wishing she had dressed more formally than her khaki skirt and leather flats. "I'm so honored to meet you, Maestro."

"Please, call me Stewart. It's a privilege I afford to my concertmasters. And we are going to be working very closely over the next months."

"I'm looking forward to it."

Stewart looked at Larry. "And this is…?"

"My apologies," said Julia. "Please meet my companion, NYPD detective Larry Somers."

Larry offered Stewart his hand. "At your service, Maestro."

Stewart raised an eyebrow. "I wasn't aware we needed police protection."

"Oh, I'm not working. I'm just Julia's groupie and chauffeur." Larry smiled mischievously. "Though I'm told the Surgeon General has warned about the effects of 'secondhand opera.'"

Stewart barely cracked a smile. "You will be a valuable asset to our season. Most of our players bring family members to support them."

"We're not quite…family," Julia said uncomfortably.

"Ah." Stewart indicated a sofa and a chair near the piano. "Please, sit, Julia. Let's chat." He shot a glance in Alan's direction.

Alan turned to Larry. "Would you like to see the rear stage area?"

"Absolutely," Larry said.

"How will I find you?" Julia asked.

Larry grinned. "Just send me a text."

"And if you get lost, ask the nearest stagehand," Alan added. "They're always lurking about."

"Take good care of her, Maestro," Larry said.

"How not?" Stewart smiled. "Looking after the orchestra players and protecting their creativity are my most important tasks."

"Well, that is a relief." Larry bowed slightly toward Stewart, then followed Alan out the door.

Julia chose the chair. Stewart sat opposite her on the sofa.

"The first thing you need to know, Julia, is that even though the players are a mix from many different ensembles across the country, like you it is their choice to be here for the summer. Some have been coming here for decades. The assemblage of different operas attracts them. That, and the opportunity to work with some distinguished conductors. Unlike you, however, most of our instrumentalists have been playing symphonic repertoire during the year, so they truly appreciate the opportunity to fulfill their 'opera cravings.' Some of them, for example, have never played the standard operatic repertoire. You have a distinct advantage in that regard."

"I've just completed my first season at the Met, so there's a lot I haven't done yet either," Julia said. "Certainly, I've never played *Lulu.*"

"You're not alone. Neither have most of the other musicians. *Lulu* is one of the 20th century's most important—and most notorious—operatic works. Presenting it skillfully is one of the best ways a company can demonstrate its musical and theatrical capabilities. Our company had the distinct honor of premiering the complete opera when the composer's widow died and the music was released for performance. All due to John Crosby's determination and savvy."

"I've heard about what an amazing force he was."

"I'm sure you are familiar with *Salome,* on the other hand, which has been in repertoire ten times over the last forty seasons. According to legend, it was Crosby's favorite opera."

Julia's brow furrowed. The mention of *Salome* evoked an uncomfortable moment backstage at the Met when she encountered the disembodied head of John the Baptist staring at her from a pedestal. It looked so real it rattled her.

"As to our orchestra, we pride ourselves on it. A critic once called it the best feature of our company. And we don't stint on rehearsal. That makes your contribution here all the more important."

Julia began to feel the reality of his expectations slowly creep into the conversation.

*So much for niceties. Now we get into the nitty gritty.*

"Not only am I very demanding of the players, but they are exacting in their expectations, both of themselves and of me. That is what makes our experience here unique. It's a very intimate atmosphere. Extremely close knit. When we reconvene at the beginning of the season, it's as if we had just finished the previous season's closing night. It's all thoroughly professional and comes together brilliantly."

"It sounds wonderful, Maestro."

*Wonderfully pressured.*

"Please—Stewart."

"Stewart." Suddenly reminded of the difficulties that lay ahead of her, Julia suppressed her anxiety and instead tried to focus on what Stewart was saying.

"One last thing you should know, Julia. As a former violinist, I feel that bowings are an important way to define what I want to express *vis à vis* the music," Stewart said. "So I've already marked the bowings in the string parts."

"Oh. Really?"

Julia was a bit thrown; bowings, the written indications as to whether a note should start with the bottom end of the bow and stroke toward the top, or vice versa, were an essential part of a string player's visual map when it came to playing notes on a page. Traditionally it was the concertmaster's job to determine which bowings would fulfill the conductor's interpretative wishes for the music. She had never heard of a conductor writing string bowings into orchestral parts.

Julia had played in orchestras since the age of ten, had learned by watching other concertmasters how to mark the bowings, and did so herself the times when she had attained that position.

*Is he trying to throw me for a loop? This is not what I signed up for. What have I gotten myself into?*

"Of course. I understand," she said, not understanding at all.

Stewart was more intimidating than most conductors she had worked with, and Julia was worried that he would be far more demanding than he had let on. His *politesse* seemed forced, as if he had to make a huge effort not to come across as high-and-mighty as he obviously was; so different from Abel's avuncular, benevolent attitude.

*If only you were here to guide me, Abel. I could really use your help right now.*

Stewart glanced at his watch. "Now if you'll excuse me, Julia, it's time for my coaching. Emilia will be arriving any moment. I've truly enjoyed our chat."

"As have I, Maestr—Stewart. I'm looking forward to *Lulu* rehearsal tomorrow."

"And I look forward to hearing you play those fiendish solos."

"I hope I can fulfill your expectations."

"I'm sure you will exceed them."

"Thank you."

Julia shook Stewart's hand, left him to his piano, and quietly closed the door behind her.

ꙮ

Alan led Larry across the stage through the rear and to the back of the theatre.

Larry pointed to an elevator-like structure moving up toward the stage between two adjacent staircases. "That looks like quite a piece of machinery."

"We call that 'B-Lift,'" Alan said. "It raises and lowers scenery to stage level and back, to and from the storage area three floors below."

"Impressive," Larry gazed thoughtfully at the apparatus. "But treacherous looking. Good thing there's that netting to keep stuff—or people—from falling through."

"Everyone here is extra cautious," Alan said.

"Always a first time," Larry said. "That's the cop in me talking."

Alan motioned to Larry to follow him up the staircase to the right of the lift. At the top of the stairs, the immense door was wide open, showing a gargantuan space with forty-foot ceilings, where a foreman was supervising eight or more stagehands in loading a brass bed on top of a piece of scenery held up by Ionic-style columns. On either side of the partial stage set, Larry could see rows of sawhorses holding enormous doors, storage units stuffed with what appeared to be plastic-wrapped mattresses, and countless other stage trappings.

"I never realized what goes into producing a stage set," he said.

"This is only a small cross section of what it takes," Alan said. "These people work long, grueling hours."

"Whatever they're doing, they look really happy doing it," said Larry.

"That's because they are keenly aware of how important their contribution is to the greater good."

ꕥ

"Are you lost? Can I help you find something—or somewhere?"

Julia was so deep into her pondering she hadn't noticed a slender young man approach, smiling broadly. He had dark curly hair and looked to be in his late twenties or early thirties.

She returned his smile. "No, I'm not lost. At least not yet. But I could use some help."

"Good. Because I specialize in rescuing damsels, especially if they're divas."

"Oh, I'm not a damsel or a diva."

"No? Then you must be…a new chorus member? No, you're much too slight. Ballet?"

"Wrong again. I'm Julia, the new concertmaster. Of the orchestra."

"Nice to meet you, new concertmaster. I'm the head stagehand. Steve Cañon."

Julia shook his hand. "That's an appropriate last name for around here."

"I'm supposedly descended from the first Spanish conquerors, diluted over the centuries into your run-of-the-mill Hispanic dude," he said, grinning. "So. What can I help you find?"

"Uh…the rear stage area?"

"Follow me, my lady."

"I wouldn't want to take you away from your work."

"Nah. Don't tell anyone, but I once left my post to go listen to a soprano. She sang like an angel. More like a 'magic flute' than a mere mortal. That's what it's like around here."

## Chapter 6

*No mysl reviinaya, chto yeyu drugomu obladat tomit menya*
But the jealous thought that she might be another's tortures me
~ Tchaikovsky, *The Queen of Spades,* Act 1

THE MENTION OF MOZART'S *MAGIC FLUTE,* ONE OF JULIA'S FAVORITE operas, brought to mind Papageno's famous aria, "*Der Vogelfänger bin ich ja,*" which had delighted her since her father had first played it for her on his violin when she was a child. She hummed it to herself as she approached the spot from which Larry and Alan were observing the stagehands moving the scenery props.

"Wow, that must be some meeting," Larry said to Alan. "Julia's still not here."

"Are you worried she might be lost?"

"If she can find her way around the Met, she can do it in an opera house surrounded by mountains."

"Of course I can."

Larry finally looked in the right direction and smiled as he spied Julia coming their way, but narrowed his eyes at her companion. "Who's your friend?"

"That's our head stagehand," said Alan.

Steve offered his hand. "Steve Cañon."

"Larry Somers. Julia's significant other."

"Steve showed me how to get here," Julia said.

"How nice of him."

Julia ignored Steve's disappointed look and Larry's displeased one. She wasn't quite sure what to make of Larry's uncharacteristic possessiveness, whether to feel flattered or annoyed. "I hope I didn't keep you waiting too long, Alan."

"Not at all. But I do have to get going and I thought you and Larry might like to see the prop shop. Perhaps if Steve has a few moments to spare…" He glanced in Steve's direction.

"Happy to, Boss," Steve said, turning toward Julia and Larry. "This way to the inner sanctum."

"Thank you for the V.I.P. tour, Alan," Julia said.

"My pleasure, Julia. See you at rehearsal tomorrow."

"Bright and early," she said.

Julia and Larry followed as Steve led them past the pit, down one flight of stairs, and another.

"I saw you frowning at Steve," Julia whispered to Larry. "You're not jealous, are you?"

"Who, me? Just because I'm old enough to be his uncle?"

Steve guided them outside to a terrace, where they came upon the back of a spacious, contemporary-looking concert hall. "That's Stieren Hall," Steve said. "Where the orchestra and singers rehearse when they're not in the theatre. Would you like to go inside, Julia?"

Julia laughed. "No, thanks. I'll be spending plenty of time in there soon enough."

When they had gone back inside and reached what looked like the bottom level, Steve said, "Here we are in Hades. Just kidding, it's really just the sub-sub-basement."

"Kind of like 'C-Level' at the Met," said Julia.

"If that's the Met's underbelly, then yeah," Steve grinned. "This barn over here is the properties shop."

Steve led his two charges to a room so cavernous that to Julia it seemed to extend beyond the limits of the theatre itself. The open door showed it was jam-packed with construction materials, immense machines and craftsmen fashioning objects out of faux substances of everything from Styrofoam to stainless steel.

Julia peeked in, squinting. "How can they work when the lighting is so dim?"

"Oh, they're used to it," said Steve. "It's all about creating art."

"That looks even more dangerous than B-Lift." Larry was eyeing the open elevator shaft that was visible off to the left.

"No worries," Steve said. "Everyone is super careful around here."

Large, gaping spaces with sheer drops generally made Julia nervous, so she focused on the prop shop. "Can we go inside?" she asked.

Steve gallantly pointed toward the entrance. "Of course, Miss Julia."

Once inside, Julia gaped at the industrious anthill of activity before her, where untold numbers of craftsmen were hammering, carving, gluing and fashioning statues and other stage *accoutrements*. Overstuffed period furniture shared space with breastplates and chain mail, masks and tiaras, swords, rapiers and daggers.

"May I take a closer look?" she asked.

"Sure, just don't touch anything," Steve said with a wink.

Julia approached a worker painting blood on a head, which she recognized as that of St. John the Baptist. As before, the image of her former confrontation with a similarly realistic looking replica at the Met invaded her memory. Though she knew the prop was a mere imitation of the real thing, she found it more disturbing than she cared to admit.

She shuddered. "What material is that made of?" she asked the worker. "It looks so real."

"If it doesn't, I'm out of a job," he said, grinning. "You can ruin the 'moment,' if you don't actually believe it's his real head. Or at least the head of the person who's singing him."

"It's positively gruesome," Julia said.

"Thank you. That's exactly what I was going for."

"How is it done?"

"There are different techniques. If you talk to Daniel, our wig and makeup director, he'll show you his approach. He has his own techniques to build these things. For me it starts with making a likeness of the singer in clay. Then we make a mold from the clay, produce a hollow fiberglass core covered with silicone. Inside the core, which is upside down, we put the blood and it comes dripping out…" He paused. "Are you okay? You look queasy."

"I'm fine," she said, suppressing a wave of nausea. "What happens next?"

"Then we put on the hair, and…" He held up the head by its hair and showed her the cut-off neck, the "blood" oozing from it dripping onto his hands.

"That is awesome," Larry said.

"Thanks," the prop worker said. "You wouldn't believe how many hours it takes. Though in all fairness, I work really closely with Daniel. We kind of combine the best of each of our own methods. You'll meet him eventually."

"I hope so," Julia said. "Thank you for the demonstration."

Steve pointed to an adjacent room. "Take a look at our newly expanded scenic shop."

Julia was happy to divert her attention to a vast space in which workers were noisily sawing and hammering. One, his head encased in what looked like a black Japanese Kendo mask with a blue mesh covering over the nose and mouth area, soldered two large metal frames together.

"Our production staff is as expert and committed as they come," Steve said proudly. "Have you two seen the 'Ranch'—the cantina, the pool, the gardens, the mountain views?"

"Thanks, but I think we'd better cut it short," Larry said. "I promised Julia a tour around downtown Santa Fe. And since she has rehearsal tomorrow..."

"Got it." Steve smiled at Julia. "If you have a minute, go back outside and check out the Stravinsky Terrace. Santa Fe was his favorite musical organization in the States."

"Really? I love Stravinsky." Julia held huge respect for the monumental twentieth century composer, whose *L'Histoire du Soldat* was one of her favorite pieces to perform.

"You're not alone. He was a major force in the early years of the company. Their godfather. He called it his family. He celebrated his eightieth birthday here. President Kennedy even sent a telegram."

"Wow. Tell me more."

"How could I refuse such a lovely lady?" Steve smiled.

Out of the corner of her eye, Julia noticed Larr grimace.

Steve smiled. "In Crosby's time they performed more Stravinsky than they did Verdi, and lots of other modern pieces. That wild Henze opera *Boulevard Solitude* premiered here in 1967, way before you and I were born."

"And I," Larry added quickly.

Julia caught Larry's defensive expression and smiled, bemused. She knew he was sensitive about the age gap between them and imagined he wasn't too happy about her capturing the attention of another, younger man.

"If you love Stravinsky, here's a great story," Steve said. "The night of that premiere, Stravinsky and his right-hand man Bob Craft showed up in lounge suits instead of dinner jackets. When Stravinsky told the security guards who he was, they made an exception for him but not for Craft. The Festival Director was so pissed he punched the gatekeeper in the eye—can you imagine—but they still wouldn't let Craft in. Stravinsky refused to go inside without Craft, so they went back to their hotel. It was in newspapers worldwide."

Julia was enthralled to think that such a story involving one of her composer icons actually took place where she stood. "That's incredible. Isn't it, Larry?"

Larry offered no response.

"But Stravinsky stayed loyal. Once when a piece of scenery got blown over in a storm, Stravinsky helped Crosby put it back up." Steve chuckled. "He probably was wearing the black beret Picasso gave him." Steve checked his Fitbit. "Sorry, folks, but I gotta get back to it."

"You work awfully hard, don't you?" Julia asked.

"Nah, it's the singers who are the hardest working people here. And the orchestra, of course," he added with a wink. "I'll peek in at tomorrow's rehearsal, Julia. See ya' around, Larry."

"You were kind of short with him," Julia said after Steve had departed. "He was really nice."

"Too nice," said Larry.

## Chapter 7

*Ed or fra noi parliam da buoni amici*
And now let's talk together like good friends
~ Puccini, *Tosca,* Act 2

LARRY AND JULIA HAD DONE THE SANTA FE CIRCUIT, GUIDEBOOK IN HAND, poking around the adobe art galleries and shops on Canyon Road, replete with tribal pottery, bronze sculptures, and characteristic Southwest-style landscape paintings. They dropped in on San Miguel Mission, and visited the Palace of the Governors, with its block-long row of Native American artisans hawking their wares under the front portico. They gazed at the monument in the middle of Santa Fe Plaza, the city's hub, honoring combatants who had died in battles with Indians over the New Mexico Territory, and at the plaque marking the original portal to the Manhattan Project.

As enthralled as Julia was by their touristic sojourn, traces of the discomfort she had felt that morning in her meeting with Blatchley still nagged at her consciousness and put a crimp in her enjoyment. She fretted about the impression she needed to make on the music director with her playing and worried that she should have spent the time practicing rather than sightseeing.

Nonetheless, she managed to rationalize that acquiring knowledge about the historical and cultural background of her new environment would enhance and inform her approach to performing at Santa Fe.

On one edge of the plaza, Julia watched a painter whisk his brush across a canvas. "The light here is exquisite," she told Larry. "No wonder Santa Fe is such a sanctuary for artists."

"'The second biggest art market in the U.S.,'" he read from the guidebook. "After Manhattan, of course."

In the shadow of the monument, youthful musicians playing guitars and drums serenaded onlookers in Spanish. Julia was struck by the difference between the street performers in New York City, who were largely classically oriented or hip in a contemporary vein, and the more historic folk-like character portrayed by their Santa

Fe counterparts. Even the street musicians in the Hispanic areas of New York City seemed to orient their performances toward a more modern spectator.

"You can see and feel the Native American and Spanish influence in so many things here," Julia told Larry. "The architecture, the art, the clothes…"

"True," Larry said. "And it's so much more laid back here. Really easy to like."

The Romanesque Cathedral Basilica of St. Francis of Assisi and Loretto Chapel impressed Julia the most. Despite having grown up Jewish, one of her best friends at the High School of Music and Art had been Catholic. Julia felt an affinity for the religion, and for the music and art inspired by it. Thus, the full Spanish name of the city at the time of its founding in 1610 held great significance for her.

Julia peered over Larry's shoulder at the guidebook. "'*La Villa Real de la Santa Fe de San Francisco de Asís*," she read. "'The Royal Town of the Holy Faith of St. Francis of Assisi.' That's so beautiful. Can we go to Assisi in Italy someday? It would make my Inner Catholic happy."

"You are a strange creature," Larry said. "We could visit the Georgia O'Keeffe Museum."

"No way I can do another museum right now. I'd rather save that for another time."

"Understood. Then how about we check out some of these south-west-themed boutiques?"

Julia felt weary, but she couldn't resist Larry's invitation to explore the shops that lined the streets forming the Plaza square. Shopping the boutiques on Columbus Avenue near Lincoln center was one of her favorite New York distractions, and she was keen to compare that experience to that of Santa Fe. One store on East Francisco Street caught her eye when she spied a pair of cowboy boots in the window that were unlike any she had seen elsewhere: mushroom-colored leather, adorned with yellow embroidery bordering the pointed toe and V-shaped top, and a purple and white flower stitched at the apex of the V.

"Ooh. Can you see me in those?" she asked Larry.

"Sure can," he said, "As long as you're not wearing anything else."

"In your dreams."

"Exactly," said Larry. "How about I get you the boots and you get me one of those William Henry knives?"

Julia studied the display. She knew nothing about knives, but she could tell from the fine craftsmanship, intricate engraving and hilts inlaid in turquoise and other expensive looking materials, that they were priced beyond her reach.

"Not going to happen."

"Okay. Then here's a different idea. Since Santa Fe is one of the most haunted cities in America, let's pop in on one of the spooky sites like La Fonda Hotel. They say the place is populated with former guests who, so to speak, never checked out. Plus, the city was built over an abandoned Tanoan Indian village. For all we know, their burial grounds are just below us."

Julia didn't want to reveal how uncomfortable she was to be reminded of her unnerving encounter with the ghost in their hotel room. "Suddenly you're an expert? Besides, I'm tired. And I haven't practiced my *Lulu* solos nearly enough to feel ready for tomorrow."

"Please? Just one."

Reality was beginning to overtake Julia's consciousness. She could no longer rationalize her absence from practicing. "Larry, perhaps you've forgotten I'm here to work?"

Larry put an arm around her. "You're right, forgive me. Just promise we'll get there before too long. I'm itching to see a ghost or two, aren't you?"

ꚙ

When Julia arrived at the opera house for rehearsal the next morning, the orchestra personnel manager, Sarah Gruen, greeted her.

"I can't tell you how blessed we feel to have you here," she told Julia. "We've recently had a big expansion of the backstage area, especially the orchestra's digs. They were more than generous with their renovations, and I'm psyched to show it to you. Follow me."

Julia, curious to compare her new surroundings with those at the Met, happily followed Sarah past the orchestra pit to a hallway with numerous doorways.

"Those are all practice rooms," Sarah said. "And here's the orchestra women's lounge and dressing area."

Sarah opened a door into an airy, carpeted space dotted with rows of lockers and benches. Julia gazed around, awestruck. After the dull grey walls of the Met's women's locker room, this newly renovated space looked sparkling, up-to-date and relatively cheerful.

"This one's yours," Sarah said, indicating a locker at the end of one row. "As concertmaster, you get the best location. Feel free to move on in."

"Julia!"

Julia turned to see an energetic young Asian woman, backpack in hand and violin case strapped to her shoulder, striding toward her. "Katie Ma! Trust you to get here at the last minute."

The woman flashed her characteristic sheepish grin. "You know me too well, girl."

Katie, also a member of the Met Orchestra's violin section, had been Julia's roommate and foster sister in their Juilliard and freelancing days. Julia still thought of Katie as her BFF, and the feeling was mutual. The upbeat young Korean woman, who had encouraged Julia and Larry's relationship from the very beginning, cheerfully found other digs when it seemed clear that Larry was going to spend more time at Julia's apartment than at his own place. Julia was thrilled to see Katie, who always brought a surge of buoyant energy to Julia's disposition.

Katie dropped her bag in a locker, gave Julia a brief hug, and turned to Sarah. "I'm Katie, most recently of the upper west side of Manhattan." She pumped Sarah's hand. "I'm ready for anything, even *Lulu*. Lead me to it."

Toting their violin cases, Julia and Katie followed as Sarah led them out the door and down a hallway toward the orchestra pit.

"Isn't it kind of unusual to start right off rehearsing with the singers on stage, rather than in the rehearsal hall?" Julia asked Sarah.

"Generally, yes," Sarah said. "But given the extreme difficulty of the orchestra accompaniment to *Lulu,* Maestro wanted to give both the singers and the musicians as much opportunity to rehearse together as possible. There's so much more work involved than in traditional operas, getting all the notes at the right length and pitch, when it's all so dissonant."

Julia didn't need to be reminded of the difficulties of serial composition and the musical challenges that lay ahead of her. "Understood. How do the maestro and the orchestra get on?"

"They have a super relationship. He's not only a true artist, but he's also likeable and bighearted. He looks out for them, too. He recognizes how integral they are to the audience's experience of opera."

*"Bighearted" is not exactly how I would describe him.*

Sarah pointed to a large black wooden shelf covering a wall near the pit entrance, with individual shelves labeled clearly in white letters. "That's where you leave your cases when you're in the pit."

Julia took note of a shelf titled, "Violins & Violas" as the future resting place for her violin case and was glad to see a black-lettered white sign taped to it that read, "Please do not place any cups, drinks, or liquids of any kind on the instrument shelves." She glanced toward the pit door where a dozen or more musicians gathered outside. Some were chatting, others were staring at their smart phone screens or sending texts.

"Some of our players have been coming here for twenty or more seasons." Sarah waved her arm to get the musicians' attention. "Everybody, this is Julia Kogan of the Met Opera, our new concertmaster," she said. "And her Met colleague, Katie Ma."

Several musicians waved back, then continued their conversations and texting. Sarah pulled Julia over to a dark-haired, friendly-looking Asian man carrying a violin case who was about to enter the pit. "Julia, meet Matt Kim, your associate concertmaster," she said. "Matt, this is Julia."

Matt flashed a good-natured smile. "I've heard so much about you, Julia. I'm looking forward to turning your pages."

Julia immediately warmed to him. "We'll see how you feel about that after the first few sessions," she said, laughing. She gestured at Katie. "Matt, this is Katie Ma, one of my Met Opera co-conspirators."

Katie offered her hand to Matt. "We're infiltrating Santa Fe. Looking to steal your secrets and root around for skeletons in the closets."

"Not many skeletons that I know of," Matt said. "Were you guys at the Met the night Abel Trudeau was shot?" he asked.

Julia felt as if she had been punched in the stomach.

Katie stepped in. "We both were. It was pretty scary. The pit was a crime scene." Katie paused. "It was really hard on Julia. Abel was her mentor."

Matt frowned. "Oh, Julia, I'm so sorry. If I had known—"

"No worries, Matt," Julia said. "I'm okay now, since they caught the guy who did it."

"Glad to hear it," Matt said. "As for secrets, you're more than welcome to explore. Though you never know what you'll find here." He lowered his voice. "They say John Crosby's ghost is still hanging around the place."

Katie's eyes widened. "Ooh, that sounds spicy, doesn't it, Jul?" She turned back to Matt. "Julia's got an advanced level of intuition. If there are any spirits around, they'll glom onto her."

Julia, reminded of her discomfiting encounter with the resident "ghost" in her hotel room, frowned deeply. "How do you know that?"

"Just a hunch," Katie said, chuckling. "Remember that psychic on the Upper West Side who said you were a medium?"

"She probably says that to everyone, Katie. Don't listen to her, Matt."

"On the contrary," Matt said. "We could use one of those in 'ghostly' Santa Fe."

Julia made a concerted effort to change the subject. "Did you play for Crosby, Matt?"

"Yes, toward the end of his tenure. He was quite a force. Hypercritical, finicky, brilliant. Sometimes aggravating, but you didn't hear that from me," Matt said. "And he was the embodiment of contradiction. His office desk was immaculate, everything in its place—including an ashtray spilling over with cigarette butts. But because of his dream, the world of opera will never be the same. He made opera a tourist attraction. We're all the better for it."

Suddenly Julia couldn't wait to start her new operatic adventure.

"Five minutes to rehearsal. Orchestra to the pit, please," came the voice from the P.A. system.

"Well, that sounds familiar," said Katie.

"Yes, doesn't it?" Julia smiled sympathetically at Katie. "It feels like we never left the Met."

## Chapter 8

*Saggia non è cotesta ostinatezza vostra*
This stubbornness of yours is not prudent
~ Puccini, *Tosca,* Act 2

JULIA LOVINGLY UNWRAPPED HER VIOLIN FROM ITS MAROON SILK DRAWstring pouch and plucked the strings. Considering the difference in climate and altitude from the instrument's accustomed home base, the strings were minimally out of tune. She had made sure to intersperse several "Dampits" in strategic places inside her violin case. These cylindrical sponges wrapped in rubber casing, moistened and kept inside instrument cases for the sole purpose of preventing excessive drying out, were of prime importance in Santa Fe's arid atmosphere.

As other musicians began to filter in, Julia reached for her violin bow, tightened the hairs and drew it across the strings, tuning each one carefully. Hesitant to attack the formidably difficult music for *Lulu* on the stand in front of her, she instead warmed up on the hushed, mysterious opening to her favorite concerto by Sibelius, while Matt listened with admiration.

Once all the orchestra members were seated, Sarah climbed up on the podium and waved her arms to calm down the cacophony of seventy-five musicians warming up simultaneously. "Please welcome our new concertmaster, Julia Kogan, fresh from her spectacular first season in the Metropolitan Opera Orchestra."

Sarah descended as Julia rose from her chair to the sound of shuffling feet and the bottom metal ends of bows clacking on the music stands, the orchestra's version of applause. She acknowledged the reception with a gratified smile and nodded toward the first oboist for the "A."

As the players tuned and warmed up on the usual arpeggiated flourishes, Stewart Blatchley snaked his way through the pit in between rows of musicians, nodded to Sarah and mounted the podium.

"Please welcome back Maestro Blatchley," Sarah called out over the commotion.

The din ceased. "Good morning, all." He shook Julia's hand and whispered to her. "Lots of foot shuffling. That's a good sign."

Julia flushed with pleasure at his gesture of approval.

*Maybe I was being overly pessimistic about him after all.*

Stewart peered at the stage, where a small-statured, barrel-chested singer was exploring his paces on the set. "Good morning, Sandor."

"Good morning, Maestro," said the tenor.

Julia remembered her conversation with Magda. "Is that the costume director's brother up there?" she asked Matt.

"Yes. How did you know?"

"I met Magda yesterday. She mentioned her brother was a tenor. He certainly looks like one."

"Typical tenor for sure, with that physique. Solidly built. Too bad the poor guy has to die on stage, violently," said Matt. "But that's par for the course in this opera."

"Hopefully I won't feel like killing myself after playing it," Julia said.

"Of course you won't." Matt lowered his voice. "But be forewarned. The guy in back of you, Lenny, is the jealous type. He seriously wanted your job."

Julia stole a glance behind her to see a long-limbed man with angular features feverishly practicing a difficult passage.

"He's been coming here for years," Matt said. "And he's not been shy about complaining that you were chosen over him. He might try to sabotage you. Be aware."

"I can handle him, Matt. I'm a feisty New Yorker. And Jewish to boot. No worries."

Julia had found herself in similar situations ever since she first started playing in orchestras as a student, when other players who envied her more advanced position exercised their right to a so-called "challenge." Whatever her current insecurities and self-doubts about her new position, overall Julia felt confident enough in her abilities as an orchestral leader and to fend off any and all such challenges.

*Just let him try to ruffle me. I'm ready for it.*

"Act 3, final scene, please," Stewart said. "Let's start right in by killing off Lulu."

Amidst snickers from the ranks, he opened his score. Julia summoned up her courage. She knew she hadn't practiced enough; despite her confidence in her orchestral leadership abilities, for the first time in her musical life she felt unprepared and insecure about the difficulty of the music.

Stewart looked up from his score at the stage and grumbled, "Harold, it's five seconds to downbeat. Where the hell is Emilia?"

Julia heard a high-pitched, heavily Italian-accented voice emanating from the wings and looked up to see a tall, dark-haired woman flounce onto the stage, followed by a disheveled man wearing glasses carrying a large book and a second, equally unkempt man waving his arms.

"*Ma…quello direttore sa niente,*" the woman complained to the bespectacled man, waving toward the second man.

Matt leaned over and whispered to Julia. "That guy with the glasses and the book is the stage manager, Harold. The other one is the director, Salman Kipinsky. And in case you didn't know, the screaming lady is none other than Emilia Tosti, Italian soprano from hell. Who else could get away with telling the director he knows nothing?"

Harold gestured helplessly. "But I thought you loved working with Salman?" he said to Emilia.

"That was before I found out he knows nothing," Emilia retorted.

Stewart waved from the podium. "Good morning, Emilia," he called.

"*Buongiorno,* Maestro," Emilia said, narrowing her eyes in the dim light. "*Ma, dimmi…*tell me how am I supposed to work with this, this…*gaffone.* Hours wasted because of his incompetence. He tells me the murder must take place offstage."

"Let's just rehearse the music, *cara,* and worry about that later."

"Yes, yes, if we must. Where is Goran?"

Goran Řezníček, a large, imposing man with wild-looking curly locks strode to Emilia and kissed her on both cheeks. "I am here, my darling."

"Goran, I cannot stomach working with this impostor. What am I to do with him?"

Goran gave Emilia a reassuring hug. "Just let him direct, my sweet."

"If I do, it is only under protest."

"Thank you, Goran," Salman said.

Julia watched from the pit, intrigued, as the mini-drama took place on stage. She had experienced enough rehearsals at the Met to have become familiar with the capricious behavior of divas, but to her Emilia seemed over the top even by that standard.

Salman gestured toward Stewart. "Good morning, Maestro." Stewart acknowledged Salman with a nod. The director addressed the three singers onstage. "As your director, I feel I should begin by laying out a few general concepts along with my own insights for this production."

Emilia rolled her eyes. Salman ignored her.

"In the spirit of the great Russian teacher and director Stanislavski, I, too, believe in the importance of theatrics for singers, as well as that of diction. Half of your success depends on it. Every word you sing must reach the audience."

"Does he think we are beginners, Goran?" Emilia said with a disdainful pout.

Again, Salman disregarded Emilia's lack of propriety. "Secondly, any tightness you keep in your shoulder, neck and jaw will cause your vocal technique to suffer, especially with Santa Fe's high altitude and exceptionally arid climate. For your own benefit and that of the audience, your bodies must be liberated from any tension that is not integral to the drama. You are instead communicating music to the audience as if it were an affirmation coming straight from the heart. In the end, what counts is what remains in their minds. Sandor..."

Salman turned to the tenor, who had been pretending to ignore the squabble between Emilia and the director. "You've just killed yourself. Resume your position on the floor, just as we did in the rehearsal room. Places, everyone. This opera has been called 'a wild journey of love, obsession, death, bloodshed and betrayal.' That says it all. Give the audience something to focus on besides the music. Now, Emilia—that is, Lulu..."

Emilia faced Salman with a disparaging look.

"Remember, you are Garbo, Dietrich, Louise Brooks. Your formidable psychic force causes you to destroy everyone in your path. Those who fall in love with you suffer or die. You have undone Dr. Schön, but you don't know that Goran is Jack the Ripper. Goran..."

Salman turned toward the baritone. "The so-called 'Whitechapel Murderer' cut his victims' throats before mutilating them abdominally, showing a knowledge of human anatomy. Thus, the parallels between Jack and his alter ego, Dr. Schön. Jack's music is softer than the harsh music of Dr. Schön, but more menacing. Dr. Schön's character is key. His desperation heightens the ambivalence of Lulu's role. The man Lulu murders is the one who murders her. He is still present after his death."

Matt leaned over and whispered to Julia. "Kind of like John Crosby, right?"

Julia shuddered.

"Ah, Marin, there you are," Salman said. "Sit down on the chaise, stage right, as we rehearsed before, yes? You must convey the perpetually distressed attributes of the Countess. When you sing *'Im Ewigkeit'* after Goran stabs you, that is your *Liebestod*."

Goran gently led the sulking Emilia to stage left, while Marin followed Salman's instruction. Julia, elated to see her friend onstage, gestured in Marin's direction. Marin waved back.

Stewart frowned. "You'd best focus your attention on your music, Julia, rather than the stage."

"I'm sorry, Maestro. It's just that Marin and I have been friends since—"

"We need to use every ounce of our collective vitality to make up for what we lack in numbers," Stewart snapped. "This music is difficult enough without your being distracted. Keep your friendships outside."

"Yes. Of course."

Julia heard a soft chortle and snuck a peek at Lenny behind her, smiling crookedly.

*Maybe Matt is right. I'd better watch out for this guy.*

As Marin seated herself, Emilia flashed a hostile glance in Marin's direction and stage-whispered to Goran, "She sings too loud. Always tries to upstage me."

Marin frowned. "I heard that, Emilia. In case you've forgotten, I'm your lesbian lover. Try to be a little kinder, would you?"

Salman suppressed a groan. "Let's just sing, shall we?"

Goran and Emilia huddled together as Marin watched their interaction.

"*Wer is das?*" [Who is that?] Goran sang.

"*Meine schwester.*" [My sister.] Emilia replied.

"*Das ist nich deine schwester. Sie ist in dich verliebt.*" [That's not your sister. She is your lover.]

"You could have fooled me," Marin muttered under her breath.

Emilia extricated herself from Goran and faced Marin, fuming. "What did you say?" She turned to Salman. "You see? She is sabotaging me."

"Could we continue, please?" Salman pleaded. "Lulu and Jack, offstage for the final dialogue."

Emilia's nostrils flared but she allowed Goran to shepherd her off into the wings. Then came Emilia's bloodcurdling cry.

"*Nein, nein!*" [No, no!]

"*Lulu, mein engel!*" [Lulu, my angel!] Marin cried in anguish. She rushed offstage, then returned, slowly backing up, eyes wide in horror, as Goran stalked on stage toward her, wielding an oversized stage knife, which he plunged into her. Having murdered two women, Goran sang:

"'*Ich bin doch ein verdammter Glückspilz*!'" [I am just the damned luckiest of men!]

Then, seizing a bottle of wine from a table, he washed off the knife with the wine, and wiped the knife on his coat.

Salman was ecstatic. "Excellent, excellent."

Julia watched, horrified, as the bloody violence unfolded onstage. She knew the singers were just acting, and the scenario was only make-believe; but the sheer awfulness of the bloody violence was so realistically portrayed, she couldn't keep her jaw from dropping.

"Pretty heavy duty, isn't it?" Matt asked.

"I...I just can't take my eyes off the action," she said, but seeing Stewart's disapproving glare she tore her eyes away from the stage and back to the music before her.

Meanwhile, Emilia had come back to life and strode onto the stage to confront Salman. "It is not most effective staging. Murder must be onstage."

Salman finally lost his patience. "It's the way John Crosby conceived it," he growled. "Take it up with him."

"But John Crosby is dead."

"Precisely," said Salman.

"Oh!" cried Emilia, her expression outraged. "You are...*bischero*! Idiot!" Fuming, she marched offstage.

"That attitude will make you even more enemies than you already have, Emilia!" he shouted.

Turning on his heel, he stomped offstage in the opposite direction.

"Harold," Stewart called out, "Tell Emilia if she shows up to the dress rehearsal less than five minutes before downbeat, she will be replaced."

Harold just stood rooted to the stage, his expression helpless.

## Chapter 9

*Contr'esso un rancore pei tristi suoi modi di noi chi non ha?*
Which of us has not a score to settle with him for his malice?
~ Verdi, *Rigoletto,* Act 1

DURING THE REHEARSAL BREAK, JULIA MET UP WITH MARIN AT THE CANtina to commiserate.

"She's a tough one," Julia said.

Marin grimaced. "Emilia? She tries to be. But mostly she's just paranoid. She thinks everyone's out to get her. Specifically, other sopranos. Me in particular."

"Why should she feel threatened by you? You're a mezzo."

"Doesn't matter," said Marin. "The size of her ego dictates that she be in the limelight at all times. She's made it quite clear. There's only one 'I' in 'Diva.'"

Julia giggled. "Sorry, I don't mean to make light of your situation. But you must admit that's pretty funny."

"Yeah. It is, isn't it?"

They shared a laugh. Then Marin's expression sobered. "Sometimes this profession is really, really nasty. Blatchley's not exactly making your life easy, either, is he?"

"I didn't expect him to. He's right, the music is already difficult enough. But, really, Abel never begrudged the orchestra players just a quick look at the stage."

"Abel was extraordinary, Julia."

"Yes, he was." Julia blinked away a tear. "Tell me about doing the role of Geschwitz. How in the world do you sing serial music? I can barely find those pitches on the violin."

"It took a long time to prepare. At first I thought, this is impossible, I can never do anything with that score. I just hated the music. I come from a *bel canto* background, and *Lulu* is not exactly *Cenerentola.* And there's so much going on with the staging. It was downright scary. But all those years of *bel canto* singing helped me evolve to the point that I could tackle this role. It's all about connecting with the world of these doomed characters who are pushed to the limit just trying to survive. These women are very layered. *Lulu* is like an Egon Schiele painting depicted in music. You see—and hear—more in it as you learn more about it. So many of Lulu's character traits, especially the disturbing ones, can be seen in those paintings. Ironically, Geschwitz is the only person in the opera that loves Lulu unconditionally. Me and Emilia. As if." She grimaced. "By the way, did you know Berg's sister was gay?"

"No," said Julia. "Did she inspire the role of Geschwitz?"

"Very heavy, right?" Marin turned. "Oh, look, there's Sandy." She waved to him. "Sandy, over here."

Sandor paid for his coffee and made his way to Marin and Julia's table. "Sandy, this is Julia, our new concertmaster. She and I were friends at the Met."

Julia noticed Sandor's overtly admiring look, but she didn't take offense. She had encountered enough European men at the Met to be familiar with the unrestrained, sometimes overenthusiastic, appreciation of feminine beauty.

"And yes, I know she's gorgeous," Marin said, "But try to be a bit subtler, would you?"

Sandor took Julia's hand and kissed it delicately. "*Örvendek,* Julia. Nice to meet you."

Julia noticed his accent was less pronounced than Magda's. "*Örvendek,* Sandor. How did you know I spoke Hungarian?"

"Magda shares everything with me. She always looks out for little brother. We are very close."

"She seems like a fascinating woman," Julia said.

"*Igen.* She has been with the company for many years."

"I'll bet she knows stories no one else does," said Marin.

Sandor nodded. "Our grandmother was costume director in Santa Fe many years ago. She was here in 1963, for first production of *Lulu.* Only acts one and two, of course. Berg's widow refused to release the last act while she was living."

"I've never quite understood why," Julia said.

"Some say it was because she hated the main character. Others say she believed Alwa was her husband's spirit *in persona,* and his dying onstage would cause the death of Berg's spirit."

"Wow, what a story," Julia said. "You get to embody Berg's spirit onstage."

"The role is a tremendous challenge musically, one of few contemporary ones I would do again if I could. It's a horrible story, but the piece is absolutely phenomenal, the impact tremendous. I get to sing, '*Durch dieses Kleid empfinde ich Deinen Wuchs wie Musik.*' Do you know what that means, Julia?"

"Of course she does," Marin said. "This girl's a linguist. Studies all the libretti."

"'Through this dress I feel your body like music,'" Julia said, unembarrassed. "How I would have loved to see that original production."

"It was superbly decadent, as a tale of obsession and death should be," Sandor said. "Sadly, it was among those productions destroyed in the 1967 fire. But in 1979, due to diligence of John Crosby, Santa Fe had the honor of giving the American premiere of the complete opera."

"Has Magda told you tales of John Crosby?" Julia asked.

"Many. And they are all fascinating," Sandor said. "Crosby was involved with every aspect of the company, every detail. He was so consumed with the place, he would rise at crack of dawn and go out to water the trees. He even had something to say to Magda about costumes."

"Really?" said Marin. "Do tell."

"In one rehearsal, he noticed a rose on one chorus lady's costume was slightly lower on her shoulder than other choristers. He insisted Magda sew it higher up to match."

Julia and Marin looked at each other, impressed.

"And his temper was legendary. Once he found a wad of chewed gum in swimming pool. He threw a fit. He didn't rest until he found the culprit. And then it was—" Sandor made a slashing motion across his throat.

Julia's eyes widened.

Sandor smiled. "Then I heard that a soprano once got so mad when Crosby supposedly ran off with one of her boyfriends, she drove a jeep into the pool."

"Seriously?" Marin laughed. "She was so bent on revenge?"

"I'm not sure. Whatever the reason, it didn't prevent her from being hired again. I've sung with her many times and liked her enormously. She was fantastic actress."

"Wow, Crosby sure was a piece of work," Marin said. "I've even heard his ghost haunts the theatre."

Julia, remembering her eerie encounter the first night at the Pueblo Inn, suddenly felt as if a cold gust of wind had swooped over her. "Is that really true?"

"It's been seen, I'm told. Wearing those same Bermuda shorts and straw hat he always wore. Some of the musicians who knew him are still working here. They visit his grave every summer, drink a toast to him and talk to him about old days." Sandor lowered his voice. "Some say it *might* have been Crosby himself who set the fire in 1967. There were rumors about him flying into a jealous rage over a lover—"

"Get out!" said Marin.

Julia, who couldn't contain her curiosity about the fire, was riveted. "I read that he was absolutely devastated over it. The fire, I mean."

"And look what happened afterward," said Sandor. "Everyone rallied together to rebuild. That's when the company really made a surge forward. Do not forget, without John Crosby, opera would not exist in New Mexico. He was not afraid to be controversial, avant-garde." He looked at his watch and rose. "Regretfully I must get back to stage. *Viszontlátásra,* Julia."

"*Viszontlátásra,* Sandor. Hope to see you soon."

He nodded at Marin, "See you shortly, Countess."

As Sandor hastened away. Marin peered at Julia. "You're just full of surprises. Hungarian?"

"There's a lot you don't know about me, Marin."

Julia was glad of Marin's interest in her Hungarian background, but she didn't want to reveal how uncomfortable she felt from the conversation that had just taken place. Her mind was reeling. Ghosts, jealous lovers, fires of mysterious origins: the company's past history was undeniably fascinating. But she was beginning to wonder if she could handle its present.

ꕤ

After the orchestra returned from their break, Julia began practicing one of her solos but was distracted to hear a commotion on stage. She looked up to see Emilia shrieking at Magda.

"These are not shoes you were supposed to order from Italy," Emilia said, her face livid. "How am I supposed to stand in these for three hours? The leather is not soft. They pinch my feet."

"*Sajnálom,* Emilia, I am sorry. They still have not arrived. I will check with wardrobe director."

Emilia gritted her teeth. "See that you do. *Nézd meg.*"

Julia was surprised to hear Emilia speak Hungarian, but her fascination with the spectacle on stage was replaced by discomfort in the pit when she felt the presence of someone leaning over the pit rail. Looking up, she was mortified to see Stewart glaring at her.

"It seems you find the stage more interesting than your music," Stewart said. "By the way, you should vibrate more on the upper note of that arpeggio. And pay more attention to the intonation. The high 'E' was a bit flat."

Embarrassed to be caught looking once again by the maestro, Julia quickly snapped her attention back to her music. "Of course. Thank you."

As she began to practice, she heard a soft snicker from behind her. Matt sat down, tipped his head in Lenny's direction and raised his eyebrows. Julia nodded and kept on playing.

ꕤ

After the grueling rehearsal, Julia packed up her violin and trudged from the pit to the exterior of the theatre. She knew Larry would be waiting for her by the box office but decided she needed a whiff of fresh air and a bit of solitude before seeing him and returning to the Pueblo Inn.

She stood by the fence opposite the B-Lift opening to the back of the stage, which overlooked the hillside dotted with brush and chaparral, and contemplated her experience so far. Not her most stellar performance, she realized, and though her stand partner Matt was friendly enough, she felt she lacked the kind of support she always could depend on from Abel and Sidney.

*Where are you two when I need you? I feel so alone.*

Julia gazed into the distance, forlorn, squinting from the intensity of the New Mexico sunlight. Then she blinked. Someone was out there, darting among the bushes. Male or female, she couldn't tell, but whoever it was wore a wide-brimmed straw hat and Bermuda shorts. Puzzled as to why anyone would be outside, exposed to the scorching sun overhead, a sudden irrational thought occurred to her.

*The ghost of John Crosby?*

Then she berated herself.

*That's ridiculous. I'm just hallucinating from the sun. Mad Dogs and Englishmen, as they say.*

Julia closed her eyes, then opened them. The figure was gone. She shook off a frightened shudder.

*It must be the altitude. Or jet lag. Or both.*

"Whoever you are," she muttered aloud, "Could you please get rid of Blatchley? Or at least get him off my back?"

Sighing, she took one last look at the empty landscape and went to find Larry. One thing she knew for certain: she would never tell him what had just happened.

## Chapter 10

*Taci crudele! Io non merto da te tal trattamento!*
Don't be so cruel! I don't deserve such treatment from you!
~ Mozart, *Don Giovanni*, Act 1

JULIA SURVIVED SEVERAL MORE CHALLENGING REHEARSALS, DEVELOPING A thicker skin, until she became mostly impervious to Blatchley's criticisms and reproaches. On the day of the opening performance, she practiced steadily from the early morning hours until it was time to get dressed and go to the theatre. By then, opening night terror had replaced her spooked reaction to the apparition she had seen on the hillside after the first rehearsal.

"Don't you think you're overdoing the practicing, Julia?" Larry was dressed for opening night himself. Julia, who as a courtesy was given a company comp ticket for him, inwardly admitted he had cleaned up rather well.

She waved away Larry's admonition. "Blatchley's been on my case since day one. If I'm not perfect tonight, he'll—"

"What? Fire you? Not gonna happen," Larry said.

"Maybe not. But between him and 'lurching Lenny' behind me I've got enemy eyes and ears just waiting for me to screw up."

"I thought you and Blatchley were buddies."

"We were—or at least I thought so, until apparently I didn't deliver what he wanted."

"You will tonight, once the adrenaline starts pumping." He grasped her left hand and eyed the painful looking indentations the strings had made on the pads of her fingers. "Meanwhile, give it a rest, or your fingers will start bleeding. This opera's already bloody enough."

She didn't need to look. "I hate to admit it, but you're right."

Larry gave her an affectionate kiss. "Wow, an actual acknowledgment of my wisdom. I knew if I waited long enough, it would happen."

"Don't push your luck." Sighing, Julia placed her violin in its case. Then she kissed him back.

ഇഗ

The opening night performance was going surprisingly well—better than Julia had hoped or anticipated. She knew from the appreciative shuffles and murmurs of her orchestra colleagues—Lenny excepted—that her solos were impeccable. But she was not at all shocked that Blatchley showed no acknowledgment or recognition of her efforts.

*I don't care. I know I hit them out of the park.*

Matt was his usual supportive self. "You sound gorgeous, Julia."

"Thanks. This story still spooks me, though."

"You think this is bad? They once did an opera here by Penderecki, based on a Huxley novel, called *The Devils of Loudun.* It was so sadistic, so sensationalistic, depraved and obscene, that it made *Lulu* seem like the story of a saint."

"Oh, great." Julia shivered. "Thanks for putting things in perspective for me, Matt."

"My pleasure," Matt said, smiling as always.

As the evening progressed, Julia allowed herself a glimpse of the twilight sky, lit with ribbons of orange and rose. She had seen countless photos of the miraculous Santa Fe sunsets emblazoning the expanse over the opera house, but the reality was even more stunning. Julia had to admit that even the dazzling crystal chandeliers rising toward the Met ceiling at the beginning of performances couldn't rival the magnificence of nature's effects in this unique outdoor setting.

The heavens darkened, and the third act of *Lulu* progressed inexorably to its violent end. Julia caught a brief glimpse of the blood-red sky. She couldn't help but think about the irony and appropriateness of its color.

A sudden gust, and the resultant whoosh of the white baffles just outside the theatre resisting the wind, made her uneasy. But a flash of lightning tearing through the crimson firmament sent tremors through her. She had heard about precipitous changes in Santa Fe weather, and how a small streak of lightning could portend a huge storm about to hit. She became more nervous when rumbling in the distance grew closer, and then resounded with a violent crack.

"That was the thunderclap from hell, right on cue," Matt murmured to her. "We're in for it. Good thing we have clips on our music to keep it from taking off in the wind."

Julia nodded. Drawing her eyes back to her music, she peeked at the stage out of the corner of her eye. Just as Jack the Ripper appeared, a bolt of lightning slashed through the sky, followed by a huge clap of thunder and the heavens opening in torrents of driving rain.

Julia gasped, terrified. Stewart glared at her. She gave him a look of apology.

"Lightning strikes at Jack the Ripper's entrance? How is that kind of timing even possible?" Julia whispered to Matt.

"It happens more often than you think here," Matt whispered back. "It seems to go with the territory. Once, in a performance of *Don Giovanni,* lightning struck just as the Commendatore's statue appeared onstage. That's the kind of 'magic' that happens here."

Julia shuddered. That was the kind of "magic" she could do without. Thunder and lightning accompanying disembodied statues' entrances onstage. Strange apparitions visible in the late afternoon sun. What was next?

The downpour ceased almost as abruptly as it had begun. Julia braced herself for the brutal *dénouement* of the opera, marveling at Marin's convincing declaration of her passionate love for the recalcitrant, clearly unlovable Emilia.

*"Lass mich nur einmal, zum letzten Mal du deinem Herzen sprechen! Erbarm dich mein!"*

[One last time, let me speak to your Heart! Have pity on mine!]

Marin fell into a delirious faint. Emilia and Goran, as Lulu and Jack the Ripper, edged toward each other on stage.

Goran: *"Wer ist das?"* [Who is that?]

Emilia: *"Meine Schwester! Sie ist verrückt."* [My sister! She is insane!]

*"Verrückt? Du sheinst einen schönen Mund zu haben."* [Insane? You have a beautiful mouth.]

*"Den hab ich von meiner Mutter!"* [I got it from my mother.]

*"Das sieht man! Wieviel willst du?"* [That is evident! How much do you want?]

Julia knew the rest of the negotiation scene dialogue by heart from the libretto she had studied:

Jack, suspicious of Lulu's wish for him to stay all night, tries to leave. He tells her he has no time to spend the night, nor enough money. Lulu protests that she needs only a token payment. Even half what she wants is too much, he tells her. Geschwitz tries to protect Lulu, clearly not her sister, but rather her beloved. "Poor creature," says Jack.

Despite having to play an especially impassioned violin melody, Julia managed to steal a furtive glance at the mesmerized audience without Stewart's noticing. Then she steeled herself for the final stage horror and played her heart out in the remaining passages, all the while listening to the music with a keen ear and visualizing the action:

A weary Lulu leads Jack offstage. He insists they not bring any light; the moon is bright enough. Lulu swears this is the last time she will enroll herself in this enterprise. The two move off into darkness, as Geschwitz languishes onstage.

Despite knowing that the violence was mere play-acting, Julia couldn't help gasping when she heard Emilia's far-too realistic shrieks emanate from the wings: "*Nein! Nein! Nein, nein!*" [No! No! No, no!].

Julia swallowed hard when Goran returned to the stage, declaring, "*Das war ein Stück Arbeit!*" [That was a piece of work!] and plunging his stage knife into Marin.

Marin cries, "*Lulu! Mein engel! Lass dich noch einmal sehn!*" [Lulu! My angel! Let me see you once more!] and staggers into the wings.

Jack pours wine from a bottle onto the knife and his hands to wash off the blood, returning his knife to his inside pocket, as the final, anguished chords resound to Marin's last off-stage words: "*Ich bin dir nah! Bleibe dir nah! Im Ewigkeit!*" [I am close! Stay close! For eternity!]

But as the curtain fell, Julia heard more shrieks emitting from the wings.

Shrieks that were too hair-raising to be part of the staging. Shrieks that could be heard over the roaring applause from the audience.

And she knew something was terribly wrong.

## Chapter 11

*L'impresa compier deve il delitto poichè col sangue s'inagurò*
The enterprise by crime must end, since with blood it was begun
~ Verdi, *Macbeth,* Act 1

To Julia, the next moments seemed suspended in time. The audience kept applauding in anticipation of the curtain calls, but none came. After a minute or two, the curtain swished to a close. The applause stopped, and patrons began murmuring amongst themselves.

Stewart had left the pit to go onstage for his bow. Julia, confused and not knowing what to do, looked to Matt for help but he seemed equally bewildered.

Then her cell phone buzzed softly. She plucked it from her handbag and stared at the text message pulsating on the screen. It was from Marin. *"Julia help me! In trouble. Come to wings."*

Alarmed, Julia turned to Matt. "I have to go. Could you put my violin in the cage?"

"Sure, but what—"

"I'll tell you later," Julia said. "My case is on the violin shelf. The blue one with the purple ribbon attached to the handle."

"Not to worry, I'll make sure it's safe."

She thrust her violin at him. "I know you will."

Clutching her phone, she raced out the door.

ℵ

Behind the curtain, the scene was chaotic. The screams had stopped. Salman and Harold simultaneously accosted Goran.

"Where is Emilia? Where is Marin? Why haven't they come onstage for their bows?" Salman demanded.

"I don't know," said Goran, his expression panicked. "It's not like Emilia to forgo her shining moment."

Then Marin staggered on stage, her face ashen, a large knife dripping with blood gripped in her palm.

Salman accosted her. "Where is Emilia? Why isn't she here?"

Marin, breathing heavily, opened her mouth to speak, but no words came out.

"Marin," Goran said, "What the hell—"

"She's dead," Marin said finally.

"Well of course she is," Salman said. "But if she thinks she can keep the audience waiting while she milks her moment, she has another thing coming. Now go tell her they will leave if she doesn't get here immediately—"

"N-no," Marin stammered. "She's…really…dead."

"What?" Goran rushed offstage. A piercing cry of, "Oh my God!" came from the wings. Salman and Harold raced toward it. Marin stood motionless for moment. Then she slowly followed them.

ꟽ

Meanwhile, Alan appeared onstage in front of the closed curtain. "Ladies and gentlemen," he announced. "There will be no curtain calls tonight. Please accept our apologies. Thank you."

Alan watched as the audience members, some grumbling, some murmuring in confusion, left the theatre. He gestured to the players in the pit. "Please wait there until instructed further."

He surveyed the confused musicians' expressions. Then he rushed backstage.

ꟽ

In the wings, Salman and Harold stared, incredulous, at Goran kneeling over Emilia's lifeless, blood-soaked form.

Marin's eyes glazed over. The knife tumbled from her hand and clattered to the floor.

Salman confronted her. "My God, Marin, what have you done?"

Marin struggled to regain her composure. "What have *I* done?" She stared, trancelike, at the red stains on her hands and dress. "I haven't done anything. I…I just found her, like that. Blood everywhere…" She fell to her knees.

Goran turned to face Marin. "Where did that knife come from, Marin?"

"I don't know. When I went offstage to sing my last line, I found it there. Next to her…body."

She began to sob. Goran rose and squeezed her shoulder. "Marin, calm down, for God's sake."

Stewart appeared and strode over to them, red-faced and ready for a battle. He stopped short when he saw the bloody scene before him. "What is going on here?" he said, tight-lipped.

"Clearly there's been a murder," Salman said.

"What?" Stewart peered at the blood stains on Marin's clothing. Seeing Emilia's body he gasped.

"Marin found her," Goran said.

"Or perhaps Marin killed her," Salman said grimly.

"Call 911," Stewart said.

Hands shaking, Harold extracted his cell phone from his pocket and dialed.

ꕥ

Julia turned up on the scene to see Marin on her knees, weeping. She rushed to her sobbing friend, knelt by her and clutched her shoulders, as Marin moaned.

"Julia! Oh, Julia!"

"Marin, what happened?"

"I didn't do it," Marin said. "I swear. I didn't do it."

"Do what?" Lifting her eyes from Marin's tear-stained face, Julia caught sight of the knife at Marin's feet and Emilia's bloodied form on the floor. "Oh, my God!"

Julia looked toward stage right to see Alan approaching from the wings. As he took in the scene before him, his face paled.

Harold hurried to Alan's side. "Thank God you're here. Things are pretty out of hand."

"I can see that. It's good you called me. The police?"

Harold nodded. "On their way."

The sound of clicking heels drew everyone's attention to a striking figure striding toward the stage from the wings.

The taps on her cowboy boots reverberated loudly on the bare floor as she approached the group. She wore a Santa Fe Police Department badge on her jacket, beside a video body cam.

"Who's in charge here?" she asked in a husky voice, her steely eyes surveying the scene.

"I am." Alan walked over to her. "Alan Reynolds, general manager of The Santa Fe Opera. And you are…?"

"Detective Stella Peregrine, SFPD," Stella replied, shaking his hand.

Stella's eyes fixed on Emilia's body, Marin and the knife, and Julia next to her. She slipped a latex glove onto her hand and carefully picked up the knife, placing it in a labeled plastic evidence bag, then sealing it. She turned toward the direction from which she had entered. "Grabowski, get over here."

A short, tousle-haired, wiry man in his early thirties sauntered over to the detective.

Stella handed the evidence bag to the young man and turned back to Alan. "This is my partner, Constantin Grabowski."

Alan shook Constantin's hand. "Alan Reynolds, general manager of the Opera."

"When did this incident occur, Mr. Reynolds?" asked Stella.

"At the end of the opera. There's a murder scene. Actually, several murder scenes in this particular opera."

Stella raised her eyebrows. "Oh?"

"But this…this incident happened during the *dénouement* at the end."

"I see." Stella looked around at the group surrounding her. "Who found the body?"

Salman pointed an accusing finger at Marin. "She did. Marin Crane. And she was holding the knife, too. She had it in for Emilia."

"Let's not get ahead of ourselves. There'll be time enough for all that when we interrogate everyone." Stella leaned over Emilia's body and scanned the damage. "Multiple stab wounds to the abdomen. Looks like she bled out." Stella turned to her partner. "CSU on their way?"

Constantin nodded in the direction of the stage. "They're here."

The CMI team entered, pushing through the gaggle of company members that had gathered onstage.

Stella turned to Chief Medical Investigator Nick Pleasance. "Thanks for getting here so fast, Nick."

"Light traffic night." Nick knelt beside Emilia's body. "Stab wounds are very fresh."

"It just happened. At the end of the opera, I'm told."

Nick grimaced. "They say opera can kill you."

"Evidently," said Stella, fighting a smile. With company members standing around, many looking shocked, the grim humor she might indulge in to deal with the horror of violent crime was absolutely not appropriate here.

The CSU techs began photographing the scene. Of the DNA and prints they would collect, some were routinely sent to the forensics lab in Las Cruces. Ultimately it was Stella's responsibility to make a case, so she watched them for a moment to make sure the team was on the ball. It was a good team, but they didn't get a case like this very often.

"Good news is, we have the weapon." Stella nodded toward Constantin. "Make sure they send it to the lab ASAP."

Constantin handed the enveloped knife to a female tech. Nick continued his examination of Emilia's body.

Stella turned to Alan. "Who else is still here, Mr. Reynolds?"

"Pretty much everyone. Stagehands, costume and wig people, singers. They're all onstage. Musicians are in the pit."

"We'll need as much space as possible to question all these folks. Do you have a large enough room to accommodate them all?"

"Of course. Stieren Hall, where the orchestra rehearses, should be spacious enough. There's also an orchestra lounge. I'll call the personnel manager and ask her to meet us there."

Stella faced her partner. "Grabowski, gather up everyone hanging out over there onstage for questioning."

The techs continued their work. Stella narrowed her eyes at the young woman clutching the quaking Marin. "And nobody leaves."

As she watched the woman help Marin up off the floor, Stella was impressed at her gentleness and look of concern.

Julia reached into her pocket, pulled out the cloth she always kept there to clean the rosin off her violin strings, and thrust it at Marin. "Here, use this for…the blood."

Marin mechanically wiped her hands. Stella gripped Marin's arm firmly and appropriated the bloodied cloth. "Grabowski, bag this hankie. Ms. Crane, you come with me. Lead the way, Mr. Reynolds."

Julia flinched as Stella pried Marin from her protective grasp. She was reluctant to let Marin go, as if relinquishing her grip on her friend would leave Marin vulnerable to the cruel realities of the cold, unfeeling world outside the protective shell of the opera house. She was horrified at the violent, shocking murder that had taken place; but she was equally convinced that Marin was blameless. And terrified that something terrible was about to happen to her..

Shaking from fear, Julia dutifully trailed behind Goran, Salman, Stewart and Harold as they followed Alan. She opened her phone and texted hurriedly,.feeling thankful that Larry was in the audience.

*"Larry. Come to the orchestra lounge. Need you…It's happened again!"*

## Chapter 12

*E tu va, fruga ogni angolo, raccogli ogni traccia*
And you, search every corner, track down every clue
~ Puccini, *Tosca,* Act 1

When Stella took a close look around the orchestra lounge, she saw a generous-sized room with several large grey sofas, two placed back to back and one positioned a few feet away. Grey metal lockers lined two of the walls, along with a bulletin board with posted announcements, mailboxes and a spacious galley with numerous cabinets, a sink and a coffee machine. One set of cabinets was placed above a countertop beneath a window that looked out over a hillside.

Stella watched as Goran, Salman, Stewart, Harold and Julia filed in behind Alan. "Nice space you've got here, Mr. Reynolds."

"Thank you. We've recently expanded it."

"The orchestra people are spoiled," Harold said.

"No, they're not." Sarah came to Alan's side. "They work tirelessly, and they're here all the time. It's the least they deserve."

Stella was not surprised to see Julia flash a gratified look in Sarah's direction. She had never belonged to a union, but Stella was familiar enough with management-worker relationships to know that on the whole, management tended to underappreciate workers' contributions, whatever the circumstances.

"Detective Peregrine, this is our personnel manager, Sarah Gruen."

"Pleased to meet you, Ms. Gruen." Stella peered around the space. At the far end of the lounge beyond a row of lockers, in a semi-darkened corner, she spied a table and two chairs. That might be doable for most of the interviewees. Behind closed doors would be better for Marin Crane.

"Would that table and chairs do?" Sarah asked.

"Do you have anything more… private?"

Sarah pointed out several doors, some with small windows in them. Taped to one door was a printed sign that read: "Orchestra Library." Yet another read, "Percussion Room." Stella's eyes narrowed when she read the sign posted on a more remote one: "DANGER! Harp Tuning Room."

"'DANGER?' What's with that?" Stella asked.

"Musicians' humor."

"I see." Stella resisted another smile. Still not appropriate. But good to know musicians dealt with stress in a similar way. "The table in the corner over there will work just fine for the most part. I would like a more private space for Ms. Crane."

"Which room would you prefer?"

"Any one will do. Though I think it would be best to avoid the 'dangerous' one."

"Of course." Sarah unlocked and opened the Orchestra Library door. Stella escorted Marin inside.

"I'll stay here in the lounge, Detective, in case you need me," Sarah said.

"After I show your partner the way to Stieren Hall, Detective Peregrine," Alan added, "I'll come back and wait here in the lounge, too, in case there's anything else you need."

"Thank you both."

Alan gestured to Constantin, who shepherded a large group of other company members. "Please follow me."

After the group had filed out, Stella turned to face Goran, Salman, Harold, Stewart and Julia. "Hang out here until I'm ready for you."

Stella waited to make sure they found spaces on the sofas, and watched as they sat down and took out their cell phones. Then she escorted Marin inside the Orchestra Library.

ꕤ

Stella guided Marin to a chair before a table and sat down on the opposite side. "Okay, Ms. Crane, can you tell me what happened?"

"What…happened?" Marin avoided Stella's gaze, instead staring down at the bloodstains on her now-wrinkled costume and twisting the material in her shaky fingers. "I…I can't remember."

Marin's lack of eye contact immediately raised Stella's suspiciouns. "Surely you can. It only just happened."

Marin managed to talk, but very slowly and disjointedly. "I just remember I was…I was trying to sing. At the end of the act. Then..." Marin fidgeted again.

"Go on," Stella said. Marin definitely was hiding something.

Marin stared into the distance. "Goran, the baritone. He murders Lulu in the story, offstage, with a stage knife. I hear screams. Then Goran comes back on stage, stabs me with the same knife. I run offstage to see Lulu one last time. When I get there…I see…oh, God."

"What did you see?"

"Blood. Blood, everywhere. And this big knife. A *real* knife. Covered with…blood."

"And you picked it up. Why?"

"I don't know. I was just…scared."

Stella peered at Marin's distraught face, unsure whether to believe her. She had never met an opera singer, but as an aficionado of "straight" theatre, she knew that thespians were highly skilled at putting on an act. She assumed opera singers possessed similar expertise.

"Did you see anyone else lurking around at all?"

"No, no one. All I could see was…blood." Marin broke down, her body quaking with sobs.

Despite her doubts as to whether or not Marin was telling the truth, Stella couldn't help but feel a fragment of sympathy for the stressed-out singer. "Let's take a break. I'll be back shortly. Don't go anywhere."

Stella peered at Marin's helpless form. Her order to stay put was superfluous. Clearly the poor woman was not about to move anywhere, anytime soon.

## Chapter 13

*Ora a te...pesa le tue risposte*
Now, as for you...weigh your answers well
~ Puccini, *Tosca,* Act 1

As Julia waited her turn to be questioned, the text messages on her phone came in precipitously.

Larry: "Julia, where are you?" ["*Orchestra lounge. Waiting for you.*"]

Katie: "Julia, I'm holed up in Stieren Hall with the orchestra. What's happening? Are you okay? They won't tell us anything" ["*Not okay. Emilia's been murdered. I'm waiting to be interrogated.*"]

Katie: "WHAT?? I'm coming straight over." [*NO. They won't let you. Wait till I find you later. I CAN'T BELIEVE THIS IS HAPPENING AGAIN.*"]

Katie: "OMG. Need to see you ASAP." [*Nothing I can do. WAIT FOR ME.* ☹]

Larry: "Opera house on lockdown. Will have to wait for you outside." [☹]

ꕤ

Stella left Marin hunched over the table, closed the door behind her and approached the two back-to-back sofas where Stewart, Harold, Goran and Julia waited to be questioned. She approached Alan, who was seated on the third sofa, and gestured toward Goran, who was still in costume. "Is that the baritone?"

"Yes," Alan said. "Goran Řezníček."

Stella motioned at Goran to follow her to the table in the corner at the end of the room, where she placed the chairs opposite each other. Goran courteously pulled one out for Stella and sat down in the other.

"You were Emilia's leading man?"

"Not the only one. In this opera the lead soprano—Lulu—has many men, many lovers."

"Oh, really?" Stella scrutinized his expression, looking for signs of avoidance. There were none. "Which one are you?"

Goran said. "The one who murders her.."

"Really." His offhand manner made Stella wary. "Would you tell me how that plays out?"

"In the last scene, I go offstage with Lulu and stab her to death. With a fake knife, of course."

"Of course. When you went offstage to 'murder' Emilia, did you see anyone else back there?"

"No. I just did the deed, she screamed, '*Nein, nein!*'—that's 'No, no!' in German—and then I went back onstage to 'stab' Marin—Marin and Emilia are lovers in the story, by the way—and Marin rushed offstage to Lulu's aid. The next thing I knew, Marin was screaming her head off. Then she came back onstage. Holding a *real* knife… dripping with blood."

"How did you react?"

"I was in shock. We all were." Goran shook his head. "I myself was devastated. Devastated."

As with Marin, Stella was skeptical. Goran seemed genuinely distressed, yet she was having a hard time determining whether he was telling the truth or whether he was giving the performance of his life. She was beginning to think opera singers were more difficult to read than any other witnesses she had ever interviewed.

"Did Emilia and Marin have conflicts?"

"Everyone had conflicts with Emilia. We all respected her voice, her talent. I myself adored her. But frankly, she was impossible to work with. Much of the time. Grated on everyone's nerves and she complained about everyone and everything."

"Like what—or who?"

"She grumbled about her wigs, her costumes, her shoes. Her co-stars—except for me. I was the only one she got along with," Goran said. "The lighting, the sets. Everything under the sun bothered her. The first time she sang here, a particularly strong gust of wind from the Sangre de Cristo Mountains blew a clump of gravel into her mouth while she was singing. You can well imagine how she reacted to that."

Stella tried to conjure up such a scenario in her mind's eye. She would have liked to be there to see that. "What about this time, the *Lulu* rehearsals?"

At the dress rehearsal, she criticized Salman—the director—mercilessly," Goran said. "Basically said he was incompetent."

"I see, and how did he respond to that?"

"Well, he didn't like it, of course. He said something about her attitude making even more enemies than she already had."

"Sounds like she had a lot of them."

"Perhaps. But Emilia didn't want to share the limelight with anybody, least of all her enemies.

Stella thought she perceived a tone of disdain in Goran's statement. Perhaps he wasn't as adoring of Emilia as he had claimed to be. "And Marin was one of them?"

"Emilia really pushed Marin's buttons in a huge way. And Marin made sure everyone knew it."

"Do you know of any reason why Marin would do harm to Emilia? Did she ever threaten Emilia directly?"

Goran hesitated for a long moment. For the first time since the interview started, Stella thought she detected a chink in his acting armor. "I...I might have heard her say something vaguely to that effect at some point."

"Do you remember what it was?"

"No, not specifically."

"I see." Stella gave Goran a long, hard look. "Don't go anywhere, in case you remember any more details. Thank you for your help."

"Of course."

Stella rose. Goran gallantly leapt up, pulled out her chair, walked back to the sofa and sat down. Stella gestured at Salman. "You're next."

ꟸ

True to Alan's description, Stieren Hall was an immense space, a long and vast gallery with windows that reached almost to the top of the high ceilings. A set of a dozen or so tall screens stood at one end of the hall. Fortunately, chairs from a recent orchestra rehearsal were still lined up. Constantin marshalled the gathering of company members into them. He gazed at the sea of faces and took a deep breath. No use trying to assess numbers. There seemed to be too many to count.

"Who wants to be first?"

A young man stood up. "Steve Cañon, head stagehand."

Constantin indicated two chairs and pulled them to the far edge of the stand of screens, out of earshot from the others. Steve walked over and sat down. Constantin was glad to see Steve looking him straight in the eye. That was always a good sign. At least this guy seemed willing to cooperate.

"Where were you when the…incident occurred?" Constantin asked.

"We generally hang out by B-Lift—that's the elevator at the back door of the house that moves up and down. We always wait there at the end of the show. For the call to strike the set."

"'Strike the set?'"

"That's 'stagehand speak' for taking the set down and moving it out when the show finishes to make room for the next opera."

"Thanks for the explanation. "I don't know much about opera," Constantin said.

"You're not alone. Most people don't." Steve smiled. "Until John Crosby founded this company, no one else here cared about it, either."

Constantin frowned. Too much information about the history of the company would muddy the waters. He needed to keep things on track. "When you got backstage, did you see anything weird going on? Anyone who shouldn't be there?"

"Not really," said Steve. "It's usually mobbed back there. But not at the end of this opera."

"What's different about this opera?"

"Well, there's no chorus, and the set is what they call minimalist. Very little to move around. When it's near the end, we—I mean the stagehands, of course—"

"Of course."

"We don't come back to the stage until we get the call."

"Okay, let me get this straight..." Constantin furrowed his brow, trying to picture what the stagehand was describing. "Then you weren't actually backstage when the incident occurred?"

"Nope," Steve said. "And we didn't think anything of the screams. We knew they were part of the show."

Constantin was skeptical. "And you didn't think it was strange not to get the call?"

"Actually, yeah, but it can happen occasionally. So, when we didn't get the call, we just went backstage when we heard the applause."

"What happened then?"

"We came onstage to strike the set. Then we heard screams. And we saw Marin in the wings, and all that blood. And she just kept screaming. That's when we knew something was amiss."

"How did everyone react?"

"Well, let's just say Emilia didn't have a lot of fans, at least among people in the company. She was difficult to work with. But still, no one would have ever thought this kind of thing could happen. To anybody. We were all kind of in shock."

"I can only imagine. And all hell broke loose after that?"

"Well, actually, no. Everyone just stood there on stage, gawking."

This was not the response Constantin expected. "That's kind of... strange, isn't it?"

"Maybe, maybe not. You never know how you're going to react in these situations. It wasn't till management—director, stage manager, conductor, along with that violinist, Julia—came rushing in. That's when things got chaotic."

"And...'that' violinist, Julia. What was she doing there?"

"Seems Julia and Marin are friends, and Marin had sent her an urgent text."

"Hold on." Constantin was beginning to think opera performers were the strangest life forms he had ever encountered. "The singer actually had her phone with her? In a performance?"

"Even singers can't live without them. They always manage to find a pocket somewhere in their costume. Ringer off, of course."

Constantin paused to tap some notes into his own phone. His screen was getting crowded with names and information. He would have to organize it all. Later. "And Julia. How do you know her?"

"We met on her first day here. I showed her around a bit when she was trying to find her way around the theatre. But I don't really know her," Steve grinned. "Though personally, I wouldn't mind. That is, if her boyfriend wasn't watching her like Papa Bear."

"Her boyfriend?"

"Yeah. He's a NYPD cop."

"Really?" This investigation was getting weirder by the minute. "A NYPD cop in Santa Fe?"

"He's just along for the ride while she plays in the orchestra. Or so they told me. Nice work if you can get it."

"I agree. Thanks for your time. You were very helpful."

"Sure. No biggie."

Steve stood up, walked back to the group waiting in the chairs and sat back down.

Constantin scratched some more notes into his smartphone, mumbling to himself. He generally wasn't the type of detective to feel easily threatened, but having a New York cop in their midst felt like he and his SFPD colleagues were being put on notice—something like what it might feel if a New York Yankee pitcher were trying to infiltrate the Boston Red Sox dugout.

"NYPD cop. Humph."

## Chapter 14

*Ohne Zweifel, wird er wieder tausend Fragen an mich stellen*
Without doubt, he will have a thousand more questions to ask me
~ Beethoven, *Fidelio,* Act 2

SALMAN SAT OPPOSITE STELLA. SHE WATCHED CLOSELY AS HE FIDGETED with his ascot. Nervous squirming in a witness frequently meant he had something to hide, or was avoiding the truth.

"About Emilia and Marin. It seems they were at odds with each other?" Stella said.

"Yes, yes," Salman said. "Extremely."

"Care to explain?"

Salman avoided Stella's gaze. Lack of eye contact was another sign of hedging.

"Marin was always accusing Emilia of acting like she was the only diva in the company and made it clear how much she resented being eclipsed by Emilia's importance—or should I say, sense of entitlement."

"You mean Marin wanted the spotlight? Maybe to even take it away from Emilia?"

Salman kept looking down. "Exactly."

His continued avoidance of looking directly at her made Stella suspect he really was hiding something. "Is it true you threatened Emilia during the dress rehearsal?"

At this, Salman finally raised his eyes. "I'm sorry, I didn't hear the question. Could you repeat that?"

"I asked if you threatened Emilia." The bead of sweat forming at Salman's brow confirmed Stella's suspicions. At first she thought he had seemed distracted. Now he looked totally panicked.

"What? You're seriously asking me that? Who told you I threatened her?"

"Just answer the question," Stella said.

"Okay. I admit her attitude made me mad. And…" He lowered his voice to a near whisper. "I…might have said something about her making more enemies than she already had. But I did *not* threaten her. The conductor, he—*he* threatened to replace her. In rehearsal, he told Harold to tell her as much."

"Blatchley? Why would he do that?"

"She was habitually late. He'd had enough."

Stella thought for a moment. Salman was being defensive. And he had motive. But whether he actually had opportunity remained to be seen. She would have to revisit this witness later, after discussing his interview with Constantin.

"I see." Stella rose. "We're done for now. But don't go far."

After Salman had walked off, Stella saw Alan perched on the sofa closest to the Orchestra Library and sat next to him.

"Mr. Reynolds, if you don't mind..."

Alan looked up from his iPad, on which he was perusing a digital version of Opera News. "Yes?"

Aware of the others close by, Stella spoke softly. "Is it true Emilia gave everyone a lot of grief?"

"There's no denying she was a diva in every sense. She was not, shall we say, hugely popular."

"How did you feel about her?"

"Detective Peregrine," Alan said, snapping shut the cover of his digital device, "Let me tell you something about being general director of an opera company. Since opera first began, people in my position have been dealing with artists who have a huge sense of self. It goes with the territory. I'm used to coddling people like Emilia. Stroking their egos, dealing with their self-esteem issues and self-images. It's my job to make sure they perform optimally, because ultimately, it's my responsibility to make sure we fill seats. We have an expression in German, "*Die liebe brennt.*" Basically, it means, 'No love lost.' I neither liked nor disliked Emilia. I simply put up with whatever behavior she felt compelled to inflict upon me, for the greater good of the company. Does that answer your question?"

Stella thought Alan's explanation was impressively succinct, if a bit glib. It was almost as if he had rehearsed his speech for a performance. Still, she couldn't find fault with his logic. He seemed like a pretty upstanding guy. "Yes. Totally. Thank you."

"Excellent. If you need anything else, please don't hesitate."

Alan reopened the iPad cover and went back to his reading. Stella motioned Stewart to follow her to the corner table. They sat down. She regarded the impeccably turned out man for a moment as she pulled out her iPad Mini.

"First, is it proper to address you as Maestro?"

"Yes," Stewart answered. "That's fine."

"Okay, Maestro, tell me. Did you have a difficult time working with Emilia?"

"Everyone did. I was no different, except that my main concern is how she performs her music. Nothing else."

"And yet, I'm told you threatened to replace her."

"Yes. That's true. But it wasn't exactly a threat," Stewart said. "I was just stating a fact. Diva tantrums are one thing, but when it comes to habitual lateness, I always make it clear that it will not be tolerated, not even from the so-called 'star' in a cast. That kind of behavior undermines the other singers, the conductor, the director and everyone else involved in trying to create art on the stage."

"How far would you go to protect everyone else's interest?"

"All the way to the general director, if necessary."

At that moment, Alan looked up. Stella watched intently as he and Stewart exchanged glances. There was something in their regard that hinted at collusion; almost as if they had rehearsed their speeches together for consistency. But for what reason?

Stella quickly tapped a note into her device.

*Reynolds, Blatchley. Something to hide?*

Then she hurried back to Marin.

## Chapter 15

*Fia lunga, sta notte*
It's going to be a long night.
~ Verdi, *Rigoletto, Act I*

WHEN STELLA OPENED THE DOOR TO THE ORCHESTRA LIBRARY, SHE SAW Marin seated on the edge of her chair, her wig in her lap. Spying the fistful of wig hairs at Marin's feet, Stella gathered that the singer had been pulling hairs out of the hairpiece, probably from worry or trepidation. Her impression was confirmed when Marin literally jumped out of her chair.

"Did I startle you, Marin?"

"I…I didn't see you coming."

Stella set a hot cup of coffee before the trembling singer. "Here," she said. "This will help." She delicately took the wig from Marin and set it aside as she resumed her own chair.

Marin stared at the cup, not drinking.

"So," Stella said. "I'm hearing Emilia was pretty hard to get along with. And people are saying you were jealous of her. Is that true?"

Marin's breathing started to come in shallow gasps. "No…I mean… yes, I had a hard time getting along with her. Everyone did. She was so full of herself."

To Stella, Marin clearly was more nervous—and, given her palpable animosity toward Emilia, probably had more to lose—than Salman, Alan and Stewart combined. "What about you, specifically? Did you feel like you wanted to share her limelight? Or maybe even take it away from her?"

"What? No, no, I would never—"

Stella sat back in her chair. She had heard such protests countless times before, and she was skeptical. "It's an emotional opera. In the heat of the night's drama, maybe you just lost it? Or maybe even planned it, kept a knife backstage because you couldn't bear it any longer?"

"I couldn't do anything so vile, not for anything!" Marin cried. "Yes, I resented her stardom. And I hated the despicable way she treated me. But I could never kill anyone! Ask anybody. Ask Julia!"

There was that name again. Julia. Stella realized that questioning the violinist would have to be her next priority.

"I'll do that, Marin. Meanwhile, sit tight."

ꟷ

In Stieren Hall, Constantin had interviewed another stagehand and was now busy questioning Magda. Her accent gave him pause. He was accustomed to interviewing witnesses with all kinds of accents but had never met anyone whose first language was Hungarian. To make sure he understood every word, he had to pay extra close attention.

"What is your job at the Opera?"

"I am costume director. I make sure all stage people have attire in good shape to look best. We must get to know the singers. We know each one very, very well."

"Oh? In what ways do you 'know' them?"

"We are, as you say, up close and personal with them. We have conversations with them, sometimes before they come here. About their special needs."

Given what he had learned from Steve about the personality quirks of singers, Constantin was not surprised. "What kind of needs?"

"In meetings, singers confide, how you say, self-esteem difficulties, sometimes with voice, sometimes with appearance. If they do not feel confident about voice or new role, it spills out in closed room with very quiet, intimate atmosphere where they have to talk about their character and their body. We are close to them in terms of self-image."

"When you say 'we'—who are you referring to? Does someone else work directly with you on the singers' needs?"

"Yes. Daniel Henderson. He is wig and makeup director."

Constantin tapped a note into his phone. *Speak to wig guy, Daniel, next.* "What was your relationship with Emilia?"

"Strictly professional," Magda said.

Constantin, who remembered Steve's assessment of company members' problems dealing with Emilia's foibles, was startled. "No conflicts? Or difficullties?"

"We all had difficulties with her. She was diva in every sense. Fussed over everything, demanded everything, expected to get what she wanted. She complained if something not fitting right. But it is my job to make singer comfortable onstage, whatever character they play. Even if director makes them ugly. Everyone understands that is how it goes in opera."

"If that's how it goes, then why would someone kill her?"

Magda shrugged. "Who can say? It is excessively stressed environment. Emotions run high one moment, low the next. Tempers flare. Rivalries common. Affairs too. Some people cannot control their emotions."

"I gather you're not one of them?"

"I survive Communist-era Hungary. I learn to keep my passions in check. Otherwise, I get into trouble."

The Communist era was something Constantin had only studied in history class, and his years at the Police Academy had pretty much obliterated any memories of mid-twentieth century events that had occurred before his birth. But being face to face with a witness to that history sparked his interest. "That must have been tough."

"It was. I escape to America with my little brother, Sandor. He is tenor." Magda pointed toward the group still awaiting interrogation, Sandor among them. He saw her and waved. "Every day we feel grateful to have job in opera."

"I can understand that." Constantin added a note to his phone: *Sandor.* "Where were you when Emilia was killed?"

"With wardrobe supervisor and wig person in dressing room area. At end of show we wait for singer to return to dressing room so we can remove costume and wig, send for clean."

"Did you see or hear anything unusual? Anyone lurking around who didn't belong there?"

"I see only stagehands and singers," Magda said. "I hear screams, but that is part of final opera scene. It did not seem anything wrong."

Constantin thought Magda's story was consistent with what Steve had told him. He was anxious to see if he would get a similar vibe from her brother. He had yet to interview any of the singers. "Thank you," Constantin said. "Please tell Sandor to come over here."

Constantin watched as Magda rose, walked over to Sandor and whispered to him. The grim glances exchanged between brother and sister as Sandor got up made Constantin even more keen to speak with the tenor. He just hoped Sandor's Hungarian accent was less pronounced than Magda's.

ꝏ

Meanwhile, Stella had walked through the orchestra lounge, bypassing the sofas where Julia and Stewart still waited, and strode through the French doors over to Stieren Hall. She stood inside the entrance, watched Constantin for a moment, then waved him over.

Constantin rose and approached Stella. "What's up?"

"Have you heard anything from Forensics?"

"Not yet."

"Let me know right away if you do."

"Sure."

"Anything interesting from the head stagehand guy?" Stella asked.

"That violinist, Julia. Her boyfriend is a NYPD cop. He came to Santa Fe with her."

"I hope he doesn't try to butt in."

"Doubtful. Those New York guys know their jurisdiction boundaries."

"You're right, I guess."

After Stella had returned to the lounge, Constantin found Sandor standing by the chairs. Constantin motioned to him to sit and scrutinized his coloring and build. With his barrel chest and light-colored hair, he saw little family resemblance between him and Magda. There was no accounting for the roll of genetic dice. "You're Magda's brother?"

"Yes."

"You're in this *Lulu* opera, too, right?"

"I play part of Lulu's lover," Sandor said. "One of many."

"Oh?" Constantin was beginning to understand why opera singers had so many eccentricities. Changing lovers from one opera to another was one thing. Being the object of affection for multiple men within the same opera was something else entirely. He wasn't familiar with many opera protagonists, but the one character he did know of, *Carmen*, changed lovers like some women changed underwear. Evidently so did Lulu. "Which of her many lovers do you play?"

"The one who truly loves her," Sandor replied. "I kill myself out of love for her."

Constantin took note of Sandor's troubled expression. His distress seemed genuine.

"Where were you when Emilia was stabbed?"

"Waiting in dressing room for my curtain call."

"Did anyone see you back there?"

"Magda. And Daniel, wig person."

Constantin flipped through his phone. This was the second mention of the wig director. He found his previous reminder, "check with wig person," and tapped in three asterisks beside it.

"How did you get along with Emilia?"

"I have no problem getting along with her."

"From what I've heard, you may be the only one."

"I get along with everyone. Especially women. I love beautiful women."

"That's good to know, but you must know of others who found her especially difficult to work with."

"Everybody complain about her. I don't care. I am just happy to have job singing. With her, or anyone else."

"You seem to be unique in that respect, Sandor." Constantin would have liked to spend more time with Sandor, but he felt he had a long way to go to make a substantial dent in his list of interviewees. "You're done for now but stay close by. Could you point out the wig person?"

Sandor rose, then pointed toward a portly man who was deep in conversation with the costume director. "That is him over there, next to Magda."

Constantin watched as Sandor approached Magda. Then sighing, texted Stella: *"It's going to be a long night."*

ꕥ

When Stella returned to the lounge, she gestured to Julia, whose eyes were fixed on her phone.

Stella cleared her throat to get Julia's attention. "You're Julia, right? Come with me."

"What?" Julia tapped a quick text into her phone, then looked up. "Sorry, I was—"

"You millennials, always glued to your screens," Stella said. "Think you can tear yourself away?"

Clutching her phone tightly, Julia rose and followed Stella to the table at the far end of the lounge. Stella regarded the pretty, petite young woman as they sat across from each other. She was possibly the youngest person in the company. And she was pale, shaken.

"What is your connection to Marin Crane?"

"We're friends," Julia said. "We worked together at the Met."

"How long have you known each other?"

"Not that long. We only just met in the middle of last season. But—"

"Yet you were onstage with her after the last scene?"

"Marin sent me a text, asking me to come."

Seeing Julia's creased forehead, Stella felt a bit rueful about following such a hard line of questioning. Unfortunately, in this situation, it was necessary. "Why would she text you?"

"She needed help," Julia said. "She's here all alone. She had no one else to turn to."

"And you didn't come to Santa Fe alone?"

"No. My partner, Larry, is here with me. He's—"

"A NYPD cop?"

"How did you know?"

"I'm a detective. I investigate, get information. It's what I do. You should know that—if your partner's a cop."

Julia blushed. "Y-yes. Of course."

Stella saw such distress in Julia's deer-in-the-headlights eyes, she was afraid the poor girl might break down completely. That was not a good thing. She softened her tone. "What did you see when you got to the stage, Julia? What kind of condition did you find Marin in?"

"I saw blood. Everywhere. And Marin… well, she was pretty hysterical. Understandably," Julia said. "She kept saying the same thing. Over and over."

"And what thing was that?"

"That she didn't do it."

Stella murmured under her breath. "'Methinks the lady doth protest too much.'"

"Excuse me?"

"Oh, sorry," Stella said. "I performed with A.R.T. when I was at Harvard Law. Shakespeare understood people so well. Sometimes he helps me think." She studied Julia's face, expecting to see confusion, but there was none. Perhaps Julia was too traumatized to connect the dots at the moment "Getting back to Marin. Did she ever confide in you about her feelings toward Emilia?"

"Well, actually, she…" Julia stopped mid-sentence. And fell silent.

"Answer the question, please. What did Marin say?" Stella paused. Despite her professional work ethic, she couldn't help feeling sympathy for this young girl. "Just tell the truth. Don't be afraid. It's better in the long run. For you—and for everybody."

"She…she did say once that…that Emilia felt threatened by her. But from what I'd heard, everything threatened or troubled Emilia. Everything and everyone. She was just paranoid."

"How did you know? Is that what Marin told you?"

"It was pretty much common knowledge. Even my orchestra colleagues told me so. On the very first day, actually."

"I see." Stella sensed she had pushed Julia as far as she could without causing a complete breakdown. It would have to do. For now. "Stick around, Julia. I may need to ask you more questions later."

"Okay." Julia rose. "Larry is outside. Is there any chance he could be let back in?"

"We'll see about that. For now, please go back and sit down."

Stella watched as Julia trudged back to the sofa and settled in. The girl was shaking. She had stopped questioning her just in time.

ꕥ

Aggravated at the thought of further grilling, Julia sank down wearily. Stella's relentless probing had upset whatever little remained of her equilibrium. The trauma elicited by the night's gruesome events had shaken Julia to her core. But it had also evoked terrible memories, the horror of which she had been trying to resist—memories of the night at the Met when her mentor, Abel, was murdered before her eyes.

She kept her eyelids tightly shut in an effort to avoid the images, but she no longer could hold back the emotional turmoil. The shocking scenario from that dreadful night still invaded her senses: *Abel, on the podium, conducting the assassination scene from Verdi's* Don Carlo*…a bullet striking him… Abel, collapsing from the podium onto the floor…Julia, jumping up from her orchestra chair, rushing to him, holding him in her arms as the life drained from his body, his blood staining her fingers…*

The feelings were all too familiar. They were not good. Not welcome.

Not at all.

## Chapter 16

*Sai quale oscura opra laggiù si compia?*
Are you aware of what dark work is done down there?
~ Puccini, *Tosca,* Act 2

DANIEL WAS PORTLY, CHEERFUL AND VOLUBLE. CONSTANTIN HOPED THAT would make him an easier interview than his two Hungarian ones. He would have liked to probe more deeply into their psyches. It was hard to peel back the layers underneath their surfaces. But there just wasn't time; there were too many others to question.

"What would you like to know, detective?" Daniel asked in a booming voice, suitable for the stage.

"You're the wig person?"

"Wig director. And makeup director."

"Where were you when the murder took place?"

"Do you mean the stage murder, or the actual one?"

Daniel's overly cavalier attitude made Constantin annoyed. "Just answer the question, please."

"I was in the dressing room area with Magda, waiting for the singers to come back, so we can remove their wigs."

"Is that a hard job?"

"It's labor intensive, but not as much as actually building the wigs. That's downright dangerous."

This was the first time Constantin had heard the word "danger" mentioned in any of his interviews. His attention became more acute. "How so?"

"We do use some tools that could be considered…hazardous. But most of the departments have at least a few of those."

"Could you describe some of these implements?"

"Well, we build the wigs out of human hair, by hand, and we use very sharp objects. Needles to tie the hair in, one by one, with thousands of knots. Or tiny little hooks you could do punctures with, and hardly even notice. Like the things they used in ancient Egypt to get the brains out of mummies," Daniel said. "If you drop one of those instruments and it goes into your leg or arm, you can really feel it when you have to rip it out. It definitely will tear your flesh."

Constantin winced.

"If that happens, you have to be really careful about pushing against it when pulling it out in order not to rip your leg or arm open," Daniel added.

Constantin glanced at Daniel's hands, which showed numerous cuts and scratches. "Is that how you get all those gashes? From working with those instruments?"

Daniel studied his numerous battle scars. "Yes. I guess you could say it's unavoidable."

"Sounds like your job is not only hard. It's also more than a little risky."

"It really is, sometimes. We work with a lot of toxic chemicals, too. Ninety-nine percent alcohol. Bleaches and colors for dyeing hair. We have to wear gloves with the acetone we use to clean the laces on the wigs. That substance seeps into your body." Daniel snickered. "We should get hazard pay."

Daniel's humor was lost on Constantin. Getting compensated for extra dangerous situations was a serious topic, frequently discussed among his colleagues. "Don't you use masks when you work with that stuff?"

"We should, in theory, but we don't always. With really fume-y things we go into the ventilation room. Then there are the wig dryers." Daniel pointed to a strange looking wooden box. "They actually go to fairly high heat. You could chop off someone's hand and dehydrate it in there."

Constantin swallowed hard. "What?"

"I'm speaking theoretically. Nothing like that ever happens, of course. This company is remarkably safe, more than most. We have yearly two-day safety seminars that everyone is required to attend, run by an industrial safety consultant. People in the audience don't know about these things, of course."

"For sure."

"With our schedule—we open two shows, one right after another, tech rehearsals every other night—people get tired, make mistakes. So we have to be careful and pay attention."

Constantin stole a glimpse of the clock on the wall opposite them. Time to focus on the matter at hand: the murder. "Let's talk about Emilia. How did you get along with her?" Constantin asked.

"Oh, she was a piece of work. A real trial to deal with."

At least Daniel was being consistent with his other colleagues' take on the deceased opera star. "In what way?"

"She gave new meaning to the phrase 'temper tantrum.' She had one in the room with me once, during a run of *Salome*."

Now they were getting somewhere. "What about?"

"She was habitually late. The director, someone a lot more high-powered than Salman, scolded her every time. At the final dress, Emilia came in five minutes before curtain and got onstage just as the curtain opened. The director told her, 'If you show up like this on opening night, you will be replaced.' When I got there the stage manager was getting impatient. He said, 'Will you be done in time?' I just said, 'I'm trying.'"

"That must have been annoying for you."

"Admittedly, yes. Meanwhile Emilia couldn't really yell at the director, so instead she had a fit, throwing stuff around the room, yelling, 'It's not my fault!'—at me. I just picked up my stuff, lobbed the head of John the Baptist onto the couch, said, 'O-kay,' and walked out. One of the other singers said to me, 'I guess I should behave.' I said, 'Yes, you should.'"

"Did you ever lose your cool?"

"Not really. I got used to it eventually. I still would never put up with it. But that kind of behavior is a very rare thing. Most of the singers are perfectly lovely. Onstage, certain divas still act out their own self-importance, like Emilia does. But that so-called ruling of the opera world by divas is mostly a thing of the past. They don't get away with it like they used to. Maybe in Europe but not here in the U.S.

There are remnants of it, but it's really the conductor and director who rule the roost. With all the fierce competition out there, and the conservatories churning out more and better singers, companies these days prefer to hire someone who seems to be a good colleague as well as able to handle new compositions that require a certain physicality. I still encounter a few nasty types, but I have ways of getting back at them—if need be."

Constantin leaned in more closely. "Oh? How?"

"Like when we do molds of the singer's head, kind of like a cast, for something like John the Baptist. That can be pretty unpleasant. The properties director has his own way, but I prefer to do it my way, where the entire head is covered with sheets that have plaster of Paris in them. The singer has to sit there for a long time, really still, with only straws in their nose to breathe. You can't be claustrophobic. So the singer had better be nice. Sopranos especially. Otherwise..." he grinned impishly. "If they give me grief, I could just plug up the straws. Not that I've ever done that, of course."

"Of course," Constantin said dryly. "Sounds like you're in a good position to get your revenge, if you wanted."

"Like I said, I have my ways. But none of them has ever involved murder."

"Let's hope so."

"I have no reason to lie. Trust me."

Constantin wasn't sure. It always brought his hackles up when someone used the words "Trust me." In his experience, it was a classic evasion tactic.

ꟾ

After she had dismissed Julia, Stella could see one of the CSU auxiliary officers waving at her from the other end of the lounge. He approached Stella and handed her a report sheet.

"Forensics came back, detective. I thought you'd want to see it right away."

Stella looked over the report, frowning.

"You're sure about this?"

"They checked and rechecked at the lab," the officer said. "They're absolutely sure."

"I see. Thanks."

Stella perused the report once more. The words on the page told all there was to know about the murder weapon. The knife revealed only one set of prints.

Marin's.

## Chapter 17

*Ma se reo soltanto è l'indizio che m'accusa?*
But what if the guilt is only in the clue that accuses me?
~ Verdi, *A Masked Ball,* Act 3

IN AN OPERA HOUSE, NEWS CUSTOMARILY TRAVELS AS RAPIDLY AS A California wildfire. Santa Fe's rumor grapevine was no exception. By the time Larry had managed to persuade the security guard that Julia needed his support, Julia already had heard that Marin was accused of Emilia's murder and been arrested. Larry appeared in the orchestra lounge to find Julia crumpled up on a sofa, her diminutive body quivering.

"No, no, no. This can't be," she moaned, shaking her head.

Larry sank down beside her and folded her in his arms.

"Julia, you poor thing. What an ordeal."

She turned her tear-streaked face up to him, her expression grim. "Those bastards have arrested Marin."

"Marin? Why on earth...?"

"That SFPD detective—"

"So you're the NYPD cop?" Larry looked up to see a woman standing before them. She was in her forties, tall and broad-shouldered, with close-clipped, raven-black hair. Her neat outfit suggested plain clothes, even with the cowboy boots. A badge on her right shoulder read, "Peregrine."

"Yes. Larry Somers," he replied. "My reputation precedes me, evidently."

"'Reputation is an idle and most false imposition. Oft got without merit and lost without deserving.' But then, we are bastards, after all," Stella said, eyeing Julia.

"Am I dreaming, or were you quoting from *Othello*?" Larry asked. He assumed that this Detective Peregrine would be aware, as he was, that people often lashed out in stressful situations. Cops dealt with it.

"Shakespeare is relevant in any situation. But never mind," Stella said. "We normally don't get visits from your kind. I hope you're not thinking of—"

"Investigating? 'Our kind' tend to know better." Maybe she wasn't dealing so well with it, Larry thought. Well, he'd continue to be civil, to try and dissipate any tension between them.

"Good." Stella regarded Julia's trembling form. "You should probably take her home. It's been a long night. For all of us."

"I can only imagine how much longer it will be for you."

"I'm sure you can."

Larry helped Julia up from the sofa. "Are you okay to go?"

"Yes…No…I don't know."

"Here. Lean on me," Larry turned to Stella. "She's been through a lot. Adjusting to the responsibilities of being concertmaster, and now this. She and Marin were quite close."

"So I've heard," said Stella.

Larry guided Julia toward the exit. "So much blood," Julia said. "So much blood."

"'Who knew the old man had so much blood in him?'" Stella murmured.

"Did you say something, detective?" Larry asked, as he and Julia passed by Stella.

"Just talking to myself," Stella said.

Julia shook her head. "I can't believe this is happening again, Larry."

"Let's talk about it later. Right now, you need some rest."

ꕥ

Once back at the Inn, Julia became increasingly unraveled as the full import of what had occurred that evening at the opera began to collide with her shattered emotions.

"Larry, what am I going to do?"

"There's nothing you can do. Except maybe ask for some time off to get over the stress of what you just went through."

The thought of further jeopardizing what felt like her precarious position in the eyes of the imperious music director heightened the degree of panic that already had begun to consume her. "I can't do that, I've barely started my job."

"We'll see about that. I'm going to speak with Alan and get you some personal time off. Even one day would help, don't you think?"

Julia shook her head vehemently. "No, no. Besides, I…I have to help Marin. I have to—"

"You have to help yourself first."

Julia felt backed against a wall. She knew Larry was right, but with her relationship with Stewart tenuous at best, and very little opportunity to prove her worth so far, she couldn't conceive of absenting herself from the orchestra. And she was frantic with worry about Marin.

A frenzied knock at the door distracted her from these dark circular thoughts. Larry opened to admit Katie, who rushed to Julia and threw her arms around her.

"Julia!" Katie said. "I heard about Marin. Are you in one piece?"

"What do you think, Katie? Pieces, many pieces. And I'm barely holding them together," Julia said. "Another murder, another friend accused. I must be cursed."

"You're not cursed. None of this is your fault."

"Maybe not. But Marin—I can't let this happen to her."

"Right now, you have to recover," Katie said. "You've been traumatized."

Larry's brow creased in tight lines. "I couldn't agree more, Katie. I'm going to ask the general director to excuse her from work for a day."

Julia's panic escalated. "But I couldn't possibly—"

Katie tightened her supportive grasp around Julia's shoulder. "Yes, you can. I'm sure Matt is ready to jump in. And I'll be there, too. We'll both support you."

"What about Lenny? This is the perfect excuse for him to undermine me."

"Screw Lenny," Katie said. "I can deal with him. He has no clue as to the power of New York females, especially violin-wielding ones."

Julia knew both Katie and Larry were right, but she stubbornly clung to her resolve, her work ethic—and her sense of justice when it came to her friend. "No, no. I have to be there. Plus, I owe it to Marin to find out what really happened. And you have to help me, Larry."

"Okay, back up," Larry said. "You just experienced a very harrowing incident. Now you're ready to investigate?"

"How can I abandon Marin in her time of need?"

"'A,' she's probably got a lawyer to take care of her by now. 'B,' you've been through this before with Abel, and look where it got you."

"It got me to his real murderer."

"At what price?" Katie said. "You were almost killed."

"And 'C,'" Larry added, "I don't have the authority to do any investigating here. Didn't you see how that detective was giving me the stink eye?"

"She doesn't have to know what you're doing."

"She's a detective," Larry said. "A damn good one, from what I could gather in the few minutes we spoke. I don't see anything getting past her."

Julia was starting to feel desperate. She couldn't see a way out, yet somehow she felt there had to be one. "Then what are we going to do?"

"I don't know about you, but I'm staying out of it. And if I were you, I'd do the same."

"I can't just let Marin down. It's not fair." Julia gazed at Larry intently, a look she knew he couldn't resist.

"Okay, you win. I'll see what I can do to find out how things operate around here. At least what kind of sentence she may be facing," he said. "But in exchange, you will follow my orders and take a day off."

"He's right, Julia," said Katie.

Julia recognized when she was defeated. "Seems I'm outnumbered."

Larry and Katie flashed each other triumphant looks. "Yep."

## Chapter 18

*Perdon, perdono...quello non sono, sbaglia costei...*
*Il delitto mio non è. L'innocenza mi rubò*
Oh, spare me, spare me...I'm not the one, you're mistaken...
I am blameless, I was only led astray
~ Mozart, *Don Giovanni*, Act 2

As a first-time suspect awaiting trial, Marin found herself imprisoned in the Santa Fe County Detention Center. The fact that the facility was only a county jail was little consolation. She was thousands of miles from home, in a town she knew little about, and accused of murder. If she were sentenced, she faced incarceration in the infamous Grants facility with the serious, so-called level three-to-six inmates. She couldn't even fathom what that might be like.

Worse, given the nature of her alleged crime, she was only allowed visitation by appointment, which meant that Julia—likely the only person Marin knew who might consider visiting—would be severely restricted by her rehearsal schedule. According to the information the ADA had revealed so far, since Julia was not a family member, a visit might even be out of the question.

But at the moment Marin had no time to contemplate visitation. A guard led her to an interrogation room, where she sat handcuffed at a table and waited until the DA arrived, with a court-appointed lawyer in tow.

"Ms. Crane, I am District Attorney Henry Cordero of the first Judicial District of New Mexico. This is your attorney, Elaine Baxter."

The attorney nodded toward Marin. "Henry, is it really necessary for my client to be restrained? She is a first-time offender. Could you please unshackle her?"

"I suppose we could allow it." The DA motioned to the guard, who unlocked Marin's cuffs. Henry tapped his foot while Elaine reached over and shook Marin's hand. Then he turned to Marin.

"I have read the reports, Ms. Crane. You are suspected of the stabbing murder of Emilia Tosti, a singer at the Santa Fe Opera, the evening of June twenty-ninth. You had a known rivalry with Ms. Tosti, were heard having heated discussions and disagreements with her previous to the incident, and were found holding a weapon that matched the stab wounds on the deceased shortly after she was attacked. The weapon was found to contain only your fingerprints. Do you have anything to say?"

"Don't say anything, Ms. Crane." Elaine turned to the DA. "It's all circumstantial, Henry."

"Not quite. We've learned that Ms. Tosti had stolen Ms. Crane's female lover right from under her nose. People have murdered for less."

Elaine's face paled.

Marin, her head lowered, avoided Elaine's gaze and that of Henry. She knew the DA's claims were true. But she was too terrified to admit it..

"You can't deny it's a high-profile case, Elaine. We will seek maximum penalty," Henry said.

Elaine recovered her composure. "You know as well as I do there's no death penalty in New Mexico."

"Premeditated murder is still a capital felony in this state," Henry said. "Punishable by life in prison, possibly without parole. Non-premeditated first-degree murder, eighteen years in prison."

Hearing this, Marin jumped out of her chair. "What?"

Elaine gently restrained Marin. "Premeditated or not, you'll have to prove it first, Henry."

"I intend to."

"And even in a felony case, with no criminal record, and no proof of drug involvement, the judge could sentence her to probation," Elaine added.

"You're dreaming," Henry said. "In any case, she'll need a super-aggressive defense lawyer."

"She's got one. Now if you don't mind, I need to consult with my client privately."

Henry motioned to the guard, who ushered him out of the room.

Elaine turned to Marin. "Okay, Ms. Crane, what really happened?"

ꕥ

Larry left Katie in charge of keeping Julia calm while he went to visit the Santa Fe Police Department headquarters. He found the building itself, located on Camino Entrada, not far from the so-called artsy "Railyard" District, non-descript: a brown flat-roofed cinder-block-shaped rectangle with virtually no landscaping surrounding it. But he was somewhat impressed with the tidy, well-organized interior, with its displays of historic SFPD photos, certificates of merit and earned honors, and even the SFPD logo-imprinted souvenir glasses and mugs for sale at five dollars each. The dissimilarity from his much older-looking precinct in Manhattan was extreme: his home base was not nearly as well-lit, and a bit unkempt and disorganized. But it still was as homey as a police facility could be, and familiar territory to him.

Still, he knew comparing home bases was not productive, nor was it the reason he was visiting the SFPD. His mission was to find out as much as he could about Marin's situation, the extent of her possible sentence and any other information that might shed light on whether there was any hope for her future, without prompting suspicion. He had his work cut out. It was a far cry from what he had expected from his vacation in the Land of Enchantment.

ꕥ

Julia, whom Katie could not prevent from frantically pacing the room, looked up expectantly when Larry returned. She knew him well enough to be able to read his experssion. Her face fell.

"Start with the bad news."

"What makes you think it's bad?"

"I know you, and your looks," she said grimly. "Just tell me. And don't mince words."

"Okay, then, I'll give it to you straight," Larry said. "It's a high-profile case, they're going for life without parole."

"What?!"

"You told me not to mince words."

Julia stopped pacing and sank down on the bed, her head in her hands. "How is this possible?"

"It's not all bad. I talked to your personnel manager, Sarah. She approved your day off."

"Forget it. I need to go visit Marin first."

"Ah. About that..."

Julia bit her lip. "What?"

"They're not allowing Marin any visitors yet," Larry said. "Even her attorney has limited access. Plus, you have to submit an application, which could take some time."

"That's positively Byzantine," Julia said. "In New York—"

"In case you hadn't noticed, Dorothy, we're not in New York anymore."

Julia moaned. "This can't be happening."

Katie sat next to Julia and grasped her hand. "What's the good news, Larry?"

"The good news is, I've booked Julia and I a night at a historic Santa Fe hotel for some R&R."

"I'd rather rehearse *Romeo and Juliet*," Julia said. "At least that would keep my mind off all of this misery."

"Too late. I've already paid for the night, and they've enlisted Matt to take your place in tomorrow's opera performance."

"A night away from the scene of the cri...the opera...will do you good," Katie said.

Julia knew that standing in opposition to either Larry or Katie was within the realm of possibility, but trying to wrangle both of them was useless.

"Okay, I give up," Julia said. "Which hotel is it?"

"It's a surprise," Larry said.

Julia looked up at Larry dubiously. "You know I don't like surprises."

"Don't worry. It will be perfect." Larry smiled. "Trust me."

ജ്ജ

Criminal Court Judge Marlo Madison of Division VII, Santa Fe District Court, was no Ruth Bader Ginsburg. She was not an opera fan; in fact, she had never seen an opera. Nor did she feel undue sympathy for female defendants just because they were female.

Elaine Baxter had warned Marin of this; as a result, Marin was deeply apprehensive about her bail hearing. Still, she welcomed the chance to get away from her prison cell and catch a glimpse of the flawless, crystal-blue Santa Fe sky, if only for a few moments, from the prison van.

The court building on Montezuma Avenue was not far from Santa Fe Plaza. As the van wound through the narrow streets, Marin kept her eyes fixed on the window. Because of an event blocking off the usual route, the van was forced to pass by famous Santa Fe landmarks she recognized from her tourist brochures: The Cathedral of St. Francis (which she had read of in Willa Cather's *Death Comes for the Archbishop*), the nearby Loretto Chapel, the San Miguel Mission; sights she had profoundly wished to see but probably never would, because of her dire situation.

Compared to the courthouses Marin had seen in Lower Manhattan, the Santa Fe County Courthouse looked astonishingly contemporary, with its square lines, adobe and white exterior, rectangular columns and state and federal flags flapping in the wind.

Such thoughts provided welcome distraction for Marin, but as soon as she was ushered into the courtroom her anxiety skyrocketed.

Seated with Elaine at a table across the aisle from DA Cordero, Marin kept her hands in her lap so as not to reveal her nervous wringing. All three participants rose as Judge Madison swept into the room, up the steps and into her chair. Spying the judge's austere expression, Marin lost all hope.

"We are seeking bail for my client, your Honor," Elaine said. "She has no record, and is an important member of the artistic community in her home city of New York. She should be released on her own recognizance."

"Your honor, we beg to differ," the DA countered. "Since the defendant has no ties to the Santa Fe community, and her home is two thousand miles away, she is an obvious flight risk."

The judge deliberated only briefly. Marin took that as a bad sign. Her heart sank.

"I believe the defendant is indeed a flight risk," said the judge. "She will be remanded and remain in custody until the trial."

"But the New Mexico Constitution guarantees that people charged with a crime have a right to be released pretrial, your Honor. Since passage of the 2016 constitutional amendment to reform New Mexico's pretrial release and detention system—"

Henry interrupted Elaine's protest. "Revisions that went into effect in July of 2017 state that district court judges can lawfully hold felony defendants in jail before trial if they are shown to be too dangerous for release, your Honor. Defendants charged with a felony are subject to pretrial detention."

"I agree with Mr. Cordero," said the judge. "My decision stands, Counselor. We are adjourned."

The judge pounded her gavel, rose and disappeared through the door from which she entered. Marin felt like her legs were about to give way under her.

Elaine exchanged defiant looks with Cordero. "This isn't over," she said.

## Chapter 19

*L'effroi me pénètre*
Fright consumes me
~ Offenbach, *The Tales of Hoffmann*, Act 3

THE RUMOR MILL WAS WORKING OVERTIME AT THE OPERA. WHEN JULIA heard that Marin had been denied bail, she was grief-stricken and found herself agreeing with Larry's plan for a brief respite from the theatre. The name of the hotel he had chosen, La Posada de Santa Fe, translated from the Spanish as *place of rest*. She needed that. Desperately.

Julia admitted this to Larry as they sat over lattes amidst the lunch crowd at the company cantina. Glancing around, it looked to her as if every member involved in the current production was frenetically trying to seize the opportunity to gobble down a few bites during their few fleeting moments of respite from work.

"So maybe it's not such a bad idea. La Posada, I mean." Julia spied Magda and Sandor at the cash register paying for their lunches, and waved. They smiled and waved back at her.

"The grounds are some of the loveliest in the city," Larry told her.

His phrasing put her on guard. It wasn't like him to sound as if he were quoting from the Santa Fe Chamber of Commerce. Or at the very least, the hotel's glossy promotional brochure. "Since when do you use the world 'lovely?' Have you got something up your sleeve?"

"Have I ever steered you wrong?"

Not only was she annoyed at his nerve to answer a question with a question—in her mind that entitlement was reserved for people of Jewish extraction like herself—she wasn't quite in the mood for loveliness; not yet, anyway. And she knew Larry was well aware of it.

"Do you really want me to respond to that?"

"Wow, two questions answered with questions. You're really bringing out the big guns."

"I'm glad you recognized that, so I'll cease my protesting. Just be aware that I'm bringing my violin to practice."

"Can't you be without it for one night?"

She gave him a withering look. "What do you think?"

ꝏ

Julia discovered that Larry had not been exaggerating. "Didn't I say it was perfect?" he said when they entered the driveway of La Posada, located just steps from Santa Fe Plaza.

Julia nodded, impressed. The property of the rustic hotel was indeed magnificent. Lush gardens with multicolored flowers and elegant fountains nestled between charming pueblo-style adobe *casitas,* all of which surrounded Staab House, the original 19th century Victorian mansion that was the hotel's centerpiece.

After the valet had taken possession of their car, Julia, her violin case poised on her shoulder, stood gazing at the façade while Larry started to recount the hotel's sad history of the mistress of the house, her untimely demise and her ostensible sporadic appearances to the hotel guests.

A feeling of unease displaced Julia's annoyance. "It's haunted? By a ghost named *Julia?*"

"Everything is haunted in Santa Fe," Larry said. "Evidently this ghost was not pleased with the modern additions to her house."

"I don't like ghosts. Especially ones with my name."

"When was the last time you saw one?"

Julia did not reply. It had been several days since her ghostly encounter at their inn, but she still felt uncomfortable at the thought of sharing the experience with Larry. That La Posada, the largest private residence in New Mexico, was one of the few hotels in the U.S. with an art curator on staff was no antidote for Julia's overall feelings of disquiet. She wondered how such a beautiful place could be haunted. Then she remembered: it was in Santa Fe.

The concierge, Peter, offered them a mini-tour of the historic section of the house. "Our porter, Eldred, has been here longer than any of our employees. His great-great grandfather worked on the architect's plans for the original Staab House, constructed by nineteenth century merchant Abraham Staab for his wife, Julia, after they emigrated from Germany."

Julia's anxiety began to escalate.

*A ghost named Julia, from Germany? This is getting too close to home.*

"Fascinating," said Larry, extracting his cell phone from his pocket and opening the camera icon. "Let's do it."

Peter led them inside. "By the way, Larry, be sure to take a photo of the mirror above the mantel in the room with the marble fireplace. The one with the marble cross positioned on top of it. When you look at the picture afterwards you'll see a blue light reflected in the mirror that's not visible when you look at the mirror itself."

"Why isn't it visible?" Larry asked.

"Because that light is Julia's ghost, which only appears in photographic images."

Julia sensed that Larry was unfazed, but her own uneasiness continued unabated. She hovered in front of the flagstone entrance to the older portion of the hotel, hesitant to enter, as Larry snapped photos with his cell.

"Julia, please don't be anxious about our ghost. Some of the musicians who perform here on weekends have had all sorts of 'supernatural' experiences here. Mysterious disembodied voices harmonizing with them, sound systems going out suddenly and then coming back on. It just adds intrigue to the atmosphere."

His insight did little to quell Julia's discomfort, but when she gazed at the dark wood entrance, with the initials "A.S." for Abraham Staab carved into the mahogany frame above the entryway, something came over her. Perhaps it was the darkened corridor with its steep wooden staircase, lit only by ancient-looking chandeliers suspended from the ceiling; or the feeling of going back in time. Whatever the reason, Julia's artist's imagination took over. She was able to envision the gas-lit chandeliers in their former glory, bearing witness to Victorian women's floor-length taffeta dresses sweeping up the steps. The idea left her completely entranced.

Just as timeworn was the look of the wizened, elderly gentleman who approached Julia and Larry. The old man's chalk-white hair encircled his face in tufts, his ancient eyes blinking in the dim light.

He reminded Julia of Frantz, the servant character from the "Antonia" act of *The Tales of Hoffmann.*

"This is Eldred," said Peter. "Eldred, these guests will be staying in Room 100."

The old man regarded Julia, open-mouthed, scrutinizing her face with a combination of tenderness and incredulity.

"Julia!" he cried. "You've come back."

Julia was stunned. "Excuse me?"

Peter leaned over and whispered to Julia. "Eldred has dementia, though it's mild considering his advanced age. Don't let it bother you." He spoke more loudly to the old man. "Take good care of our guests, will you?"

Peter exchanged bemused glances with Larry and walked off. Julia, unnerved, avoided Eldred's gaze.

"I always knew you would come back, Julia," the man continued. "Great-grandfather said so. You're just as beautiful as he told me you were."

Julia remained confused. "But—"

"Just go along with the old gent," Larry murmured.

Waving away her concern, Eldred gently took her arm. "Come, Julia, let me show you what remains of your house's former glory."

Larry followed, continuing to snap photos, as Eldred guided Julia through the portal into the hallway by the stairs. "Here," he said, pointing to two gold-framed black and white vintage photos. "Remember when the house had three stories, the way your husband Abraham first built it, before the fire?"

Not waiting for her reply, he led her into a room, its walls lined with mahogany bookcases, between which stood a marble fireplace topped by an enormous wood-framed mirror alongside two matching red-upholstered Victorian-era sofas that faced each other.

An elegant mahogany bar several feet long dominated the adjoining room. Above the bar, five wood-framed glass cabinets displayed panoplies of colorful liquor bottles.

"It was you who insisted Abraham build the bar to such massive proportions."

Julia was speechless.

"But nothing can equal the magnificence of this mantel," he said, steering her to the next room, where another large gilt-framed mirror hung above a marble fireplace and an additional antique chandelier adorned the ceiling.

Julia stared in amazement at the marble cross entwined with elaborate carvings positioned on top of the mantel. She couldn't argue with the old man; the entire effect was splendid.

Larry, as per Peter's suggestion, took multiple photographs of the mirror behind the cross. "You see, Julia, there's no blue light. Nothing to worry about."

"I have never quite understood the presence of the cross on top of the mantel," Eldred said. "Considering that you and Abraham were Jewish."

"Jewish?" Julia echoed. She flashed a look of disbelief at Larry, who at this point also was beginning to look a bit spooked. He nonetheless persevered with his photography.

"Come, Julia, I'll take you to your room," Eldred said.

Julia trailed Eldred up the staircase in a fog, followed by Larry. Reaching the top, Julia gazed downward to the bottom of the stairs. Then, looking to the left, she saw a windowed alcove with two leather chairs, which served as a sitting room. In front of her an open door led to a room labeled, "Julia Staab Suite."

Julia whispered to Larry. "Did you know the ghost's name was Julia?"

"That was part of the surprise."

"That's not a surprise. It's sabotage," she said through her teeth.

Julia inwardly admitted that the room's past-era furnishings were exquisitely tasteful: the four-poster bed with its pristine white linen coverlet, sheets and pillowcases; the vintage-tint gilded-frame photos hanging above the bed, with its two matching tables and lamps on either side; the shiny mahogany desk and Louis XVI chair positioned in front of a lace-curtained window; the jacquard rose pattern-upholstered "courting" settee in one corner.

"You always had discerning taste," Eldred said.

But Julia was entirely unprepared for what she saw above the mantelpiece: a portrait of a beautiful woman with wavy, chin-length brunette hair, ebony eyes gazing into the distance, dark, finely arched brows, lips the color of a fine claret pursed together in the all-knowing yet unknowable smile of a strong-willed woman.

It was as if she was looking at herself.

## Chapter 20

*Sola, sola, in buio loco, palpitar il cor io sento*
All alone in this dark spot I feel my heart is throbbing
~ Mozart, *Don Giovanni,* Act 2

"I'M NOT SPENDING THE NIGHT IN THIS ROOM," JULIA TOLD LARRY AFTER Eldred had left them alone.

"If I were you, I'd be flattered. Julia Staab was a stunning woman," said Larry. "Surely you're not going to let a few coincidences spook you?"

"Coincidences? Seriously, Larry." Julia opened the brochure she found on the desk blotter. "Listen to this. 'It is said that Julia went into a deep depression after the loss of her last child, shortly after its birth, and thereafter took to her room and spent most of her time there. Unhappy with her home becoming a hotel, her ghost has been seen at the top of the stairs on countless occasions, and her footsteps heard. People report the sensation of being watched, feeling cold streams of air even though windows are closed. Outside doors to the inner courtyard are violently opened. Lights unexplainably being turned on or off. A piano mysteriously being played. Julia's ghost blows past employees and guests. Trays fall over, drinks are spilled. A vintage, non-connected telephone rings. A voice answers…speaking Yiddish.' For God's sake. That's what my grandmother spoke!"

"It's all urban legend," Larry said. "You don't believe in that stuff, do you?"

Julia was still staring at the brochure. From the time she and Larry had started dating, she had tried her best to make him understand the depth of her connection to her Eastern European roots; but his ancestors literally crossed the Atlantic Ocean on the ship following the Mayflower, and he didn't quite get what it felt like to come from much more recent and far-flung immigrant ancestry.

"You have to admit, it seems more than coincidental. The same name as mine. She was Jewish, came from Germany like my ancestors did. And she was a musician. It's creepy. For all we know, she may have burned the place down herself."

"I think it's kind of intriguing. How about we go for a drink at 'Julia's - A Spirited Restaurant and Bar?'"

Julia flung the brochure at him. Had she seen his photos of the mirror behind the marble mantle, she would have been even more taken aback. The bizarre blue light that Peter had forewarned them about appeared in every one of them.

ꟸ

That night, Julia was restless. She was miffed at Larry for springing the surprise on her, and spooked that the ghost of a woman with the same name and religious background, who came to a violent end, was trolling the halls—perhaps even watching as they slept—in the "place of rest" Larry had chosen for Julia's supposed R&R away from her traumas at the opera house.

Then there was the creepy old man who had insisted Julia was the reincarnation of the former mistress of Staab House one hundred-fifty years previous.

Julia couldn't fathom the significance of the whole encounter. It was almost a *Somewhere In Time* scenario. Julia envisioned the 1980 film, starring Jane Seymour and Christopher Reeve, which told the story of a writer who becomes fascinated with a beautiful woman from the turn of the twentieth century after seeing a photograph of her in a hotel and goes back in time to meet her—with tragic consequences. The mere thought made her apprehensive.

That night, Julia made sure to close their bedroom door as tightly as possible. Eventually she fell into an exhausted sleep, but dreams haunted her: of Marin, her hands stained with blood; of prisons and prison guards, lawyers and prosecuting attorneys.

Around four a.m. Julia awakened to the sounds of the door opening and closing and footsteps in the hallway. She tried to attribute the noises to her overall state of anxiety, but when a sensation of being watched and a sudden feeling of cold overcame her, she cautiously opened her eyes.

*Did I leave the window open?*

Squinting to adjust to the darkness, she glanced across the room and saw that the window was still closed but that somehow she had left her violin case open on a chair. Despite her fear, she started to peel herself off the bed to close the lid when a familiar sound filtered into her ears: her violin strings being plucked. G, D, A, E, individually; then a G major chord. She peered into the darkness.

*Am I dreaming?*

But it was no dream. She could hear the overtones of the strings' vibrations. Terrified, she roused Larry who, as usual, was sleeping soundly.

"Larry, wake up."

He stirred. "What the hell, Julia?"

"Somebody is playing my violin."

Now she had his attention. He opened his eyes halfway. "That's crazy talk."

"No, it isn't. Listen."

"I don't hear anything."

By now the strumming had stopped. "I don't care if you believe me," Julia said insistently. "I heard the strings being plucked."

"You've been reading too many ghost stories. Go back to sleep."

"I can't."

"I suppose you think it's Julia's ghost?" Larry said.

"It's the troubled souls who stay around," Julia said. "And she was a musician, after all."

Larry sighed. "My grandmother had a saying, Julia. 'The dead can't hurt you, only the living can.'"

Julia rose and approached the violin. There was no evidence that the strings had even been vibrating. She clicked the case shut.

*Maybe I am crazy after all.*

Seeing that Larry was beginning to show signs of consciousness Julia kept talking, if only to keep her nerves from fraying further. "Okay, maybe I imagined the violin. But I can't stop thinking about Marin in that horrible place. What if they send her to the penitentiary? I read that one of the most violent prison riots in the history of the American correctional system, was in the New Mexico State Penitentiary in 1980. Thirty-three inmates died."

"Marin's not in the State Penitentiary, Julia, she's in county jail. The Northwest New Mexico Correctional Center. Or maybe the New Mexico Women's Correctional Facility, or Western Women's Correctional Facility. They've renamed it a few times."

"Whatever facility it is, I'm sure it's unspeakable. And she has no one else here but me. What if, God forbid, they transfer her to a maximum-security prison? No, I have to get in to see her."

"But the county jail's way far away."

"I don't care. If I don't do something, I will go crazy for real."

"Okay, okay." Larry forced himself awake, rose and sat at the desk in front of his iPad. He opened the browser, Googled the "New Mexico Corrections Department" website and scrolled down until he found "SPECIAL VISIT REQUEST APPLICATION."

For the first time since they had checked into La Posada, Julia felt relieved. At least she was doing something to alleviate her anxiety. Checking out of this hotel would be the next step.

## Chapter 21

*Il carcere mi ha dunque assai mutate?*
Prison, then, has wrought such a great change in me?
~ *Tosca,* Act 1

Since Marin had no family close by, Julia's application was fast-tracked and approved by the Assistant Warden sooner than she and Larry had expected. The day after the two had checked out of La Posada and, to Julia's great relief, returned to their original abode, a tech rehearsal was scheduled and the orchestra was off, leaving Julia free to visit Marin in prison.

The visiting directive Julia had received via the hotel desk specified a lengthy list of restrictions that Julia found daunting. No physical contact was allowed, nor controlled substances of any kind. The Dress Code for Visitors was strictly adhered to: no short skirts, shorts or sweat clothes; undergarments required, and no tank tops or see-through clothing. Julia was more than willing to comply with any requirements that would result in her being able to show her support for Marin, who Julia sensed was receiving no other moral encouragement from the outside.

Julia and Larry drove south from their hotel, through barren desert landscapes, crossing over from one Indian reservation to another, until they found themselves in an isolated area with low hills and little in the way of vegetation but scrub bush and chaparral. It was even more desolate an environment than Julia had imagined. Her first glimpse of it was not reassuring.

"To think she's in that overcrowded place, with drug addicts and violent criminals with tattooed heads and GEDs. It's the pits," Julia said as they pulled up in front. "It got one star on Yelp."

"I have to admit that's not a great recommendation," Larry said. "What did they say?"

"They said it's totally run down. And the food is inedible. It's been called the 'Santa Fe weight loss center."

She peered at the foreboding entrance with its flat-roofed adobe-looking buildings and fences and suppressed a shudder.

Julia and Larry passed through the entrance and arrived at the reception desk. "Only one visitor allowed," the shift supervisor told them. "You'll have to wait here during the visit."

"No problem," Larry said. "I'm just her escort."

Larry observed as the shift supervisor had Julia sign the Visitor Statement of Understanding, in which she acknowledged she might be searched, filled out a questionnaire and surrendered her driver's license, which the shift supervisor scrutinized closely.

"I need to make sure you're over eighteen, otherwise you'd have to take a drug test," the supervisor said.

"Does she look like a minor?" Larry asked.

The supervisor ignored his question. "I'll also need your cell phone, as well as whatever cash you have on you over twenty dollars. Do you have any other electronic devices, Ms. Kogan?"

Julia shook her head.

"The metal detector is over there," the supervisor said. "Are you afraid of dogs?"

Julia glanced at a large German shepherd hovering nearby. "Not generally, but this one doesn't look too friendly."

"He's there to sniff for drugs," the supervisor said.

Julia quelled her impatience. "I don't take them, but if I did I certainly wouldn't bring any here with me."

"You'd be surprised what people try to smuggle in here," the supervisor said.

Julia flashed a look of stupefaction to Larry. He countered with an encouraging smile as she stepped through the metal detector.

ꟾ

The prison was less dank than Julia had expected. Bright fluorescent ceiling lights illuminated the cavernous rooms. The walls, instead of battleship grey, were a much lighter cream color. The inmates wore blue shirts and black pants instead of orange jumpsuits.

Still, Julia felt the heaviness of the somber atmosphere weighing on her. The gloomy mien of the security guard who led her into the visiting room emphasized the solemnity of the situation.

When Marin trudged in, Julia had to restrain her shock. The singer, whose figure was usually on the ample side, looked diminished. Her normally round face was drawn, her complexion sallow. She attempted to smile, without success, as she sat down opposite Julia.

"I didn't think they'd let you come."

"I admit it wasn't easy getting in here. But more importantly, Marin, are you all right?"

"Do I look all right?"

Julia hesitated.

"It's okay to be honest, Julia."

"No. You don't."

"That's what I thought."

Marin's grimace heightened Julia's feelings of panic. "Marin, I'll do anything I can to get you out of here. Anything."

"Is that true?"

"Of course it is." Julia tried her best to steady her nerves. She didn't want to reveal the extent of her distress to Marin, and risk causing her friend more anguish. "I know you didn't do this. The question is, who did?"

Marin leaned in closely toward Julia. "Talk to Deborah."

"Who's Deborah?"

"She's one of the apprentices. Emilia's understudy," Marin said.

Julia had heard much about Santa Fe Opera's famed apprentice program, which was run by Rob Cheever, a former Met Opera tenor who now lived in Santa Fe full time. An impressive fifteen hundred singers had been through the program under Rob's direction. She was anxious to learn more, but the present circumstances weren't exactly the most favorable ones.

"Wait a minute," Julia said. "I know an apprentice can get their big break here, but…murder?"

"Just talk to her. She desperately wanted a chance to sing Lulu. And she was acting funny during rehearsals, especially around Salman. She was practically throwing herself at him." Marin lowered her voice.

"Which is weird, considering she was also sleeping with Emilia."

Julia gasped. "You're kidding. That sounds like a twisted 'Three Faces of Eve' scenario. Does that still happen?"

"For sure," Marin said. "Some people would throw a singer off a cliff to get a crack at a role here. Or 'accidentally' shove someone into the pool and give them a cold so they'd have to cancel. Or make sure they get the most belligerent horse."

Julia was puzzled. "What?"

"It's happened," Marin said. "Riding is a popular leisure pursuit here. I'm told one singer had to cancel after being thrown."

"I can almost comprehend that kind of competitiveness," Julia said. "But killing someone? That's...well, I can't imagine it."

"Just talk to Deborah, about her rivalry with Emilia. And to Rob, too. He knows more about the apprentices than anyone," said Marin. "Will you do that for me?"

"Of course I will." The more Julia studied Marin's tortured face, the more worried she became. "Marin...is there...something else you need to tell me?"

"I..." Marin hesitated. "I was sleeping with Deborah, too. Until Emilia lured her away," she murmured softly.

"Oh, my God. Does anyone know?"

"My attorney. And, unfortunately, Detective Peregrine and the DA." Marin bit her lip. "He's charging me with premeditated murder. If I'm found guilty, I could get life in prison. Possibly without parole."

Julia was stunned. Just a few days before, she and Marin were chuckling over their lattes. Now Marin was facing a prison sentence that was unthinkable. It didn't seem possible.

The security guard appeared at the door. "Time's up."

Marin rose and moved with great effort to the door. Then she turned back to Julia, her expression grave. "Even non-premeditated, I could get eighteen years. *Eighteen years.*"

"You can't be serious."

"Believe it. If that happens, Jul, I'm toast."

"It won't happen," Julia said. "I won't let it."

"Thank you, Julia. You're a true friend."

Julia watched with trepidation as the guard led Marin away. She was at a loss as to how to obtain justice for Marin. She wasn't sure if she deserved to be called a true friend, but truth be told, at this moment, she suspected, to her chagrin, that she was Marin's only friend.

## Chapter 22

*Certo moto d'ignoto tormento dentro l'alma girare mi sento, che mi dice...cento cose che intender non sa*
I feel some strange suspicion stirring in my breast which tells me...a hundred things I don't understand
~ Mozart, *Don Giovanni*, Act 1

With two major roles suddenly vacant due to Emilia's demise and Marin's incarceration, an emergency "cover dress" rehearsal with piano, to take place in one of the small outdoor studios, was called for all the apprentices involved as understudies in *Lulu.*

Julia, who thought it a perfect opportunity to surreptitiously corner Deborah and question her, as Marin had advised, asked Stewart if she could sit in on the rehearsal. To her surprise, he didn't inquire as to her motives. She figured he was too preoccupied with such game-changing re-castings to argue with her. He even offered to introduce her to Rob Cheever.

"Rob has been in charge of the apprentice program for over three decades," Stewart said. "He performed in the chorus of Hindemith's *Cardillac* premiere the night before the theatre burned down in 1967."

Considering his protracted history with the company, Julia thought Rob looked fairly young and energetic. He certainly did not seem old enough to have performed with the company in 1967.

"I've been listening to your solos in *Lulu,*" Rob told Julia. "Absolutely gorgeous."

"Thank you." Julia felt vindicated, especially with Stewart standing right next to Rob, but she suppressed a desire to say anything to that effect. She just smiled graciously.

It was Rob who flashed a meaningful glance at Stewart. "Recognition where it's due."

Stewart excused himself, walked over to a small podium facing the stage, opened his score and began studying it.

"Whatever his shortcomings, Julia, you can't fault Stewart for not being thorough," Rob said. "Is this your first time hearing the apprentices?"

"Yes."

"Well, you're in for a treat. They're always looking for chances to sing real roles." He leaned close to Julia. "Some of them sing better than the people they're covering. But you didn't hear that from me."

"Of course not. I think your faith in them is inspiring."

"They also love to do outside events, like the ones we've held in Whole Foods, where I usually wheel in an electric keyboard and the apprentices sing a forty-minute program. I always tell people it's going to happen in Bread." He chuckled. "But seriously, when you're an apprentice, all eyes are on you. And you quickly learn that solo singers are *not* prima donnas. That's an important lesson, because the so-called 'real' opera world is not so friendly."

"I've noticed that." Julia peered at the stage and saw another young, extremely attractive female singer to whom Salman had directed his attention. "Who's the other singer?" she asked.

"That's Lorelei Forman," Rob said. "She's covering Marin's role."

It never had occurred to Julia that she not only might want to talk to Deborah, who had a vested interest in usurping Emilia's role, but also to the singer who might have wanted to get Marin out of the way.

"Come sit, Julia. I have to stay close by Andrew, but you can park yourself right behind me."

Julia had heard of Andrew Stillman, one of New York's most influential, high-profile impresarios. Over the previous four decades Andrew's go-getting organization had represented the world's most celebrated opera singers. Up until recently he had been called "The Harvey Weinstein of Opera," but given the infamous ongoing sexual harassment controversy surrounding the film producer that sparked a spate of similar revelations in the Hollywood industry, not to mention elsewhere, Andrew was anxious to divest himself of that association.

On the small stage, Salman was giving directions to an attractive young female singer, whom Julia assumed to be Deborah, while a group of young apprentices stood by and observed.

Julia sat down and, trying not to be too obvious, took a quick glimpse at Andrew. Pale blue eyes twinkled behind wire-rimmed glasses that framed his wide face, with its neatly trimmed, sand-colored beard and mustache. His stout body was almost too ample for the undersized folding chair in which he positioned himself. To her eyes, he was unquestionably an authority figure.

Glancing around her, Julia saw a number of other company members in attendance, some of whom she recognized.

"Who are all these non-singing people?" she asked Rob. "I met Magda in the costume shop, and Steve, the stagehand, on my first day, but I don't know any of the others."

"They're all here to get a jump on what might be needed for the actual performance," Rob told her. "Magda always comes to rehearsals, even the cover ones, to study a person's movements and how she can dress them most efficiently. She's an expert at knowing how best to build a costume so it allows the singer to move the way the director wants them to. Next to her is Daniel, the wig and makeup director. It saves him time to watch the singers in action so he can build them the best possible wigs."

Stewart checked his watch, then signaled the pianist. "It's time we began. Act 3, Scene 2."

Julia gave an involuntary shiver as the familiar dissonances of the opera's brutal, final murder scene filtered into her consciousness. She was taken aback to see Andrew making conducting gestures along with Stewart, waving at Deborah and leaning over to comment to Rob while Deborah was singing.

"Fabulous, right, Rob?" Andrew said. "No problem, eh? Who needs Emilia?"

Rob simply nodded and kept watching. Julia couldn't see his expression, but she was appalled at Andrew's callous chattering about the deceased diva, whose body had scarcely had time to grow cold. She felt that even nasty people deserved a modicum of respect after their demise.

"Yes indeed," Andrew said, waving to Deborah. She's going to make a magnificent Lucia, too."

*Lucia, too? Marin was right. I really need to talk to this gal.*

As the rehearsal broke for a ten-minute interval and the singers came offstage, Julia set her Fitbit to signal a two-minute alert. Then she quietly rose and approached Deborah, taking in the young singer's appearance. Deborah's build reminded Julia of so many other sopranos she had seen perform onstage: what the Germans called *saftig*—lush, to put it politely, or juicy in more contemporary terms; not the typical look for the role of a *femme fatale* such as Lulu. But Deborah's face, its olive skin and coal-black eyes framed by thick black hair cascading to her shoulders, showed remarkable beauty and intensity. Her air of confidence reflected her awareness of it.

"Hi, Deborah. I'm Julia, concertmaster of the orchestra. I've been enjoying your performance."

"I'm impressed that you would come to a piano dress, Julia."

"All part of the job," Julia said. "Especially since this is my first time here in Santa Fe. Is this your first year as an apprentice?"

"Yes," Deborah said. "It's like a dream come true to be here with the program. There's so much competition to get in."

"Quite a plum assignment for your first time, singing the part of Lulu," said Julia.

Deborah hesitated. "Yes…it is."

"It must be difficult for you, to fill Emilia's shoes with so little notice."

Deborah shrugged. "We're trained for that. Though she did have a rather large shoe size, if you get my drift."

Deborah's cavalier attitude gave Julia pause. "Sounds like you had some issues with her."

"Everybody did. She was notorious."

"So I've gathered. Was there a specific rivalry between you two divas?"

"I don't consider myself a diva," Deborah said. "I haven't reached that status yet."

Julia, not wanting to arouse suspicion in her motivation for questioning Deborah, decided to change gears by showing some interest in the singer's artistic side. "I'm curious…as just a musician and not a singer. How would you define that status? Does it have to do with what they call the applause meter?"

"According to the great mezzo Christa Ludwig, it's not so much about how much applause a diva gets but more about how she receives that applause. No names mentioned, but one soprano would fall to her knees, arms raised, milk it for what seemed like hours, and then rise very slowly. People would think of her as a diva, without question. They lapped it up."

"That sounds familiar. I've seen more than my share of that at the Met. And I think Christa Ludwig is incomparable as an artist." Christa Ludwig's recordings had represented the benchmark when Julia had first started listening to opera. She was impressed that Deborah had used the famous mezzo as an example. "Did she have anything to say about the difference between 'diva-dom' and 'stardom'?"

"She did say that being a 'star' isn't something you think about, you just become it. Though in her case she claimed she was lucky that her 'rivals' at the time were either too old or too young. I think she was much too modest."

"I agree," Julia said. "In any case, you must be thrilled to be able to play the part of Lulu, even under such difficult circumstances."

"Of course. I am. Who wouldn't be?"

Julia's Fitbit flashed its two-minute alert. Time was running out. She would have to accelerate her pace, Deborah's possible suspicions notwithstanding. "Were you backstage the night of the opening?"

"We always have to be in the house when we're covering a role," Deborah said. "But space is limited backstage. They don't like anyone hanging about who doesn't belong. We usually wait in the dressing room area."

"Did you notice anything or anyone unusual there?"

Julia could see a sudden change in Deborah's expression and manner. The singer shifted uncomfortably and her voice became clipped. "I'm afraid I have to go warm up now. Enjoy the rest of the rehearsal, Julia."

Deborah hurried away. Julia watched, intrigued, as the singer approached Salman and began to whisper in his ear.

*No question that he's totally flattered, getting attention from a young, pretty singer. Whatever her sexual persuasion.*

Julia shook off her feelings of disquiet. She watched with interest as Magda took Deborah aside and adjusted the shoulder pads on her filmy black blouse and the pleats on her gauze skirt. Magda acknowledged Julia's wave with a nod, then went back to fussing over Deborah.

Julia spied Rob chatting with Lorelei and moved toward them.

"Julia, have you met Lorelei Forman?" Rob said. "Lorelei, this is Julia Kogan, our new orchestra concertmaster. She came here all the way from the Met."

Lorelei gasped. "Really? Oh, I just love that orchestra. They're just the greatest opera orchestra on the planet. It must have been so exciting to perform with them."

"Thank you," Julia said. "It was, absolutely. And you must be so excited to be playing Geschwitz. Have you sung the role before?"

"Are you kidding?" Lorelei said. "Who gets to do that, except here in Santa Fe? Unless you're, like, Jennifer Larmore or something."

"Or Marin Crane," said Julia.

Lorelei frowned. "Right."

"That's why you kids come to Santa Fe, just to have a crack at those rarely done roles. Right, Lorelei?" Rob said.

"Um-hmm." Lorelei paused for a moment. "It's a real a shame about Marin, though."

Julia couldn't tell whether Lorelei was being sincere, or just trying to be polite. But when the assistant conductor called an end to the break she realized her window of opportunity had closed.

"By the way, Lorelei," Julia said, "Were you in the theatre for the opening?"

Lorelei flushed. "Well, I—"

"The apprentices generally are required to attend every possible event," Rob said. "They're here to learn, after all."

"Of course," Julia said. "I can't wait to hear you nail that last scene, Lorelei. Break a leg."

Lorelei mumbled flustered thanks and rushed off. Julia resumed her spot behind Rob and Andrew. She felt gratified to have been able to ask at least a few questions of the two singers.

ꕥ

Stella initially thought Constantin's suggestion that she attend the cover dress was a useless exercise. All those temperamental singers and backstage people. Nothing about her background in straight theatre had prepared her for the temper tantrums and self-important attitudes of opera folks.

But she soon discovered, as she observed unnoticed from a rear corner of the studio, how fascinating, and potentially useful, it was to watch the inner workings of an opera company in such a close, intimate setting. Seeing a conductor lead a piano instead of an orchestra was eye-opening. The attention paid to a lead singer by directors, costume and wig people, and even the portentous impresario's ceaseless background prattle, amounted to an education in why divas were so full of themselves. She was completely mesmerized.

What she didn't expect was to see Julia, putting two of the singers on the spot with questions. That clearly was unacceptable.

## Chapter 23

*Cielo! Sempre novel sospetto*
Heavens! Always some new suspicion
~ Verdi, *Rigoletto,* Act 1

ONCE THE COVER DRESS HAD FINISHED, REHEARSALS STARTED IN EARNEST for the next production: Gounod's *Roméo et Juliette,* which the company had added to their repertoire for the first time in 2016. Julia had performed the opera in her debut Met season and, as was her habit, had studied the libretto to enhance her understanding of the work. She found all of the music inspiring, but the Act 2 fight scene, resulting in Romeo's heart-wrenching exile, always caused empathetic shivers to flow through her easily-affected psyche.

Still bent on helping Marin, however, Julia made a point of picking the brains of her orchestra colleagues about the night of Emilia's demise. Before one rehearsal she hovered outside the pit door among a group of gossiping musicians.

"Wish I'd been here for that," said one harpist. "I missed all the excitement."

"How come you weren't?" Julia asked.

"There's only one harp in *Lulu,*" the harpist said. "Second harp misses the good stuff."

"Well, I was here, and believe me, it wasn't pretty," said an oboist.

"Did you see anything suspicious?" asked Julia. "Anyone lurking around you'd never seen before?"

"I wasn't exactly looking," the oboist replied. "But I don't think that mezzo-soprano, Marin, did it."

Julia's ears perked up. "Really? Why?"

"I don't know exactly. She just doesn't seem the type."

"Maybe the ghost of John Crosby did it," said the harpist, winking. "He did have some issues with divas, didn't he?"

Several musicians laughed, but Julia felt supremely uncomfortable at the memory of the mysterious apparition she thought she'd seen bustling among the scrub bush behind the theatre.

"I've actually seen his ghost," said Paul, a flutist.

"What are you, Paul, some sort of medium?" the harpist asked.

"I'm not the only one who has."

"Some say they can still feel his presence," Julia said. "Are you one of those company members who visit Crosby's grave every summer?"

Paul did not respond but held her gaze. Suddenly uncomfortable, Julia was relieved to hear the orchestra call over the P.A.

"Five minutes. Orchestra to the pit for *Roméo et Juliette,* Act 2."

As the musicians shuffled into the pit, Julia felt someone grab her arm from behind. She whipped around to see Stella, and immediately sensed the detective was not happy.

"You seem on edge, Julia," Stella said.

"Who wouldn't be, given what's been going on?"

"Oh, I don't know. Maybe everyone else who isn't snooping around, interrogating company members."

Julia squirmed inwardly but tried not to show it. "Is there something on your mind, detective?"

"Actually, yes," said Stella. "Word has gotten back to me that you've been asking people in the company all kinds of questions, none of them having to do with music, I might add. That's not acceptable. It's my job to investigate, not yours."

"I'm not investigating, I'm just…naturally curious."

"Spin it however you like, Julia. You're interfering with my inquiry. And need I remind you what they say about curiosity?"

Julia did not respond.

"I thought as much." Stella turned to go, then faced Julia again. "Back off, Julia. I'm not going to tell you again."

Stella stomped off, her cowboy boots clicking on the concrete floor. "'O cursed spite, that ever I was born to set it right!'" she muttered.

Julia heaved a large sigh and climbed the stairs into the pit.

ꕤ

After rehearsal, Julia returned to her room at the inn and placed her violin case on the floor next to her side of the bed, where Larry, deeply immersed in a Wikipedia article on *Lulu* on his iPad, glanced up at her.

"Did you know Berg was a symmetry freak?" he asked. "The whole opera is like a palindrome. Act 3 is a mirror image of Act 1, only by contrast. Luxury vs. squalor, husbands played by the same singers as her johns. And the music for the film interlude is an exact palindrome of itself."

He turned to see Julia flop onto the bed. Her desultory expression was impossible to miss. "What happened? Blatchley again?"

"No. He's bad enough, but now Stella is on my case. And it's all your fault."

"Me? What did I do?"

"You know very well. It was you who pushed me into investigating the murder."

"I didn't push. You were the one who was so concerned about Marin. And I'm not allowed to do any meddling, remember?" He put the iPad down on the bed and looked at Julia with concern. "What exactly did Stella say to you?"

"Oh, nothing. Just to back off or else."

"Or else what?"

Julia turned over on her side and clutched a throw pillow to her chest. "She didn't say."

"I know, sweetie. You don't need more turmoil right now."

"First Blatchley, now Stella is giving me grief. Not to mention Leaping Lenny breathing down my neck. I'm going to have to toe the line."

Larry lay down next to her and gently stroked her hair. "Anything I can do to make it better?"

"Take over the questioning for me."

"You know I can't."

"If you do it discreetly, no one will even notice, at least hardly." She turned to face him. "Please. I'm slowly losing my mind here. And Blatchley is pressuring me."

Her irresistable pout, which he knew would put any Parisian *jeune fille* to shame, made him smile.

"Audacious hussy. You know I turn to mush when you fret so engagingly."

"You wouldn't want me any other way."

"Damn straight," he said, pulling her to him and not letting go.

ᘓᘐ

*A little girl stood in front of a music stand lowered to her diminutive stature. The violin tucked under her chin, a gift to her cash-strapped family from a benevolent donor, was too big for her tiny, ten-year-old frame—so big that she had to stretch her left arm to the max to hold it. Perched on the stand was a piece of music by a composer named Pietro Mascagni: 'Intermezzo' from an opera called 'Cavalleria Rusticana.'*

*Next to the girl, a man with a shock of wavy grey hair, also holding a violin under his chin, was regarding her critically. He tapped his bow on the music stand, nodding his head in rhythm.*

*The girl creased her forehead, trying her best to understand the music. Tears began to stream from her eyes. All she wanted to do was escape, to run from the room. But she knew she couldn't; her father would never forgive her.*

*Finally, she could not take it any longer. She stopped playing. "I hate this music," she cried. "I can't do it."*

*Her father lowered his violin and looked at her tenderly. "Yes, you can, Julia. You must."*

*"But why, Daddy?"*

*"Because it is great music."*

*"I'll never play it the way you want me to. Why are you so hard on me?"*

*"I just want you to be the best, my darling, as I know you can be."*

*"No, no. I'll never be as good as you think I should be. I'll never live up to your expectations."*

*"You will, Julia. I believe in you."*

ᘓᘐ

Julia had slept very little that night. In the brief moments when she did manage to sink into oblivion, images she couldn't shake—of herself as a ten-year-old, practicing violin with her father, who was relentless in his insistence that she play the violin to perfection—dominated her slumber. She always had felt incapable of achieving the goals he set for her. Clearly she still felt incomplete in that regard.

She sat up in bed and revisited the scene in her now-conscious mind. It wasn't until she had grown up, long after her father had been caught in the crossfire of an attempted bank robbery on Broadway across from Lincoln Center, that she realized he not only had wanted her to be the best; he wanted only the best for her.

Not a day went by that she didn't miss him. He was her guiding light, one that had been snuffed out that day when he placed himself in the path of a streaking bullet to save her from being killed.

"Larry, wake up." Julia kept prodding Larry until he grudgingly opened his eyes and looked at the digital clock on the night table.

"Julia, what the hell. It's four a.m."

"I know, but I couldn't sleep. I had that nightmare again."

"The one about your dad? We've been down this road before."

"Yes, but I…I suddenly grasped something really important. About Blatchley. Why he's so tough with me."

"Really? And why is that?"

"It's because he wants me to be the best. Just like my dad did. He wouldn't be so demanding if he didn't think I had what it takes."

"Wow, that is eye-opening. For once you're making perfect sense, Julia. I'm proud of you."

"Really?"

"Would I exaggerate?"

Larry's condescending attitude was beginning to annoy her. "Yes, actually, you would. You do it all the time."

"Well, not this time. Any breakthrough of yours is one for our home team." He kissed her on the cheek. "Any more revelations? Or can we go back to sleep now?"

"We can." Julia, deciding to give him the benefit of the doubt, returned his display of affection. "Thanks for being there for me."

"To quote Otello, '*per sempre.*' But in the good sense."

## Chapter 24

*Ma vegli'l sospetto sui perigli che fremono intorno, ma protegga il magnanimo petto a chi nulla paventa per sé*
But may suspicion of the lurking dangers awaken to protect the magnanimous soul which fears not for itself
~ Verdi, *A Masked Ball,* Act 1

THERE WAS NO QUESTION IN JULIA'S MIND THAT *ROMÉO ET JULIETTE* WAS French grand opera at its most glorious. The music was sublime and, from what she had seen thus far, the production was sumptuous. Julia had gotten permission for Larry to attend a stage rehearsal.

"Love comes to Santa Fe," Julia told him as they entered the theatre.

"I think we've proved it's already here," he said.

She ignored his provocative smile. "I wasn't expecting the surtitles to be both in English and Spanish. I guess that's because it's co-produced with Barcelona."

"Don't they speak Catalan there?"

"True. But how many people in Santa Fe do?" She always welcomed the opportunity to challenge Larry's somewhat annoying questions, but tried to do so with an affectionate look.

"In any case, I'm happy to expand my foreign language skills."

"Why am I not surprised?" Larry grinned. "I can't wait to see you find cognates from Hungarian to Spanish."

"Watch me," she said.

Julia was glad to see both apprentices and former apprentices were slated to perform in secondary roles, including Lorelei as Juliette's nurse. Julia had extracted a promise from Larry to subtly question Lorelei about her ambitions regarding taking over Marin's role in the run of *Lulu* performances.

But as Julia approached the pit, she noticed Larry hovering in the background, chatting with a neatly bearded young man who was holding two rapiers in one hand. She approached the men and whispered in Larry's ear.

"I thought you were going to speak with Lorelei."

"I will later, no worries. This guy is much more interesting," he whispered back. "Julia, have you met Sam Chapman, the opera's fight director?" he said for them both to hear.

Sam extended his free hand. "I loved your solos in *Lulu*."

She shook his hand, her eyes focused on his swords. "Thanks, I really appreciate that. I'm not so sure Blatchley's happy, though."

"He'd be foolish not to recognize how awesomely you handled those. I can only imagine how difficult they are to play," he said, smiling. "But I'll make my opinion known to Blatchley, just to make sure."

Julia warmed to him immediately.

"Would you believe Sam says the swordplay in Act 2 is so realistic, even he was scared of some disastrous mishap in rehearsal?"

"Not quite," Sam said. "But since Shakespeare's time audiences have expected lots of audacious swagger and adrenaline-charged combat, and that's what we want to deliver. We're really fortunate to have a few members of the Wise Fool New Mexico troupe as supers. Those folks look like they've been doing this since they were kids."

The thought of men with swords blithely cavorting around a stage made Julia apprehensive. "Maybe they have been."

Sam laughed. "You could be right, Julia. Most of all they just love being a part of the opera. They're doing a great job helping the chorus members look as true-to-life as possible with their sparring."

"How do you make someone seem like they're stabbing somebody when they're actually not?" Larry asked.

"And aren't they afraid of someone swinging a sharp blade at them?" Julia added. "Or having it pointed right at their face?"

"Stage blades are never sharp, we make sure of that," Sam replied. "It's my job to generate the illusion of danger while keeping everyone as safe as possible. Ultimately, after much rehearsal, it should be about as safe as a dance. We even call it fight choreography." Sam pointed at the practice stage. "Even so, I admit having all twelve of those fencers the composer called for with their foils simultaneously at play onstage could potentially be dangerous. The trick is to keep sufficient distance between each of them so that no one's ever really in harm's way. Together with Wise Fool we've been rehearsing outdoors on the opera campus, working with the chorus and other supers, for several weeks. On the grass, no weapons at first, slowly working up to speed. By now they're all pretty much experts."

"I wouldn't mind being a super myself," said Larry. "Do you need any extras?"

Julia shot Larry a threatening glance. She didn't like to think of his getting involved in swordplay, even while playacting. "Most people steer clear of fight directors. If they're smart, that is. I know I would."

"I'm not most people."

Julia tried to hide a smile. Larry's uniqueness was one of the characteristics that first had attracted her to him. She just didn't want to be too obvious about her appreciation of it. At least not too much of the time. "Clearly. And evidently not that smart, either."

Sam laughed. "We have fifteen minutes till rehearsal starts. If you'd like, I can show you two a few stage combat moves."

"I appreciate the offer but having just said I steer clear of fight directors, I should stick to my words," Julia said. "Besides, I have to warm up."

"Oh, come on, Julia, it'll be fun," Larry said. "And you don't have any solos in this opera to worry about. So you're off the hook there."

Julia, who couldn't argue with Larry's logic, decided to let him have this one. Sighing, she followed the two men outside to a large, open space near the white baffles.

"On the topic of handling a sword, have you visited La Fonda Hotel?" Sam asked as they walked.

"No," said Larry. "Why?"

"In 1940, when Errol Flynn was here for the premiere of his film *Santa Fe Trail,* he was staying at La Fonda. After the opening, he went back to the hotel and knocked back a few too many Margaritas. He started leaping between balconies, perching on balustrades, fencing with an imaginary adversary and quoting lines from his movie, *Robin Hood*. Evidently, he thought he was back on his Hollywood set. The happening has become legend."

Larry whistled. "Very cool, but not my style," he said.

Julia was fascinated. As a kid she had loved watching vintage action movies based on adventure novels, which evoked her inner Sir Walter Scott.

Sam handed a rapier to Julia and one to Larry and showed them how to position their fingers on the narrow handle. "Keep a tight pincer grip. It should move freely in your hand. The cup hilt will protect your fingers. Especially important for you, Julia."

Julia weighed the handle in her hand. "Definitely heavier than a violin bow."

"You'll get used to it quickly enough," Sam said. "First thing you need to know is that it's natural to feel apprehensive holding the thing. You can get past it by thinking of this as a ballet rather than an adversarial battle."

"Oh, we're used to those. Adversarial battles, that is," Larry said with a wink.

Julia flashed him a mock threatening glance. "Suddenly I'm feeling like I want to learn how to use this thing after all."

Sam smiled. "I can only imagine. Now, holding the swords in front of you, turn so your sides face each other. That's the narrowest part of your body, so you present the smallest target. Extend your arms. This is called taking your measure, it's for safety. At this distance, you can see that you can't actually hurt each other. Larry, thrust your foil as if you're going to skewer Julia. When you see that threat, Julia, raise the tip of your sword and sweep it over and around Larry's blade." Sam demonstrated the movement he was describing. "Now step through, Julia, like this, and turn, so you're shoulder to shoulder with Larry.

"Nudge his shoulder with your sword arm. Remember, this is pretend, it's just for show. Be careful not to hit Larry's shoulder too hard, you can jar the nerve and make his arm go numb.

"With your other hand, slap your own thigh on the side the audience can't see—that makes a sound we call a knap—and it will sound like you hit him pretty hard. Remember, just a nudge.

"Larry, sell the blow by acting like she really walloped you. That's it.

"Lastly, Julia, beat his blade aside, right here, like this...knocking it out of his grasp."

When they had blocked out the fight, Julia, who had studied ballet even before she had started playing the violin and was proficient at movement as well as at following directions, executed Sam's instructions seamlessly. She parried Larry's thrust, quickly closed the space between them, turned, shouldered Larry, and then, sure enough, smacked the sword smartly, right out of Larry's hand. It clattered to the floor.

Julia was amazed and pleased. "Wow. You were right, Larry. This is fun."

"Beginner's luck," Larry muttered.

"I disagree, Larry. I think Julia's got a real gift. She's impressively light on her feet."

Julia could see that Larry was trying, with little success, not to acknowledge her gratified smirk.

"Eight minutes," came the call from the P.A. "This is your eight-minute call, ladies and gentlemen."

Julia handed her sword to Sam. "I hate to leave you two warriors, but I actually have a real job," she said, and marched triumphantly toward the hall.

Sam turned to Larry. "I have to go, too. A few last-minute tweaks to the combatants before the music starts. Keep at it."

He walked off, as Larry continued to practice his thrust and parry.

Julia returned to the theatre in time to watch Sam make his last-minute adjustments. She was impressed with the way Sam put the choristers and supers through their paces, showing them how to make imitation kicks and punches look real. He clearly was a real pro.

"No contact to his knee, okay? Here, let me show you."

Sam demonstrated how to simulate touching another person. "It's really a "para" punch, but we have to hear the 'knap'—the sound of it. One way or other, the other guy has to end up on the floor. And the audience has to feel that the end result is going to be death."

The super in question followed Sam's instructions. Sam nodded his approval. "Well done. And I know you're having fun, but stop smiling," he said with a grin.

He turned to the two singers who were playing the dueling rivals, Tybalt and Mercutio. "Remember, Mercutio, you're out for his blood. You can almost taste it," Sam said. "That's it! Fantastic. Your fencing is as dazzling as your singing."

After Julia had tuned the orchestra and taken her seat, she saw Larry wave to her from about midway back in the orchestra section. She mouthed the word "Lorelei" to him. He nodded and gestured a thumbs-up.

Stewart climbed up to the podium. "Act 2," he announced. "Fight scene."

Julia was trying not to watch the skirmishes as she negotiated the aggressively difficult violin part. But between the slashing and stabbing onstage and the powerful, goose bump-inducing music, both in the orchestra and from the singers, she was having a hard time concentrating.

*Capulets, Capulets! Montaigus, Montaigus! Race immonde! Frémissez de terreur!*

*Que l'enfer seconde…Sa Haine et sa fureur!*

[Capulets, Capulets! Montagues, Montagues! Vile clan! Shake with terror!...

May hell assist our hate and our fury!]

Unable to restrain herself despite what she knew would be Stewart's ire, Julia chanced a look up at the stage. At the very back, at the far limit of her sight line, a shadowy figure who was not in costume and clearly not part of the action crept in the background behind the players.

*What…who…?*

From the person's attire—Bermuda shorts and a straw hat—Julia could tell he or she was not a player or stagehand. When she blinked, the figure disappeared. Puzzled, she shook her head and turned her attention back to the combat scene, wincing as she saw Mercutio throw Tybalt to the floor with all-too convincing violence.

Tybalt scrambled to one knee and, as Mercutio came to offer him a hand up, vengefully ran Mercutio through.

A grief-stricken Romeo confronted Tybalt.

*Tybalt! Il n'est ici d'autre lâche que toi! À toi…!*

[Tybalt, you're the only villain here now! To you…!]

Romeo drew his sword from his scabbard to fight Tybalt. He swung it once in a furious "*en garde.*" As he did, Julia was horrified to see the blade suddenly separate from the hilt. Even more terrifying, the blade was flying full force toward the pit.

And it was coming straight at her.

## Chapter 25

*Mir sträubt sich schon das Haar...mir fällt kein Mittel ein!*
My hair stands on end...I see no way out!
~ Beethoven, *Fidelio,* Act 1

A COLLECTIVE GASP EMITTED FROM BOTH STAGE AND PIT AS PERFORMERS watched the blade hurtle through the air, graze the left side of Julia's rib cage and crash onto the pit floor with a loud thump.

With only a split second to react, Julia, far more worried about potential damage to her instrument than to herself, instinctively clutched her violin to her chest.

Larry leapt up from his seat in the hall, tore down the aisle to the pit and leaned over the rail. "Julia, what happened? Are you all right?" Seeing the gash in her torso, he drew in a deep breath. "Oh, my God, you're hurt!"

Not waiting for a reply, he rushed to the backstage area, climbed up to the pit door, threw it open and pushed his way through the music stands and musicians to Julia's desk. Her slight body was shaking.

Matt, hovering over Julia, murmured to Larry. "She doesn't seem as agitated as I'd expect. Maybe it's because she's in shock. In any case, they've called 911."

Julia, her arms still wrapped protectively around her violin, murmured through tight lips. "It's just a scratch. I'm fine."

"You definitely are not. You're bleeding," Larry said.

"Doesn't matter, as long as the fiddle is okay." She looked down at her left flank and frowned. "Good thing I wore red today."

"Wow, you're right, she really is in shock," Larry whispered to Matt.

Julia looked up to see that two EMTs had appeared by her side. She held the violin more tightly. "What are you doing?"

"We're taking you to the hospital, ma'am," one of them said.

The other EMT turned to Larry. "There's a stretcher waiting in the hallway. No room for it in here. I'll have to carry her out."

Julia was beginning to feel the pain from her wound but was determined not to show it. "I don't need a stretcher. I'm fine."

"You're in shock," Larry said. "Just let them take you to the hospital, okay."

"But…my violin—"

"Give it to me," Matt said. "I'll make sure it's safely put away."

He reached for the instrument, but Julia still gripped it tightly. "No, no. There's no reason. I'll just put it in my case myself."

Larry gently pried the instrument from her grasp and carefully handed it over to Matt.

"Let Matt take care of it. You know can trust him, right?"

"Yes, yes. I just…Oh…" She started to swoon. "I feel a little… spacey."

The EMT caught her before she keeled over. Julia reluctantly let go of the violin, relinquishing it to Matt, as the EMT held gauze against her torso.

Sam rushed to her side, panicked. "Julia! I'm so sorry. I don't know how this happened. We've never seen anything like it before. We'll find out who's to blame for this, I promise."

"It's…it's…not your fault, Sam. But…" She struggled to catch her breath. "Didn't you say that the…the blades weren't sharp?"

"They shouldn't be." Sam picked the blade up from the floor and inspected it. "This one doesn't look like one of ours. It's too sharp. And the plastic tip is missing. It's almost like someone has tinkered with it."

"It was John Crosby," Julia said. "I'm sure of it. I saw him lurking around at the back of the stage during the fight scene."

Julia looked from Larry to Matt to Sam and Back to Larry. She guessed the concern etched into their faces was genuine. Then she passed out.

The second EMT carefully lifted Julia up, swiftly carried her out of the pit, making sure to avoid bumping into any music stands, and placed her on the waiting stretcher outside the door.

Larry followed the other EMT out of the pit. Matt stayed behind, Julia's violin firmly in his grasp.

ᐅᐊ

At the hospital ER, Larry watched as the resident cleaned and dressed Julia's laceration. "She was very lucky. It's just a superficial flesh wound, no stitches required," he said. "But she'll have to be careful about keeping it clean." He handed Larry a sheet of discharge instructions. "She should follow up with her PCP."

"No can do," Larry said. "We're from out of state. Just here for the summer."

"Then be extra careful about changing the dressing. Watch for fever above 101, swelling or excessive draining. And bring her back here in two days for a follow up."

"That we can do." Larry turned to Julia. "Are you good to go?"

"Of course," she said, but without her usual conviction. "I need to get back to rehearsal."

The Resident shook his head. "I'm afraid no violin playing for you till after your follow up. At least for the next couple of days."

"But…they're expecting me to work."

"Not after what you've just been through." Larry turned to the doctor. "Thanks for your help."

With his arm held firmly around her waist, Larry led the sulking Julia out of the ER, and toward the hospital entrance.

"I'm going to find out who's responsible for this," Julia said, with as much conviction as she could muster in her weakened state.

"Are you delirious? You just asked me a while ago to take over questioning for you. Now you want to start investigating again?"

"How can I not?"

"Easy," Larry said. "Let the SFPD handle it."

"They've already got their hands full," Julia said. Her resolve was flagging.

"And so do you. Healing your wound." Larry helped Julia into the Uber car awaiting them in front of the hospital. "No arguments."

"I do appreciate your trying to take such good care of me, Larry, but—"

"But nothing. Taking care of you, not to mention keeping you from embroiling yourself in yet another heap of trouble, is one of the worst tasks on the planet. You're lucky I'm here to do it."

Julia brooded for a moment, her eyes fixed on the car window. She wasn't ready to give up just yet. She turned back to Larry. "And what about Marin?" Julia said. "She's still in trouble. I promised her to do everything I could to help her cause. I can't give up now."

"You're injured," Larry said. "She'll understand."

The car sped through the streets. Julia didn't even try to hide her discontent.

## Chapter 26

*Dalla sua pace la mia dipende...È mia quell'ira, quel pianto è mio*
On her peace of mind my own depends...her anger and her sorrow are mine
~ Mozart, *Don Giovanni,* Act 1

JULIA WAS STILL FRETTING WHEN THE CAR DEPOSITED HER AND LARRY IN front of the inn. But worry turned to surprise when she saw Sandor seated in the lobby by the fireplace.

When Julia and Larry entered, Sandor rose and approached the couple. "Julia, I was so distressed when I heard what happened to you. Is there anything I can do?"

Despite her debilitated state, Julia felt deeply touched by his concern. "Sandor, you didn't have to come all the way here to check on me. I'm fine."

"It's no trouble. I needed to know you were not in danger. The maestro also wanted me to let you know not to be concerned about work. He said just to take your time and heal."

"That's very big of him," Julia said, surprised and a bit wary.

Sandor indicated a large, comfy leather sofa. "Might you have a moment to talk?"

Larry waved a hand in protest. "She's supposed to rest. Doctor's orders."

"I have two days to do that, Larry. I want to hear what he has to say," Julia said. "It's not every day Blatchley shows signs of sympathy."

Julia wearily sank into the sofa. Larry scowled but made no attempt to argue. When all three were seated, Sandor took Julia's hand and looked into her eyes.

"You've had a difficult time since you've been here, and I feel terrible about it. I wanted to offer a suggestion to help you cope."

"After what I've been through, I'm open to anything."

"I've been living here a long time and am familiar with the stresses of performing in the company," Sandor said. "We are all a family, a tribe if you will, devoted to our way of life and to one objective. The highest possible standard in every undertaking. That was Crosby's ideal."

"I'm certainly aware of it by now." Julia's interest was piqued. She wondered what he was getting at. "And?"

"We've followed that principle at Santa Fe Opera ever since Crosby first guided his modest but daring troupe of freethinking artists in a tiny open-air theatre our first season. He kept on that pathway in all his efforts, whether leading from the podium or planting flowers and bushes in the gardens. He didn't care if some critics called his more contemporary operas unsingable or decadent. If Maestro Blatchley is tough with you, it's only because he is committed to maintaining that paradigm."

"What's your point?" Larry asked.

"Creating art is a gift that comes from a greater being. As artists, we have the 'divine afflatus,' that spiritual element we are attuned to that helps us access our highest selves, feeds us and propels us into creative realms we couldn't conceive of ourselves. I think we have the ability to be in touch with that afflatus, to reflect it upon those around us." Sandor paused. "I remember when I was preparing to sing Apollo in *Daphne,* a tough role. It felt fine working on it, but when I got out there and started to struggle I thought, 'What's going to happen here?' Then something came over me and suddenly I was in total control. I surprised myself how well I sang. Moments like that... for a performer they happen without necessarily knowing how they happen."

"Creative people are not always the nicest to be around, though." Given her recent experiences, Julia was well aware of that fact.

"True. But when we get out of our own way, the afflatus makes us respond to its own spiritual harmonies and wonderful things happen, especially in the extraordinary atmosphere of Santa Fe," Sandor said. "I strongly believe in the spiritual energy of the early indigenous people here. It gives us beauty, mystery, and feeds the art. I have a friend, Miles, a Navajo shaman and spiritualist, who leads one-day vision quests up in the mountains. I think he can help you heal, physically and spiritually."

Larry's expression darkened. "What makes you think she needs spiritual healing?"

"Most of us need our sprits fed. With our high, dry climate, azure skies, mountains and canyons, we live in one of the most restorative environments in the world here," Sandor said. "Julia has been through a lot of difficulty in a very short time. She might benefit from resetting her spiritual outlook, to help overcome her traumas, to live fully in the present. It might help you, too, Larry."

"Me? It's not in my DNA."

"If you have questions, Larry, I'm happy to answer them," Sandor said. "Let me give you my cell number. You can send me a text whenever you like."

"If you insist."

"Thank you." Sandor tapped his number into Larry's phone.

"Sandor's right, Larry." Julia was beginning to see wisdom in Sandor's assertions. "I have been dealing with a lot since I've been here. I need to sort things out, in a different atmosphere away from here." She turned to Sandor. "I'm in."

Larry grimaced. "Julia, you can't be serious. The doc said you need to rest."

"Relieving my stress will benefit me more."

"Suit yourself," said Larry. "But count me out."

Julia countered Larry's skeptical gaze with her own challenging one. "I don't think so."

## Chapter 27

*Ah, quelle est cette voix qui me trouble l'ésprit?*
Ah, what is this voice troubling my spirit?
~ Offenbach, *The Tales of Hoffmann*, Act 3

JULIA AND LARRY MET MILES ON A HIGH DESERT MESA IN THE SANGRE DE Cristo Mountains, ninety miles northeast of Santa Fe. To the east lay the western border of the Great Plains; to the west, the eastern edge of the Taos Plateau. Ponderosa pine forests, rocky ridges, valleys and meadows were visible in all directions. The setting was undeniably exquisite.

With his rugged, weather-worn face, waist-length ebony hair and broad shoulders, Miles gave the impression of being older and taller than he was. To Julia he seemed exceedingly serene and otherworldly, despite his work shirt and frayed jeans; the dreamcatcher hanging from the rearview mirror of his van, its image of a drum encircled by eagle feathers, was a tipoff to his mystical nature.

The first thing he did was hug Julia and Larry. He took note of Julia's surprise and Larry's discomfort. "It's normal for some men to feel awkward at a stranger's hug," Miles said, smiling.

"That's not the only thing that makes me feel uncomfortable here," Larry said.

"I understand, Larry. Some people are reluctant to connect with their higher selves and to believe in the concept of becoming one with the Spirit."

Miles pulled a photo from his shirt pocket. It showed a handsome Native American man in an army uniform. "This is my dad. When he came back from Vietnam his PTSD was so severe, he lost his way in a haze of alcohol. He found himself again by doing vision quests. He never drank again." A faint smile crossed his lips. "Then one of our Navajo brothers taught Dad to make traditional pottery. Now his work is considered some of the most authentic being sold at the Native American market in Santa Fe Plaza. The Opera has also commissioned this year's poster art from him."

Julia remembered the Navajo artisans displaying their earthenware in front of the Palace of Governors shone. It did her heart good to feel a personal connection to what she had seen. "What an inspiring story."

"Thank you, Julia. I think so, too." Miles gently clasped Larry's hand. "Our ancestors called this land *Dancing Ground of The Sun*. New Mexico's most magnificent mountains surround us, mountains whose crystalline rock core is five-hundred-seventy million years old. The ley lines that crisscross Santa Fe create a special energy vortex, heightening the spiritual and psychic vitality of our terrain. As the day evolves you will comprehend the worth of our journey."

The shaman reached inside his van and pulled out three highly ornamented drums and three colorful pueblo style blankets. He offered Julia and Larry each a blanket and a drum.

"Sandor tells me you've come from New York to perform with the Santa Fe Opera here, Julia," Miles said. "As a kid growing up, I watched dress rehearsals from their Pueblo Opera Program, where they bused us in to the theatre from the reservations. I was skeptical at first, but then I became hooked on opera. Now I am eternally grateful for that opportunity."

Miles seated himself cross-legged on the ground, wrapped a blanket around his shoulders and gestured to Julia and Larry to do the same. "Julia, Sandor told me about your recent traumas. Would you like to know more about what the Holy Spirit has in mind for you?"

Julia, sitting on the ground beside Miles, was beginning to feel drawn to his fervor and to the dynamism of his personality. She nodded. Larry took a seat beside her and stayed close.

"In our wilderness ceremony," Miles began, "we learn unifying lessons of love that have eluded us since leaving childhood, by forming a meaningful relationship to human nature and Mother Earth and removing the masks we wear that distort our normal ego consciousness. This broadens our limitations and deepens our connection to Nature, beckoning us to reconnect with our ancient tribal roots. It is a deeply transformative journey of self-discovery that is woven into our indigenous culture. The wisdom and experience of our Native

American ancestors, especially the Anasazi cliff dwellers, will help us on our path."

"How do I know if it will help *me*?" Julia asked.

"Mother Earth does not exclude anyone," Miles said. "Thus, all are invited to experience our native transformative ceremony to discover their own power, as we are surrounded by the geologic wonders of our lands. That is why we use these ancient shamanistic tools. A vision quest will guide you to physical and spiritual healing,"

Larry stared down at his drum and muttered under his breath.

"I can see you're wondering about the rationale behind our drumming, Larry," Miles said. "Rhythm has been a part of our makeup since we were conceived. We are created from it. Drumming connects us with larger cosmic rhythms—of the seasons, the planets, the galaxy. And most importantly, with the mountain ranges and diverse cultures of the Pueblos around us. The Tiwa people of the Taos Pueblo pray the sun up daily. Look around you and you will see the petroglyphs of the Pueblo peoples etched into many boulders."

Julia turned her head and spied a rock escarpment with symbols engraved on it. She motioned to Larry, who raised his eyebrows in acknowledgment.

"As you drum, think of yourself as unbound from your mental turmoil." Miles demonstrated a slow, gentle rhythmic tapping. "Clear your body and mind, that you can contemplate who you are and who you have always wanted to be. Remove the toxins from your soul. All things around you—rocks, trees, air, birds, even your blankets—are alive, mindful, and voicing their being to you."

Miles continued to drum. He nodded to Larry.

"You try, Julia," Larry said. "You're the musician."

"We are all musicians of the spirit," Miles said. "And Mother Earth responds most generously to collective communication from all of us."

Julia imitated Miles's example. After a moment, Larry tentatively joined them. Soon the sounds of their beating punctuated the mountain air.

"A mind preoccupied with thoughts and worries will hinder your understanding of the Spirit. Divest yourself of the debris that litters your mind, Julia. Think about your traumas. Not only the recent ones but those from times past. What hunger at your soul level needs to be satisfied?"

As Julia further immersed herself in her drumming, she became cognizant of her obsession with her work responsibilities. Visions played in her mind: she with her violin; Abel, her father, and Sidney, all hovering over her, love and caring in their regard. An unanticipated emptiness began to ache inside of her. She was grieving: for the loss of her father, of Abel, of Sidney. She felt broken. Then a desire to connect more deeply with Larry overcame her. Profound sobs that seemed as if they would never end surged up from her core.

"Be in touch with your pain, Julia," Miles said. "Give it back to Mother Earth."

Larry stopped drumming and glared at Miles. "This is not helping. You're making her upset."

"On the contrary, Larry. It is all part of the process. By healing herself she is healing the Earth, returning the Earth's gifts to the living creatures around us."

Julia, eyes closed, was so engrossed in her personal experience she was barely aware of the conversation. In her mind, she could see an approval in her father's and Abel's expressions that soothed her soul.

*We're always with you.*

Then the specter of a man in a tuxedo holding a baton entered the image and gave her a penetrating stare. At first she was confused, but when she recognized him from the photos she had seen of John Crosby in his conductor's attire, she gasped.

*Is he trying to tell me something? Is he distraught over all the violence in his opera company?*

The true identity of the mysterious figure she had seen lurking in the shadows behind the opera house still eluded Julia, but whether or not it actually had been the ghost of Crosby seemed less important than the message that came across to her:

*Find the killer.*

ꕥ

After what seemed like hours, Julia's visions started to fade. She felt profound sadness, but ultimately was filled with a tranquility deeper than any she had ever known. The wound in her side no longer hurt. Her fears and feelings of desolation were replaced with what seemed like the Spirit that Miles had described. She knew she was well on her way to healing and would be ready for anything life was going to hand her from that point onward. Then she opened her eyes to the most exquisite sunset she had ever seen, a golden orb that seemed to melt into the horizon.

"When the Native Pueblo Indians briefly overcame the Spanish in the Revolt of 1680," Miles said, "A dying Spanish priest prayed to heaven for a sign. The radiance of the sky as it turned crimson symbolized what he had yearned for. He died with the words, *Sangre de Cristo,* 'The Blood of Christ,' on his lips. That's how these mountains got their name." Miles stood up. "Let's join hands and thank Mother Earth for her endowments."

He hummed softly for a long moment. Then he let go of Julia and Larry's hands and handed them each a small red stone. "This is a gift of your retreat. Keep it as a reminder of the love and constant presence of the Spirit."

He gave them each another hug. Julia wasn't sure, but she thought that the hug she received from Miles was longer and more intense than the one he gave Larry.

She knew she wasn't imagining it when she recognized the look of jealousy in Larry's eyes.

## Chapter 28

*Ich glaube, es ist schon lange hier, dass er gefangen ist? Er muss ein grosser Verbrecher sein!...oder er muss grosse Feinde haben*
I believe he has been in prison for a long time? He must have committed a great crime! Or he must have a great enemy
~ Beethoven, *Fidelio,* Act 1

ELAINE SAT BY MARIN AT THE TABLE IN THE COUNTY JAIL INTERROGATION room opposite the DA. Elaine was worried about Marin, who had lost so much weight that her prison scrubs hung off her body. And just today, Elaine had informed Marin that Henry had fast-tracked the trial date in order to obtain swift sentencing.

What Marin didn't know was that the DA had been coordinating with Stella Peregrine, who had been frequenting the forensics lab at the New Mexico Department of Public Safety, making note of their results and consulting with them about providing their expert testimony in Marin's trial. Stella also had questioned Deborah, who had confirmed Marin's deep-seated resentment about Deborah's transferring her affections to Emilia.

Elaine had been conferring with the DPS lab, and with the lab's assigned analyst, to keep track of the case's status and to arm herself with as much information as possible, with anything that might mitigate Marin's situation.

Unfortunately, there was little evidence to favor Marin. Subsequent testing confirmed initial findings, and no other evidence was available. The Latent Print Unit had processed the knife and the crime scene for the presence of invisible prints. Elaine knew they used the latest scientific chemical and illumination techniques in their search efforts and, when relevant, also used the Automated Fingerprint Identification System to compare prints with other records in their database. They would also offer testimony if needed.

The Biology Unit had analyzed the weapon and the scene for DNA and compared it with Marin's. The fact that no trace of Marin's DNA was evident on Emilia's body was the only factor in Marin's favor.

Other than that, there was nothing to help plead Marin's case, other than her being a first-time offender.

With so little to go on, Elaine was at a loss when Henry made his plea offer.

"Twenty-five years to life," he said.

"You've got to be kidding, Henry. Marin has never so much as killed a cockroach. Five years and a fifteen thousand dollar fine."

"What you're suggesting is a sentence for a first-degree felony. She's committed premeditated murder, a capital crime."

"You'll have to prove it first. The jury will side with her for sure."

"What makes you think so? She bumped off a famous opera singer, with whom she had a known dispute resulting in heated discussions on more than one occasion."

"Marin's famous, too. Or have you forgotten?"

"Don't forget her jealousy over the stolen lover," Henry added hastily. "Whose identity, by the way, we've confirmed."

Marin's hands began to shake. "Excuse me, I'm here, you know."

"She's right, Henry. It's very insensitive of you to ignore her presence." Elaine placed her hands over Marin's to calm the tremors. "And no judge is going to sentence a woman as severely as you're proposing."

"I disagree. Women's incarceration rates have exploded over the last few years," Henry said. "If she takes the plea, at least she'll have the possibility of parole."

Elaine flashed an inquiring look in Marin's direction.

Marin shook her head. "I'm innocent," she said, through her teeth.

"I know you are," said Elaine. "We're done here, Henry."

"Suit yourself, Elaine. But don't wait too long. The offer will get cold before you know it."

ꕥ

By the time Julia returned to work, she already had missed two days of rehearsal for *Lucia di Lammermoor.* When she arrived backstage, Julia received warm greetings from her orchestra colleagues, with the exception of Lenny who, predictably, looked none too thrilled to see her.

Matt was especially attentive, smiling and squeezing her shoulder in sympathetic gestures. Larry had gotten permission to attend the rehearsal to support Julia.

As the musicians entered the pit, Paul, the flutist who had claimed to have seen John Crosby's ghost, whispered to Julia. "I'm surprised to see you back so soon. How did you manage such a speedy healing from your injury?"

Julia thought for a moment. She didn't know Paul very well and wasn't sure if she should confide in him. But he did seem more open to so-called "spiritual" phenomena than the other orchestra members.

"I went on a vision quest," she said softly.

"Wise choice. I applaud you," he said. "A vision quest is the best way to neutralize negativity."

Somehow she wasn't surprised. "You've done it?"

"Many times. A lot of us musicians have outside interests to handle the stresses of performing. The second clarinetist studies astronomy and archaeology. The timpanist likes to solve math problems in his extra time. The first trombone likes to fish. And of course, we have our softball matches. For me it's vision quests. They really can help you cope. Especially if you're sensitive to the spirits haunting this part of the world. And there are too many to count."

Julia winced as she remembered her unsettling encounters, both in her room at the Inn and in La Posada's "Julia Staab Suite", not to mention her sightings of what looked like Crosby's ghost.

"I've...seen a presence," Julia whispered.

"I see," Paul said. "Do you want to talk about it?"

Julia hesitated.

"Most ghosts are easy, benevolent. Nothing to be afraid of, Julia," Paul said. "If you'd like to share any of your experience, I'm happy to listen."

"Some other time. But thanks for asking."

Luckily there were no violin solos in *Lucia,* so Blatchley did not seem annoyed at Julia's absence from work. In fact, she was surprised at how solicitous he was to her.

"Are you all right, Julia? Not in too much pain, I hope?" he asked when she sat down in her chair after tuning the orchestra.

"I'm fine, Stewart, thank you for asking. Two days off were all I needed."

"Good, good."

*Well, that is an unexpected relief.*

Stewart turned to the assembled musicians. "Act 2 Sextet scene, please."

*Lucia* was not Julia's favorite Donizetti opera. She much preferred the composer's comedies, especially the captivating *Don Pasquale,* which, she had been told, was great diva Beverly Sills' swan song at the Met.

However, Julia had been a huge fan of Sir Walter Scott's evocative novels when she was growing up. Scotland's flamboyant—and admittedly bloody—history fascinated her. She had heard that the greatest operatic legend to sing Scott's *Lucy of Lammermoor* was Dame Joan Sutherland. Julia wished she had been around to see Sutherland and Sills perform.

Alejandro Fernandez, the production's South American director, made his wishes known to the ranks. "Places, please. Harold, collect everyone, if you can."

The stage manager shepherded chorus and ballet members who had been randomly peppering the stage. Alejandro then arranged the players in formation for the wedding reception scene.

"Chorus, make this a celebration to remember. The contrast between it and the tragedy to come must be startling."

Julia was quite surprised when she looked up at the stage to see Deborah take her place as lead soprano and protagonist Lucia.

"Deborah, again?" Julia said to Matt. "Isn't that unusual for an apprentice, even for Santa Fe?"

He nodded. "She's been understudying everything. Her success story as apprentice-suddenly-turned-diva will go down in the annals of the company."

That seemed a bit over the top to Julia. "I wonder what Rob has to say about that."

"Just ask him. I'm sure he'll fill your ear, as always. In her defense, she did jump in at the eleventh hour last season as Norina in *Don Pasquale,* and did a fantastic job. They really appreciate that sort of thing here."

"So I've learned." Julia watched a male singer move close to Deborah. "Who's that?"

"Adam Conrad, the *comprimario* tenor who plays Lucia's arranged husband, Arturo," Matt said. "Strangely enough, he's not an apprentice."

Julia lowered her voice to a confidential whisper. "He's terribly cute. I can't imagine this 'Bride of Lammermoor' could object to being married to him, whether it's diplomatically advantageous or not."

Alejandro steered Adam and Deborah toward the apron of the stage, where Julia was close enough to catch the drift of the two singers' conversation.

"SFeO's catchphrase for *Lucia* is 'A wedding to die for,'" said Adam.

"Well, that's what the lead tenor Edgardo gets for going off to France to flirt with French girls and leaving me in the lurch," Deborah said, with a tinge of haughtiness. "Although a guy as hot as you could do worse, all things considered."

"And yet you reward me by stabbing me to death?"

Deborah chortled. "How else would I have an excuse to lose my mind in front of two thousand people?"

## Chapter 29

*Proschai, pokoi!*
Farewell, peace of mind!
~ Tchaikovsky, *The Queen of Spades,* Act 1

THE OTHER FOUR SINGERS GATHERED AROUND DEBORAH AND ADAM FOR the sextet.

"Remember, Deborah, you are a woman on the verge of a total emotional collapse, who cannot bear your present reality," Alejandro said. "You're torn between forbidden love and family duty. This scene foreshadows your impending withdrawal into complete insanity."

Stewart tapped his baton on the podium, bringing the orchestra to attention. Julia followed his downbeat, leading the stream of string *pizzicati* in the opening phrases. She listened as the principal tenor expressed his fury.

*Chi mi frena in tal momento, chi troncò dell'ira il corso?*

[Who holds me back at such a moment, who stemmed the flood of my anger?]

As the plucking morphed into a soaring melody, Julia had to admit the sextet was pleasurable, both to play and to hear. Donizetti was not her favorite composer, but he certainly could write tunes on a par with the best. Plus, he was astonishingly prolific: the melody brought to mind an image she had seen of the composer with a pen in each hand, writing simultaneously with both.

"Very good, everyone," Stewart called out as the piece ended. "Act 3, Mad Scene, please."

Julia watched Alejandro reposition the players onstage, shuffling them about like a deck of cards, and moving Deborah, Adam and the other soloists off.

The chorus sang of their exultation over the grand celebratory wedding reception.

*D'immenso giubilo s'innalzi un grido, corra la Scozia di lido in lido, e avverta i perfidi nostri nemici che a noi sorridono le stelle ancor.*

[Let us raise our voices in wild jubilation, to rouse Scotland from shore to shore and warn our perfidious enemies that fortune smiles on us still.]

Alejandro wove through the hordes of choristers and approached the apron of the stage. "Maestro, may we take a break now? I'd like to give the chorus some notes before we proceed to the Mad Scene."

"Absolutely." Stewart placed his baton on top of his orchestra score. "Fifteen minutes, please."

Adam tapped Alejandro's shoulder. "Will you be needing me after the break? I could use a coffee. I'm dying up here."

"Not literally, I hope," said Alejandro.

He and Adam shared a laugh. "We may be doing the Sextet again. Don't go too far."

"Whatever you say, *Capitano*."

Matt leaned over to Julia. "I can't wait for the Mad Scene. That glass harmonica makes the atmosphere positively eerie."

Julia shuddered. Notwithstanding her fascination with Sir Walter Scott, she didn't like being reminded of ghostly encounters, past or present.

ೞೞ

Adam stretched out on the chaise in his dressing room with his latte, eyes closed, lights dimmed, feeling totally relaxed.

His role was a small one, but playing it in Santa Fe was akin to performing it in paradise.

The physical beauty surrounding him enriched his creativity. Cute bunnies cavorted around the lawns while birds chirped agreeably in the background; glorious melodies resounded from every corner; children's laughter emanated from the swimming pool. And stunning, multihued sunsets brought the idyllic days to a close. It was almost like something out of Disney, except more real.

Life was good.

Adam heard the door open, but was too blissed out to acknowledge the person entering. He assumed it must be one of the dressers bringing some accessory for his costume.

"Felipe, is that you?"

Opening his eyes, Adam could see someone approaching him in the semi-darkness, carrying what looked like a small object. "Is that the missing pommel from my sword?"

There was no response. He had no time to put down his latte. The cup fell from his hand and splattered on the floor as the sharp point entered his torso and tore his flesh. He uttered a brief cry—of surprise, of pain—before collapsing back onto the chaise in a glossy, wet patch of crimson.

The unending parade of dramatic *agita* onstage never ceased to amaze Julia, who knew from studying the libretto that Lucia's troublemaking brother orders the crowd to stop their merrymaking. Having heard terrifying moans emitting from the bridal chamber, he has discovered Lucia clutching the dagger with which she has stabbed her bridegroom to death.

*From exultation to murder. That's opera.*

Right on cue, Deborah staggered in, clenching the weapon, her expression crazed, her pristine white wedding gown soaked with scarlet.

*Il dolce suono mi colpì di sua voce!... Ah, Edgardo, io ti son resa.*

[I was stirred by the sweet sound of his voice! Ah, Edgardo, I am yours again.]

Then Alejandro, his face as pale as Deborah's gossamer gown, appeared behind Stewart and whispered into the maestro's ear.

Stewart grimaced. "But we just had a break."

Alejandro whispered something else and rushed off. Stewart stopped conducting. Confused whispers circulated among the musicians.

Julia looked at Matt, puzzled. He mouthed the words, "I have no idea."

Rising to her feet, Julia stood on her tiptoes, trying to get a better look at the stage to sense what was going on. In the wings, she could spy chaos: Harold, Alejandro, Deborah and several stagehands were involved in a heated discussion. It was all but inaudible to Julia, but clearly they were highly distressed.

Stewart placed his baton inside his orchestra score and turned to Julia. "I'm afraid I have to go backstage to try and help control a calamitous situation."

"Calamitous situation?"

"Harold found Adam in his dressing room. He's been stabbed to death."

## Chapter 30

*Egli è là...morto!*
He's there...dead!
~ Verdi, *Rigoletto,* Act 3

Reports of Adam's demise quickly circulated among company members. Some were sanguine: accounts of senseless violence were all too frequent in the U.S., and many people had become inured to such tragedies. Others panicked. Julia was among the latter.

"How is this possible? How can it be happening again? How?" Julia said to Katie as they sat together on sofas in the orchestra lounge. "I suppose we'll have to wait till they interrogate us, like last time. Once they're done, I'm out of here."

"Me, too."

"No," Julia said. She knew she would have to be blunt and exceedingly clear to make Katie understand the true significance of what she was about to tell her. "I mean really out of here. I want to go home."

"Back to New York? But you. . .you can't."

"Oh yes, I can. Face it, Katie, the vibes in this place are unreal."

"They're not worse than the Met, if you remember," said Katie.

"Is that supposed to make me feel better?"

"I think that was the general idea." Larry had appeared by Julia's side. "At least Katie's trying."

Larry settled in next to Julia, placed his arm around her shoulder and smiled ironically. "If there's anything we found out at the Met, it's that opera can kill you."

Thoughts came flooding back to Julia. Of her inadvertently placing herself in jeopardy trying to get to the bottom of Abel's murder. Of how close she came to losing her life in the process. "That's not funny." She pulled away, annoyed. "And it definitely doesn't make me feel better."

"On the bright side, you rose to meet adversity," Larry said. "Have you forgotten that your investigative efforts at the Met were responsible for finding the real killer?"

Suddenly an apparition from her vision quest, of Crosby telling her to find the real killer wreaking havoc in his opera company, popped into her mind. She shook off the unwelcome image. It was the last thing she needed right now. "That's exactly what I was talking about. Thanks for reminding me that once is enough. I'm still going home. To New York."

"Are you sure? After I finally convinced Stella that you're the person she needs to consult with to get to the bottom of these murders?"

"You *what*?" Julia was appalled. "Why would you do that?"

"Because I could really use your expertise."

Julia looked up to see Stella hovering nearby. "I'm afraid you're laboring under a misconception, Detective."

"On the contrary. Once Larry filled me in on the details of your tireless work in uncovering the truth behind the Met murders, I realized you could be a valuable asset."

"I'm done with investigating." Julia lifted the hem of her T-shirt to reveal her bandaged torso. "I think I've already sustained enough damage in the line of duty here."

"That was an accident," Katie said.

"Or not."

"You think someone had it in for you, Julia?" Larry asked.

"'Sigh no more, ladies, sigh no more,'" Stella said. "I know I've been a bit hard on you, Julia."

Julia frowned. "You think?"

"And I apologize. I'd really like to team up with you."

"Which means you're not going anywhere," Katie said.

"Just think about it, Julia," Stella said. "We really could use your skills. For now, Grabowski is backstage interviewing cast and crew. An enormous task. Meanwhile, I have to get started on the orchestra." She sat down next to Julia. "And you're first on my list. So where were you when the fun began?"

&

Constantin heaved a sigh as he entered Stieren Hall and spied the throngs of stagehands, choristers and soloists waiting to be interviewed, Harold, Alejandro and Stewart among them. In contrast to

*Lulu,* this *Lucia* opera had a cast of thousands—or at least hundreds.

The detective decided to begin with Harold, who repeatedly pushed his glasses higher up on his nose. To Constantin, that kind of fidgeting was a clear tipoff to the stage manager's overall state of agitation.

"You found the victim?"

"I...I went to his dressing room to tell him that Alejandro—the director—was calling him back for notes after the scene was finished. He...he was all...bloodied. And when he didn't move..." Harold shuddered. "Oh, God."

"Did you see anyone in the hallway outside the dressing room?"

"Just the usual people. Stagehands, costume people, the wig person."

"Was there any sign of a weapon anywhere?"

"No, no, there was nothing there except...Adam's...body." Harold broke down and sobbed.

"Okay, that's all for now. Don't go anywhere."

Constantin moved on to Stewart and Alejandro, who were huddled together in a corner.

"It's beginning to feel like *déjà vu,* isn't it, Mr. Grabowski?" Stewart said.

"Can't argue with that, Maestro. But this time it happened in rehearsal instead of a performance."

"I suppose we have to count our blessings, such as they are," Stewart said.

Constantin thought Stewart's tone was a bit flip, considering the gravity of the situation. Maybe it was just the British accent that made it sound that way. "Another opera with a stabbing as part of the action. Is that normal?"

"Aside from comedies, most operas contain some element of violence," Stewart said. "But in this case, clearly some psychopath has infiltrated our ranks and is using our venue—and our particularly... violent slate of repertoire—to perpetrate his or her malicious agenda."

The word "psychopath" surprised Constantin. In his experience, witnesses rarely used the kinds of specific descriptive terms that usually were within the realm of investigators. He turned to Alejandro. "Would you say that's accurate?"

"Yes. This opera season we have an especially, shall we say, bloody program."

"Any particular reason?"

"Not really," Alejandro said. Constantin wondered if all stage directors spoke of violence in such an offhand manner. "Our general director chooses repertoire based on what he thinks the audience will most enjoy."

"And buy tickets for," Stewart added.

"As director, do you decide whether those bloody scenes take place on or offstage?"

"In *Lucia,* it's specified in the libretto that the murder takes place offstage."

"But not, as I understand it, in *Lulu.*"

"That was an artistic choice," Stewart said.

"I see."

Constantin glanced at his watch. Too many other interviewees waiting in the wings. He thanked Stewart and Alejandro. Next would be Magda and Daniel. He was all too familiar with them. From the last murder.

ꕥ

Having satisfied a modicum of her quota of orchestra members, and found out little of what she had hoped to discover, Stella entered Stieren Hall with Julia in tow and brought her over to Constantin. Julia immediately noticed his quizzical look.

"It turns out Julia here helped solve some murders at the Met Opera. Given the massive scale and numbers of people to interview in this case, I've asked her to tag along," Stella said. "Another pair of eyes and ears, if you will."

Julia was worried. Now that Stella had outed her participation in the Met investigation, Julia would have to live up to the expectations of both detectives. She also was concerned that Constantin might feel threatened by her presence. Upon reflection, she decided he probably had enough on his plate not to be bothered by her addition to his team. He may have even welcomed any assistance she might provide in dealing with the huge task before him.

"Meanwhile, Grabowski," Stella continued. "Did you find out anything significant?"

"That depends what you think is significant," Constantin said. "I did find out from the director…" he said, pointing out Alejandro, "… That this opera has yet another stabbing scene."

"Oh, great." Stella grimaced. "You tell him that until further notice, I myself will inspect all weapons, whether onstage or off, before they're used."

"You got it, boss."

"And make sure you talk to that singer, Deborah, the one with the bloodstains on her dress. Maybe she had it in for the tenor. She was offstage when he was killed, so she had opportunity."

"But not motive."

"We don't know that yet. See what you can find out. And have the bloodstains on that dress tested. We need to find out if they're real or fake."

"Sure thing." Constantin walked off.

"I'm sure the bloodstains aren't real," Julia said. "They use fake blood, like in the movies."

"We don't know that for sure. Grabowski will get the skinny. You talk to that costume lady."

Julia frowned. "Magda? What about?"

"Just see if you can get any information out of her. She's always behind the scenes."

Julia was flattered but uncomfortable at the responsibility entrusted to her.

*What was I thinking, signing up for this?*

Julia was pondering Stella's assignment when she glimpsed Stewart coming toward them. Worried he might interpret her presence in some negative way, she girded herself.

"I've heard you might wish to leave us, Julia."

Julia was taken aback. "How…how did you…"

"Nothing passes me by when it comes to this company. Not even orchestra scuttlebutt." He gave her a conciliatory smile. "But, please, Julia, don't worry. I completely understand how you feel. And I do realize how demanding I've been of you in your work. But if I have, it's only because I believe in your abilities. I do hope you will stay on with us. It would mean a great deal to me personally, and to the company."

Julia wasn't sure whether to be flattered or suspicious. "I…I don't know what to say."

"Don't feel obligated to say anything. Whatever your decision, I will be totally onboard with it."

"Thank you, Stewart."

After he had walked away, Julia turned to Stella. "Wow, that was a surprise. Totally uncharacteristic of him. I'm in shock."

"It's in his interest to make sure important talent stays with the company. To manage that, he has to do everything he can, explore all possibilities to get to the bottom of these acts of violence," Stella said. "And we'll be needing all the help we can get. Not to worry, I'll coach you in some of my time-tested techniques. So…can I count on you?"

"I guess I don't have any choice."

"Good. What are your thoughts so far?"

Julia's first thought was to visit Rob and try to gain some insights from him, especially about the apprentices, but she didn't want to mention that to Stella; at least not yet.

"I'll need some time to process everything that's happened. But one thing is for certain, Stella, there's a murderer on the loose," Julia said. "And it's not Marin."

## Chapter 31

*Dunque l'onta di tutti sol una, uno il cor, la vendetta sarà*
The dishonor of one unites all, our hearts are bent on revenge
~ Verdi, *A Masked Ball,* Act 3

Julia was ecstatic when Stewart allowed her to take off the next morning's *Lucia* rehearsal to deliver Marin from her captors. Marin was waiting by the front entrance when Julia and Larry drove up in front of the county jail. Larry waited in the car while Julia raced to Marin and hugged her tightly.

Julia tried not to reveal her shock at Marin's haggard look as she ushered the battle-weary singer into the back seat. "I've made a brunch reservation at Clafoutis," Julia said.

"Yeah, you look like you could use a decent meal," Larry said.

Julia glared at him. "You could try to be a little subtler."

"That's okay, he's right," said Marin. "But right now, I'm feeling like I don't want to be around people. Could you just take me back to my hotel?"

Larry revved the engine. "You got it."

Julia slid into the front seat next to him, turned to Marin and eyed her anxiously. "What are your plans? Are you going back to New York?"

"Not a chance," Marin said. "I'm sticking around here till they find out who set me up."

"Wise choice," Larry said, and took off, leaving a cloud of Santa Fe dust in his wake.

ꕥ

Julia made sure to text Rob before invading the Apprentice Program office. She was elated when he invited her to pay a visit, though she didn't reveal her reasons for doing so.

She was surprised to see how small and cramped his quarters were. The outer office was just big enough for his desk, with his assistant's equally tiny space located in a room adjacent to his. Through an opening behind his desk, Julia could see another small area filled with shelves.

"Those are the opera archives," Rob said. "Shall we take a look?"

Julia followed Rob through the doorway and into what struck her as an embarrassment of musical riches. Every inch of the floor-to-ceiling steel racks was packed with opera scores and chorus materials, some standing upright, others arranged alphabetically in file boxes: from Bellini to Bizet, Massenet to Mozart, Donizetti to Puccini. Materials that didn't fit on the shelves were stacked on the floor in cardboard boxes.

Julia had never seen such a sanctuary; it was an operatic nirvana. "Wow, how do you keep track of all of these?"

"Believe me, I know every sheet of music and where it can be found," Rob said. "It's my haven when I don't want anyone to find me," he added, laughing.

"It definitely is very private back here." She explored the crammed room, trying not to bump into anything. There was barely enough space for her to step between the shelves.

"Perfect for, like…a romantic tryst or two?" she asked with a sly smile.

"It hasn't been part of my experience," Rob said. "But I can only speak for myself."

"Mind if I take a closer look?"

"Have at it. I'll be in the next room."

Rob went back to his desk, leaving Julia at liberty to examine the materials more closely. A box labeled "Berg" caught her attention. She carefully pulled it out and scanned its contents. Wedged next to a vocal score of *Wozzeck* was one marked *Lulu*.

Julia's curiosity was piqued. She extracted the *Lulu* score and flipped through the pages, shuddering when she came to the passage where Jack murders Lulu. It looked as frightening on the page as it did onstage.

Terrifying associations came hurtling back to Julia's memory, and she quickly closed the manuscript. As she did so, she noticed two pages stuck together. She debated as to whether she should attempt to separate them; perhaps that was best left for Rob.

But Julia's natural inquisitiveness overcame her better judgment. As she gently pried the pages apart, a minuscule scrap of paper dropped out and fluttered to the floor. There was such a scarcity of space in the room that when she stooped down to retrieve the paper one of the shelves started to teeter, threatening to collapse on top of her.

She managed to stop it just in time. "*Merde*!"

Rob called out from the next room. "Everything okay in there?"

"No worries."

Julia examined the paper and the few words that were scribbled on it. It took her a moment to recognize the language in which they were written.

Hungarian.

She pocketed the scrap, returned the box to its rightful place and headed out the door.

ꟸ

In order to drop Julia in front of the theatre before the opening performance of *Roméo et Juliette,* Larry had to drive through throngs of tailgaters in the opera parking lot with their overflowing wicker baskets, enjoying pre-performance repasts on tables bedecked with fancy linens, candelabras, colorful dinnerware and champagne flutes.

Julia, who watched wide-eyed through the car window, was struck by the revelers' creativity in attire. Some wore denim and cargo pants; but many of the women wore formal gowns, their escorts were decked out in black-tie tux and red cummerbund regalia, and they all sported elaborate masks made of colorful feathers. Julia, fascinated, felt as if she had happened upon a New Orleans Mardi Gras celebration.

Glancing up toward the terraces, Julia spied a number of operagoers taking in the breathtaking mountain, desert and turquoise sky views. The entire scene was an affirmation of the best of all possible operatic worlds, true to the most idealistic descriptions of life at Santa Fe Opera.

Once she had taken her place in the pit, Julia was reluctant to play full-out because of her wound and gingerly held back during the opera's first act. But when she discovered that even with aggressive playing she felt not a twinge from the gash in her left flank—a testament, she thought, of her mountaintop experiences with Miles—she gradually resumed her usual leadership mode, until the scene in Act 2 where the sword incident had occurred during rehearsal. At that point she began to tremble, her bow shaking as she drew it across the strings.

Blatchley noticed Julia's look of trepidation and smiled his encouragement, but the memory of that moment of terror took control of her rational mind and she feared she would have to stop playing. Just as she was about to lower her violin and bow, a voice entered her head.

*Divest yourself of the debris that litters your mind…Give your pain to Mother Earth.*

She tried mentally to return to her vision quest, making a supreme effort to clear her mind as Miles had instructed her, and to visualize the scene in which she had felt at peace. As suddenly as her fear had overcome her, an immense calm pervaded her being, her bow ceased to quiver and her strokes became strong and steady.

*I'm fine. I can do this.*

Finally, in the last scene, as Julia watched the young lovers' tragic self-sacrifice, she imagined their souls ascending to heaven. The music was heartbreakingly sublime, but she suppressed the fountain of tears that were threatening to gush forth. If she were to loose her emotions from their restraints, it was best done away from the curious stares of her orchestra colleagues.

As Blatchley motioned to the orchestra to rise and acknowledge the audience's applause, Julia heard a soft buzz from her cell phone and stole a surreptitious look at the screen.

*Stella: meet me tomorrow at Café Pasqual's, 8 am. Breakfast and interrogation instruction.*

When she had investigated Abel's murder at the Met, Julia was operating totally on instinct. This time, she had an opportunity to hone her skills under the tutelage of a professional. Whatever Julia could learn from Stella would make her probing more sophisticated and efficient.

There was no time to waste expressing opera-induced emotions. She had work to do.

## Chapter 32

*Warum denn nicht? Ich habe Mut und Kraft!*
Why not then? I have the courage and strength!
~ Beethoven, *Fidelio,* Act 1

SQUEEZED INTO A CORNER TABLE AT THE ALWAYS PACKED CAFÉ PASQUAL'S, just off Santa Fe Plaza, Stella and Julia chatted over lattes and bowls of red quinoa with berries, toasted almonds and grilled figs topped with coconut milk.

Julia thought the dish was pricey but worth every penny. "I've never tasted anything so good," she told Stella.

"Now you know why this place is perpetually jammed," Stella said. "Although I almost expected you to go for Julia's Wild Salmon Gravlax."

"Seems my name is ubiquitous in this town, given her presence here and at La Posada. But Cognac-cured Salmon is a bit much at eight o'clock in the morning. Plus, I'm allergic to dairy and potatoes and vinegar. So, no *Gruyère,* Potato Cake, *crème fraîche* or lemon vinaigrette."

"Aren't you the hothouse flower. For me, it's all good. Far as I'm concerned, if 'Music be the food of love,' then food is music." Stella chuckled and scarfed down a large mouthful of quinoa. "Okay, here's your crash course. How to get the whole truth from victims, witnesses, and hopefully perps. Ready?"

Julia reluctantly put down her spoon. Still chewing, she extracted her phone from her bag and brought up her notes app.

"Number one," Stella said. "They have a 'tell,' like in a poker game. They fidget—touch their nose, pull an ear. Two, and this is tough if you aren't familiar with how they normally act. If they don't look you in the eye, they're probably lying. Or at least couching the truth."

Julia tapped as fast as she could. Luckily, as a millennial, she was practiced in tapping rapidly with two thumbs. But she also knew she had to be careful about overuse: trigger thumbs and fingers, often a consequence of too much playing, especially for string players, were to be avoided at all costs.

"Three. They'll talk so fast you can barely understand what they're saying. They do this on purpose to avoid being heard."

Julia was puzzled. "Really? Why wouldn't they want you to hear what they've said?"

"They might have something to hide. And sometimes they'll repeat the question to stall you while they think of a lie that sounds believable. They'll say something like, 'Hold on, is this for real? Let me make sure I heard you right.'"

Julia's touch screen had never seen so much action. "Wow, I never knew."

"Most people don't," said Stella. "One more thing. They'll try to sidetrack you by switching the topic. Don't fall for it. Got it?"

"I think so." Julia put down her phone and swallowed another mouthful of berries. She wasn't sure if the food tasted so good because it was organic, or because her body was still healing from her injury. Whatever the reason, she was almost tempted to order another bowl.

Evidently, Stella was on a similar wavelength. "I'm still hungry. Think I'll try some of Julia's Gravlax. You?"

"No thanks, I'm good."

Julia was astonished. Either Stella's large frame required a great deal of nourishment, or detective work made one especially hungry. In any case, she was looking forward to putting the detective's valuable recommendations to good use.

Holding up her menu, Stella motioned to a nearby waiter, who hurried over. "Yes?"

Stella pointed to Julia's namesake dish on the menu. "I'd like one of these. And another latte. Oh, and a chile cheeseburger." She looked up at Julia. "They put chiles in everything here. There are, like, two dozen different kinds of peppers."

"Red or green?" said the waiter.

"How about both? I'm feeling adventurous today."

The waiter moved off. Stella turned to Julia. "So, what have you got so far?"

"Not much, I'm afraid. Just this." Julia pulled out the scrap of paper she had found in the archives and handed it to Stella. "I found it in the archives in Rob's office."

"Rob?"

"The head of the Apprentice Program."

"Oh. How have I not met him yet?" The detective scrawled a note in her phone. Then she stared at the words on the paper. "What the hell language is that, anyway?"

"Hungarian."

"I should have known. Do you know what it says?"

"It says…" Julia struggled with the pronunciation. *"Hívja… azonmmal…a…rendörséget!"*

"And that means…?"

"I have no idea. But I know someone who does."

## Chapter 33

*Ora facciam la recita!*
Now let's do the show!
~ Leoncavallo, *Pagliacci*

GETTING THROUGH THE OPENING NIGHT OF *ROMÉO ET JULIETTE* HAD BEEN a huge relief for Julia. The enchantment of the surroundings—mountains glowing in the distance, the iridescent sunset, and the crescent moon floating among the stars when the sky turned inky black—fueled her motivation to give the best possible rendering of the music.

The entire performance had gone off so smoothly, Julia began to wonder if she had been hallucinating, especially when Stewart uttered some generous words of praise to her afterward. She shared her amazement over Blatchley's appreciative remarks to Katie.

"That's the first time he's said anything positive to me about my work. It's like a dream."

"Take it and run," Katie said, in her usual nonchalant manner. "Gift horse and all that."

"I guess you're right," Julia said. "Do I dare hope that all this opera-induced adversity is now in the past?"

"Believe it, Jul."

Hoping Katie was right, Julia accepted her friend's wisdom and began to feel like she could handle resuming *Lucia.*

At her first rehearsal, Julia was surprised to see Sandor onstage in Adam's place. She knew his voice range and timbre were well suited for the role, but she still felt bewildered as to why he would be performing so frequently.

At the break, she and Katie set off to the cantina, where company members hovered together at tables, deep in discussion. It seemed to Julia that the members' passion for their art was boundless; they constantly hashed out details about the productions in which they were involved, whether over lunch on the terrace, hanging by the pool, or pausing on the lawn to admire Donna Quasthoff's distinctive *Orpheus and Eurydice* sculpture.

Julia and Katie found Sandor in line at the cash register, paying for a green tea. "You sound great, Sandor," Julia said.

"Thank you, Julia."

Katie took note of Sandor's admiring glance directed at Julia. "I second that," said Katie. "I think you're perfect in the role of…what is he called?"

"Arturo," Sandor said.

"I knew that," said Katie. "Hey, want to join us?"

The three of them found a table in a far corner of the crowded outdoor space.

"I didn't know you were understudying Adam's role," Julia said, sipping her latte.

"Oh…" Sandor cautiously tasted his tea so as not to burn his tongue. "Actually, I wasn't. But the apprentice understudy didn't feel prepared, so they asked me to step in."

Julia thought Sandor seemed caught off guard by her comment. "Magda must be happy about that."

"No one is happy, after what happened to Adam. But Magda is always pleased to see me onstage."

"Of course she is," said Katie. "Her kid brother being so talented."

"Magda is gifted, too. When we were growing up in Hungary, our father encouraged both of us to follow our dreams of being opera singers. But Magda always put my career ambitions first. She said she inherited our mother's sewing abilities, but I inherited our father's musical ones."

"Well, I've never heard her sing," Julia said, glancing admiringly at Sandor, "But judging from what I've heard of you, she may have been right on track."

"She is much too selfless. There is nothing she wouldn't do for me. I never feel I am worthy, or that I can repay her properly." Sandor paused, squeezing the last drops of water from his tea bag. "You know, Julia, you should stop by the costume department and say hi to Magda. I'm sure she would be delighted to see you."

"You're right. I haven't talked to her since my first day." Julia paused. "I'm just curious...what range was Magda's voice?"

"It was..." Sandor hesitated. "High dramatic soprano."

"Like in *Lulu*?"

"Yes."

"Wow, that's amazing. What a talented family you have. How well did you know Adam?"

"Not very." Sandor idly stroked his nose with his free hand. "I'd better get back. They'll be wondering what happened to me."

"Of course. I did have a favor to ask of you, though." Julia reached into her purse and removed the scrap of paper with the Hungarian words written on it. "I was looking through the scores in the archives and found this inside one of them. Could you translate it?"

Sandor quickly scanned the words, frowning. "The handwriting is difficult to read. Do you mind if I get back to you?"

"Not at all. *Nagyon szépen.* Thanks, Sandor. *Köszönöm.*"

"*Szívesen.*" He pocketed the paper and rushed away, clutching his tea cup.

Julia murmured under her breath. "Not looking me in the eye. Changing the subject. Fidgeting. Even opera singers have 'tells.'"

"What did you say, Jul?"

"Oh, nothing." Julia realized she had to be more careful about thinking out loud. Much as she loved Katie, she grasped the importance of keeping her collaboration with Stella under wraps, even when it came to her best friend.

"Did you see the way Sandor was looking at you? He really has a thing for you," Katie said.

Julia was glad Katie had switched topics. "Don't be silly."

"Mark my words," said Katie. "I know a major crush when I see one."

"I'm sure you do, but you know I'm spoken for."

"Right. Poor Julia. So many men, so little time." Katie grinned over her cup of coffee.

ꟾ

Sandor panted as he scurried along the path from the cantina to the theatre. What he had read on the piece of paper troubled him. He couldn't fathom what Julia was doing with a piece of paper that said, "Call the police!" in Hungarian.

But he knew it did not bode well.

ꟃ

Notwithstanding Stella's assignment, Julia found herself looking forward to talking to Magda again. At their first encounter Julia had found the woman fascinating; even more so, now that Sandor had revealed some of the Kertész family background.

When she arrived at the costume shop, Julia peeked inside to see Magda, alone, in front of a mannequin. She quietly entered and approached Magda from behind. As she drew closer, Julia could see that Magda was adjusting a costume on the figure. She recognized it as the white wedding dress and veil from the Mad Scene in *Lucia.*

Julia quietly cleared her throat. Magda turned around abruptly. "Who's there?"

From Magda's irritated tone, Julia realized she had interrupted Magda's concentration. "Oh...*Bocsánat,* Magda! I'm so sorry."

"Oh, it's you, Júlia. I apologize if I sound a bit impolite. I am focusing so hard on my work."

"I completely understand. You must forgive me, I didn't mean to interrupt. I saw Sandor at rehearsal, and he reminded me that I haven't seen you since my first day. I just dropped by to say hello." Julia smiled. "But I see you're quite busy. I can come back tomorrow."

"No, no, it's kind of you to visit. I can take a brief respite."

Magda repositioned a straight pin on the dress and turned back to Julia. "I heard you were injured in *Roméo* rehearsal. Are you all right?"

"Oh, it was nothing, just a superficial wound. I'm fine now. Thank you for asking." Julia jockeyed position to get a better glimpse of the garment. "Is that the wedding dress from *Lucia?*"

"Yes. But it is replacement. Police took possession of original one for investigation. It is my responsibility to build new one, exact duplication of original."

"That must be difficult. And time consuming."

"*Igen.* Yes. It is true. With much beading and lace detail on dress, and especially delicate veil, it necessitates exceptional care. I must handle it personally."

"I'm not surprised. But I'm sure you will manage it very adeptly. You are so meticulous."

"Thank you for saying so."

"Is *Lucia* one of your favorite operas?"

"It is. Her character is so vulnerable, so complex. Her grief at losing her mother, her longing for forbidden lover, her madness when she thinks he has betrayed her. Her entire world crashes down around her. A world with no benevolence. As is ours."

Julia was amazed at Magda's perceptive take on an operatic character that she herself did not consider as particularly deep. She thought Magda's analysis of Sir Walter Scott's tragic heroine was impressive in its astuteness.

"I never thought of Lucia that way. You are very insightful."

"*Köszönöm.* I try to think of every opera character in this way. It helps in my work. I have been closely linked with opera my entire life, in Hungary and in States," said Magda. "Of course, Sandor's talent far surpasses mine. All that matters for me is his success. I truly believe in him."

"With good reason. He sounded fantastic today."

"You are kind to say, Júlia. *Köszönöm.*"

"He told me you both came from a musical family."

"*Igen.* Our father studied piano with Bartók at Liszt Academy."

Julia was dumbfounded at the thought of someone actually rubbing shoulders with one of the musical geniuses of the twentieth century. "No! Really?"

Magda nodded. "Father told us it was frightening experience at first, in class with living genius. But Maestro never raised his voice, always spoke softly and slowly. He had unforgettable big, piercing eyes. You have played his opera *Bluebeard's Castle?*"

"Not yet." Julia studied the nostalgia in Magda's eyes and decided it was a good idea to probe the costume director's emotions. "I don't know the opera at all. Tell me about it."

"Is extraordinary. Rich and expressive. Colorful and strange. Thrilling. Librettist Balázs, friend of Bartók, influenced by Freud and Strindberg, based story on French folk tale. Begins with only one person onstage, speaking Hungarian. Then music. Deep psychological meaning. One of greatest pieces of music I know."

Julia, scrutinizing Magda's faraway expression, thought the piece sounded downright sinister and unsettling.

"It must be getting late," Magda said, seeming to come back to reality. *Hány óra van?*"

Julia checked her Fitbit. "Three o'clock."

"I'm sorry, I must go back to work."

"Of course, I've taken too much of your time." Julia said. "Might we talk again?"

"*Beszéljünk máskor is.*"

"I'll look forward to it, too. *Köszönöm,* Magda."

Magda waited until Julia had left. Then she resumed her adjustments.

Julia lingered outside the door, deep in thought. Magda's observations reminded her that opera was brimming with panicked heroines. *Lucia* portrayed one of them, a woman on the verge of a total breakdown, as did Bartók's *Bluebeard's Castle,* the story of a wife in constant fear of her creepy, murderous husband. In fact, all of history was laden with terrified women, like Julia's namesake at La Posada, who suffered profound emotional torment.

However, there was something about Magda that brought to mind opera characters other than Lucia or Bluebeard's wife, Judith. Strong female protagonists with an intensity as deep and profound as Magda's: Carmen. Tosca. Turandot.

Lady Macbeth.

## Chapter 34

*Non ci stanchiamo: il cor mi dice che trovarlo dobbiam!*
We must be tireless: in my heart of hearts, I know we'll find him!
~ Mozart, *Don Giovanni,* Act 2

STELLA HAD NEVER BEEN IN AN OPERA STAR'S DRESSING ROOM, AND Deborah's seemed as good a place as any to interview the singer, though the detective was learning more about the role of Lucia than she really wanted to know. She would have preferred to persuade the singer to open up about her activities on the day of Adam's murder.

"Lucia is my favorite *bel canto* role, the absolute benchmark for the highest level of coloratura singing. I can't tell you how gratifying it is to sing. The relationships and issues portrayed are universal. Forbidden love, family duty. The story could be set anywhere, any time. And without a doubt, one of the bloodiest operas ever. Scotland did have a rather, shall we say, 'colorful' past. Look what happened to Braveheart, and Mary Queen of Scots."

"For sure," said Stella. "And the 'Mad Scene?'"

"A real showpiece, one of the most demanding in opera, technically speaking, with all its pyrotechnics. Dramatically challenging as well."

"They say opera is like true life on steroids. 'All the world's a stage,' and all that," Stella said. "How seriously do you take your part? Do you ever get so into it that you lose touch with reality? Like Sarah Bernhardt, just living the character? Go a little mad yourself?"

"It's true that it's easy to get lost in the moment, especially in the Mad Scene, where Lucia is so deluded she retreats into insanity rather than face an actuality too horrible to contemplate. And yes, she's trying to escape. But if you're implying that I could possibly do what she does—"

"I'm not implying anything," Stella said. "I'm just curious about how actors get into character. *Modus operandi,* if you will."

"As thrilling as it is to take chances onstage, you can't get too emotional. You have to know where to draw the line. Stay balanced, not go too far," Deborah said. "If I let myself get carried away, my throat could close up. That's the worst possible disaster for a singer."

"Of course." Stella took a different tack. "It must have been tough to adapt to *Lucia* when you just sang the title role in *Lulu*."

"It's true the roles are poles apart. The music in *Lulu* is wickedly difficult. So is the *bel canto* coloratura in *Lucia,* but it requires an entirely different approach. I was happy to make the transition. My voice was tailor made for *bel canto.* It's what made me want to sing opera."

Stella reflected on the egos of opera singers. She was beginning to realize that everything she had heard, both positive and negative, about them and their heightened sense of self, was true. Artists like Deborah were divas; of that there could be no doubt. How the lower echelons of opera hierarchy were able to put up with singers' egotistical nonsense eluded her, as surely as Lucia's mind had become unhinged.

"And to sing such roles here, in Santa Fe, where even the weather has its own drama, is mind-boggling," Deborah added. "You could be dying of consumption onstage, and a storm rolls in, literally thundering your demise."

"Forgive me, but I have to ask. Where were you at the time of Adam's murder?"

"In my dressing room, changing into my bloodstained dress. I wasn't anywhere near Adam. You can ask my dresser, Felipe."

"I will." Stella tapped a note into her phone.

"Now if you'll excuse me," Deborah said, "I have to go rehearse with Adam's replacement."

"So soon?"

"'The show must go on,' as they say in the circus. The ringmaster must keep things going so the company won't panic. In this case, it's the director's responsibility. I'm just a 'poor player.'"

"Of course," Stella said. "Thank you for your time."

"I'd like to say it was my pleasure, but unfortunately it was anything but."

Deborah swept out of the room. As to Deborah's veracity with regard to Adam's demise, Stella had her reservations.

ꕤ

Julia silently thanked Larry for his prescience in gifting her with a Fitbit. While she wasn't totally hooked on using its technology to the max, she loved its sleek design and especially, at the moment, its flashlight feature.

The last thing she had anticipated in coming to Santa Fe was exploring the isolated hallways and recesses of the opera house as she had done at the Met. Yet here she was, virtually breaking into the costume shop late at night, looking for clues. She had talked to Magda as Stella had delegated her to do, but felt disappointed at not having uncovered any compelling information. Maybe if she had a closer look at the white dress Magda had been working on…

She had tried all of the many doors providing access to the shop, to see if any had been left unlocked. Her patience was rewarded when she found one side door handle that was unfastened.

The light emitting from Julia's Fitbit provided adequate but unobtrusive brightness. Guided by its illumination, she crept through the room in semi-darkness, dodging the corner edges of the huge worktables. But she wasn't familiar enough with the layout of the room to avoid running into a metal table leg bolted to the floor.

"Ow!"

Julia rubbed her offended shin. She looked around, anxious, but realized there was little likelihood that someone other than the night security guard had heard her outburst. And if he or she came to investigate the noise, she felt sure she could think of an excuse for her presence.

She found herself imagining for a moment what the previous shop must have been like: a small, dark hole, cramped and claustrophobic, with its tiny windows and lack of air conditioning.

*It must have made people working here feel irritated, to say the least.*

Chastising herself for allowing distracted thinking, she tried to determine the location of the dress. Even if she could remember where it was, the rest of the room was even darker than the area in which she stood. In the pitch blackness it was difficult, if not impossible, to see anything, even aided by the light from the Fitbit.

*Ah, maybe that's it.*

Spying what looked like a mannequin, she shone her light in that direction and cautiously stepped toward it, carefully avoiding any further collisions with inanimate objects. Using her cell phone as a backup for the light from her Fitbit, she could see that the mannequin was indeed draped in the white dress from *Lucia*. She held both mechanisms in front of the dress and moved the light from top to bottom, but to her chagrin she couldn't see anything that looked unusual.

*A useless, amateurish attempt, Julia.*

"What are you doing here?"

Julia recognized the distinctive accent. Now it was time to come up with the excuse she had been so sure of inventing. But she felt too panicked to think clearly. She turned to face Magda.

"I'm sorry, Magda, I didn't mean—"

"I think you had best to leave. Allow me to provide you some light."

The sudden, glaring brightness from the ceiling fluorescent lamps that Magda switched on made Julia squint with discomfort. There was nothing more she could do or say. She couldn't exactly ask Magda what she herself was doing there. It was, after all, her territory; her ire was justified. And since Julia had been caught in an egregious transgression in what was clearly Magda's domain, retreat was her only option.

ꕥ

The Santa Fe DPS Forensics Lab was all but Stella's second home. She kept the number for the Office of the Medical Investigator and of the Chief Medical Investigator on her speed dial.

Nick Pleasance never insisted on Stella's coming to the OMI at the University in Albuquerque; he was happy to meet her at the SFPD lab on Cerrillos Road in Santa Fe, unattractive though it was, to escape the UNM campus. In his opinion, forensics had less to do with academe and more to do with hands-on professional investigation closely linked to the on-site work of the SFPD. Notwithstanding the crime lab's daunting backlog, the high-profile goings-on at the city's venerated opera company were being given top priority.

The initial CSU findings had not been surprising. Much like the previous murder at the opera, the perpetrator had left a pristine crime scene: no prints, no DNA, no blood spatters. The blood on the wedding dress had tested as stage blood. And since the weapon used was not a firearm, there were no casings or traces of gunpowder to look for.

The autopsy findings Nick had collected for Stella were similarly unspoiled. "Some of the cleanest work I've seen," Nick told Stella as the two investigators hovered over the body of the deceased tenor. "This perp is meticulous. Picky, very hard to please. A real fussbudget. What's that thing they say about neat vs sloppy psychopaths?"

"You think it's only one? No accomplice?" Stella asked.

"No, this guy knows too many cooks spoil that soup. He—"

"Or she."

"Or she—is too smart not to work alone," Nick said.

"Same perp as last time?"

"Possibly. Though last time we had a weapon."

"Right. It was obvious from the beginning that the knife caused the fatal trauma," Stella said.

"This time there's even less to go on," Nick said. "But you might find this surprising." He pointed out the wound site. "Unlike the other stabbing, this cut is jagged. The weapon we're looking for isn't a dagger or a sword, or even a knife. This one was much smaller than any of those."

"Still a sharp object, right?"

"Definitely. But like something you'd use to rip stitches from a piece of clothing, only much sharper, spikier, and jagged. Hooked, even. Sharp enough to rip your flesh."

## Chapter 35

*Diesmal hast du zuviel dir aufgeladen...*
This time you have taken too much upon yourself...
~ Beethoven, *Fidelio,* Act 2

JULIA TRIED TO HIDE HER GLUM FEELINGS FROM LARRY ABOUT HER CONfrontation with Magda. She had failed in her mission to obtain any significant information from the costume director or from the costume shop and felt reluctant to share her experience with him. But she also suspected he would recognize her dispirited demeanor when she trudged into their room at the Inn.

"I blew it, Larry. Two for two," Julia said sullenly.

"Don't feel so overwrought, Julia. I'm sure Stella's expectations are not as high as you think."

"I came away with no evidence, and I got caught. Some detective I am. I'm no better than a musical Nancy Drew."

"First of all, you're not a detective. You're just trying to help out Stella, which in my opinion is above and beyond. You didn't have to do that. Second, you're too hard on yourself. Save it for your violin playing. And Nancy Drew rocked. Plus she wasn't trying to be two things at once."

Larry's efforts at consoling her didn't help Julia's desultory mood. She set her violin case on the bed and flopped down next to it, crossing her legs Indian style on top of the duvet. She was faintly aware of his admiring glance at her legs peeking out from under her broomstick skirt, but she was used to it. "Is that supposed to make me feel better?"

"Yes, and I fully expect you to act appropriately grateful."

Julia couldn't resist a smile. "Exactly how do you mean?"

"Contrary to what you might think, not everything about me has to do with sex."

Julia peered at him skeptically. "You brought it up, not me."

"However," he went on, "Since the next opera is *Salome,* I thought you might like to prepare for it by practicing the 'Dance of the Seven Veils.'"

"Seriously?"

"I meant the orchestral part, not the actual dance. Though I wouldn't mind."

She gave a little laugh. "I'm sure you wouldn't."

"Give me a little credit here. The piece is ten minutes long, the only strictly orchestral one in the opera. Knowing you, you'd want to practice the living daylights out of it, like a concerto. Wasn't an excerpt from it on your Met audition?"

"You remembered!" Julia was pleased at Larry's continued interest in the subtler details of her musical life. "But since when are you so concerned with my musical practice habits?"

"I did my homework on this one," Larry said.

"I'll bet you did."

"Seriously. I'd really like to hear you play it."

Julia extracted a sheet of music from the zippered pocket in her violin case cover, opened the case and positioned the music to stand up perfectly in front of the bow holders on the inside. "*Salome* is right up your alley," she said. "Erotic, violent, severed heads—maybe the bloodiest opera ever written. Certainly, the most sexual." She turned to a passage marked "Violin solo."

"It's not just about that," Larry said. "This production takes place in turn-of-the-century Vienna, the time of Freud and Richard Strauss. Biblical Christianity meets erotic decadence, with blood and gore. The conscious, preconscious and unconscious. Fascinating stuff."

Julia was impressed. "You *have* been doing your homework."

"I told you it wasn't all about sex, didn't I?" Larry flashed a knowing smile. "And timely, too. Jochanaan warns everyone that the end is nigh, if you get my drift."

"I do. I've been feeling that way since November of 2016."

"You're not alone. On the bright side, *Salome* was John Crosby's favorite Strauss opera, maybe his favorite opera, period. This is the eleventh time they've programmed it in the last fifty years."

"Given all your newfound knowledge, I'm sensing you've found out why Crosby loved Strauss so much?" Julia asked.

"*Ja, mein professor.* I've discovered that Crosby's mind was a lot like Strauss's music. Convoluted, intricate and analytical. He was meticulous about examining every facet of those works. He got more pleasure conducting them than any other composer's operas. While he was general director, he produced thirteen of them, six of which were American premieres."

Julia paused for a moment to contemplate the apparitions of Crosby she had encountered since coming to Santa Fe. Her experiences during her vision quest had dispelled any doubts she had had about the realism of those visions. Now, with the prospect of rehearsing and performing Crosby's favorite Strauss opera looming before her, she was starting to feel concerned about the effects of his psychic presence; almost as if he wanted to bring attention to the abysmal state of affairs in his opera company the same way Jacob Marley's ghost had forewarned Scrooge.

"I know that look, Julia. What's on your mind?."

"I'm really worried. After all that violence we've suffered through in the three operas so far, I'm afraid something horrible might occur again in this one."

"Another murder? I don't think anyone would dare. The SFeO campus is crawling with cops and plain clothes," Larry said.

"I'm not sure it's going to help."

"You better believe it will."

Julia remained doubtful. "I hope you're right."

"Have I ever steered you wrong?"

"You've got to be kidding me. Do you really want a response to that?"

"Now that's more like you. It's been a while since you've answered a question with a question."

"I'm getting ready for *Salome.* There are five Jews in the first scene."

Larry laughed. "Okay, you've outsmarted me as usual. But having done all this research, I'm really curious to see how this opera ticks.

After all, the audiences here are so sophisticated and knowledgeable, some people go to the same opera multiple times to learn as much as they can and compare casts. And I'm beginning to think a lot like they do. Surely you could get me into one stage rehearsal."

"I'll see what I can do."

"Great. Now how about that *Dance?*"

꩜

With two murders in quick succession, and such a plethora of company members to interrogate, Stella had found little time to compare notes with Constantin. After Julia's report of her failure to come up with evidence from the costume shop, Stella knew she would need to revisit Magda. But from the results of her consult with Nick, Stella also determined it was time to assess where things stood with her partner.

Stella met with Constantin over lattes at a large, round table in a secluded corner of the cantina. It was late in the day, and no one else was around. Only the sounds of children laughing and playing in the pool just below them punctuated the hushed atmosphere.

Stella thought she saw clear signs of battle weariness in Constantin's demeanor. Against the backdrop of the rosy New Mexico sky and what promised to be a spectacular sunset, Constantin's pallid face looked washed-out and sallow. His shoulders drooped, and his eyes held none of their usual inquisitiveness. He barely touched his beverage.

"You okay, buddy?"

"Dunno. These cases are making me crazy. So much killing. And so many people to question, we might as well put them all in a football field and point randomly."

She gave him a sympathetic look. "I hear ya. 'There is nothing either good or bad, but thinking makes it so.'"

Stella sensed Constantin was feeling too put-upon to react to her Shakespeare quote. Not waiting for his response, she opened a folder stuffed with files containing dossiers and photographs of opera singers, directors, conductors and others who had participated in the first two operas and placed it in front of him.

"Take a big drag on that coffee, partner. We need to go through and update our list of possible suspects."

"Right." Constantin took a huge hit from his cup. "What have we got?"

Marin's file lay at the top of the stack. Stella put it aside and opened another one. "Goran Řezníček, baritone."

"He had opportunity but no motive," Constantin said. "The only one who didn't have a beef with Emilia. Thought that in itself could be suspicious."

They looked at each other for a moment, then they both shook their heads.

"Right." Stella placed Goran's file on top of Marin's. "Deborah Alley, Emilia's understudy. She was in the house that night."

"Plus she stood to gain from Emilia's murder."

Stella found a separate space on the table for Deborah's file and opened another one. "Steve Cañon, head stagehand."

"He was hanging out by B-Lift with the other stagehands while the murders were going down."

Stella stacked Steve's file on top of Goran's. She and Constantin went through the rest one by one, placing them in one pile or the other. When they were almost finished, the "active suspect" heap contained files of Deborah, Magda, Sandor and Lorelei. There was just one more.

Stella drained her cup. "Daniel Henderson. Wigs and makeup."

"Right. I remember him describing those instruments of torture they use for making wigs."

"Wait a minute. What? I don't remember your telling me about that."

"Didn't I? I thought I did," Constantin said. "Why, what's up with that?"

Stella revealed the results of Nick's autopsy of Adam.

Constantin suddenly perked up. "Jagged wound? Sounds like it could have been done by one of those implements Daniel uses."

Constantin fired up his cell phone, swiped through his notes with virtuoso speed, and read from the screen. "'*If you drop one of those instruments and it goes into your leg or arm, you can really feel it when you have to rip it out. It definitely will* rip your flesh.'"

"Go on."

*"You have to be really careful about pushing against it when pulling it out in order not to tear your leg or arm open.'"*

"We'd better pay Daniel another visit," said Stella. "'Lord, what fools these mortals be!'"

## Chapter 36

*Quanto fuoco! Par che abbiate paura di tradirvi*
You protest too much! It seems you might be afraid of betraying yourself
~ Puccini, *Tosca,* Act 2

When Julia found out from Stewart that he would not be conducting *Salome,* she thought it ironic. Now that she finally had proved her worth as a concertmaster to the music director, she would have to do it all over again with the new maestro, Giovanni Molinari.

On the plus side, she was already well prepared. In the past she had studied *Salome* and its libretto in great detail—partly in preparation for her Met audition, but also because she found the opera hugely intriguing. She adored the writings of Oscar Wilde, who had created the original story on which the opera was based. Its Freudian undercurrents fascinated her, and she found its protagonist as riveting and alluring as any in opera.

More importantly, Julia found Strauss's score superb in its brilliance. The music was demanding in a way that made her want to keep examining and practicing every technically challenging passage and subtlety of phrasing. The violin solos were especially beautiful—and as difficult as any concerto written for the instrument.

Still, Julia felt puzzled over the concept of an Italian conductor for a Strauss opera. She knew that Toscanini was famous for his Wagner, and that Strauss's tone poems had been part of his vast repertoire. But she was unsure if the iconic Italian maestro had conducted many of the composer's operas.

Being Jewish, Julia was keenly aware that Toscanini was famously anti-Nazi, but Strauss's connections to the Third Reich were somewhat ambiguous. She had read that Toscanini was quoted as saying, "To Richard Strauss, the composer, I take off my hat. To Richard Strauss, the man, I put it on again." She made a mental note to learn more about Strauss's World War II background.

Nonetheless, Julia was glad of the opportunity to practice her Italian with Molinari, who was known for his Verdi and Puccini, composers whose operatic works she literally worshiped.

At the beginning of the first *Salome* stage rehearsal, Sarah stood on the podium to address the musicians. "Please welcome for the first time, directly from La Scala in Milan, Maestro Giovanni Molinari."

The players respectfully tapped their bows on their music stands. Francesco took over Sarah's place on the podium and leaned over to shake Julia's hand.

*"Benvenuto, Maestro,"* Julia said.

*"Grazie, Signorina."* Smiling, Giovanni faced the orchestra and spoke articulately, albeit with a pronounced accent. "I am humbled to follow the footsteps of the great John Crosby, whose interpretation of this opera was hailed by critics as conveying the feeling that *Salome* was 'one of Strauss's greatest tone poems.' I only hope I can come close to replicating Maestro Crosby's achievement."

The director, a diminutive Frenchman named Achille Boivin, stood at the apron of the stage and gestured to Giovanni. *"Buongiorno, Maestro."*

*"Buongiorno,* Achille. Anything I need to know before we begin?"

Julia had no clue how the company kept track of their many different conductors, directors and constantly revolving repertoire. She had observed plenty of these fluctuations at the Met, but their season was months longer than that of Santa Fe. She was filled with admiration for the efficiency of the administrative staff of SFeO, and made a mental note to mention that to Alan the next time she ran into him.

Achille responded to Giovanni's query with an obsequious smile. "If I may, Maestro, I would first like to say a few words to my singers."

Giovanni returned Achille's smile, albeit with more sincerity. *"Allez-y."*

*"Merci."* Achille addressed "his" singers, not by their given names, but by their character names. "Jochanaan, I'd like to see perceptive singing with subtle gradation. Not the pompous barking so often seen in this character. Salome, dear, *je vous en prie...*" He modulated his tone for the soprano. "Do not just flaunt your high notes. Allow the

music and its inherent drama to emanate naturally, from the depths of your soul. You are not only a sexually charged teenager but a complex personality. Now, Herod, Herodias, and the others—cut through the layers. Focus on the preconscious and unconscious thoughts below the surface that are too terrifying to contemplate."

Matt leaned over to speak *sotto* to Julia. "These French directors know how to lay it on thick, don't they? Notwithstanding their spotty reputations."

Julia, silently practicing a difficult solo passage by tapping her left-hand fingers on the fingerboard, nodded absently. "What do you mean?"

"They tend to come unprepared, and they keep changing their minds on staging," Matt said. "Opera singers have been known to walk out on them in protest. The last French director we had insisted that the baritone playing Papageno in *Magic Flute* sing the opening aria running all over the stage. He had just flown in and was still adjusting to the altitude. He was so out of breath that he had to take hits from the oxygen tank backstage in between arias."

"Poor guy. Maybe Boivin's the exception," Julia said optimistically. "After all, Jean Pierre Ponnelle was one of the all-time great directors."

"Don't get your hopes up. Boivin is no Ponnelle. In France, they hire theatre directors to direct operas, but too many of them have never even directed an opera—and never should," Matt said. "Boivin's great success as a theatre director doesn't mean he has a clue about dealing with an opera with massive amounts of ensembles in it."

"Well, with a name like 'Boivin' he probably knows his wine. Or at least drinks a lot of it. And he certainly is well versed in how to slather on the charm."

"But that's no guarantee he can figure out how to get singers situated on a stage."

"Agreed." Julia was beginning to see Matt's point. "Where is Ponnelle when we need him?"

Unlike Stewart, Giovanni didn't seem to mind faint chatter among the orchestra's ranks. He raised his baton. "Beginning, please."

Julia wasn't surprised at Giovanni's heavily accented English, but she admired the sensitivity with which he initiated the upbeat for the very delicate opening of the opera. She followed his lead, gesturing with her violin, to which he responded with a gratified smile.

*Notwithstanding the French director, this might not be so bad after all.*

A shimmering sound emitted from Narraboth, the tenor who sang the initial phrase.

*Wie schön ist die Prinzessin Salome heute Nacht*!

[How beautiful is Princess Salome tonight!]

Glancing subtly in the direction of the stage, Julia was astonished to see that Sandor was also playing this key role. She was happy for him, and he sounded wonderful, but seeing him cast in yet another role, and in such quick succession, left her wondering if this was a normal occurrence, even in this truly unique opera company.

It also occurred to her that in *Salome*, Sandor's character Narraboth, like Alwa in *Lulu* and Arturo in *Lucia*, comes to a bad end. Such was the fate of *comprimario* tenors.

ഀ

When Daniel looked up from setting the timer on the wig dryer to see Stella and Constantin coming toward him, he sensed trouble. He had never been involved in a crime investigation, but even the most mildly interested television police procedural aficionado knew that a second interview was not a good sign.

His efforts to hide his anxious demeanor proved fruitless. "What can I do for you, detectives?" he asked shakily.

"Could you show us that instrument again—the one you use to hook the hairs on the wigs?"

"Of course." Nodding to Stella, Daniel walked to a table overflowing with plastic containers and trays holding makeup, hair brushes and other implements. From out of one of the trays he lifted a small cylindrical object with a metal tip and a tiny fish hook at the end and held it up. "As I mentioned last time, this is what we use to tie the hair in. The little hook here grabs the hair. Is this the one you're referring to?"

"I think so," said Constantin. "I seem to remember you saying it was quite sharp."

"Yes, very. Sometimes if you drop it and it goes into your arm or leg, it can be quite painful to get it out if you're not careful. But I already told you that, the last time you questioned me."

"Does anyone else have access to these tools?" Constantin asked.

"No. Except for my assistant, who only can use them under my direct supervision, I'm the only one who works with them," Daniel said. "And I secure everything in a locked cabinet at the end of the day."

"Do you count them up at the end of day to see if any are missing?"

"Well, no, I don't. We all know and trust each other here. We've been working together for years. It never occurred to me to count them. Just what are you getting at, Detective?"

"According to the medical investigator's findings, the fatal wound on the body of that singer, Adam, was made by a weapon that's exactly the size and shape of that tool," Stella said.

She turned to Constantin. "Grabowski, call CSU and have them come in to check the tools for any traces of blood."

"Right." Constantin tapped a note into his phone and turned to Daniel. "Where were you when Adam was murdered?"

Beads of perspiration formed on Daniel's forehead. "I was placing wigs in the dressing rooms."

"Was one of those in Adam's dressing room?" Stella said.

"Yes. It was."

"Did anybody see you?"

"No, I was alone back there."

Constantin exchanged glances with Stella. "I think we should continue this conversation down at the station," he said.

Daniel began to tremble. "But I didn't do anything."

"Then you can tell us all about it," Stella said.

Daniel continued to protest as Stella and Constantin led him away, followed by the bewildered stares of dyers, seamstresses and craftspeople.

"Whether or not we like him for this murder, we still haven't found a perp for the first one," Constantin whispered to Stella.

"He's the only thing we have to go on right now," she said. "We'll find out if he's 'a man more sinn'd against than sinning.'"

## Chapter 37

*Non tel diss'io, che con questa tua pazza gelosia ti ridurresti a qualche brutto passo?*
Didn't I tell you that your stupid jealousy would get you in trouble?
~ Mozart, *Don Giovanni,* Act 2

When the orchestra break was called, Matt stayed seated to practice a passage from the *Dance of the Seven Veils.* Julia stood up to watch the stage as the director showed the soprano the large, ornate rectangular platter on which the severed head would be placed.

"You have the most difficult job, of all, my dear," Achille was saying. "You dance savagely for ten whole minutes. And it's not just performative. It must be erotically compelling, highly sexual. Terrifying. And you end by singing the most arduous music in the entire opera."

Julia felt a strangely ambivalent fascination for the entire concept. To be sure, she found the idea of a bloodied head gruesome. But her study of the history of the opera had revealed some enthralling details, especially about Olive Fremstad, the soprano who sang the ill-fated debut of the role at the Met in 1907. Fremstad, who ostensibly lived for the stage, had visited the Manhattan morgue to try carrying around a few decapitated human heads in order to determine how to look when she was holding that of Jochanaan. Julia, who held immense respect for such a passionate commitment to one's art, tried to imagine what it must have been like to watch Fremstad perform.

"That soprano is pretty darned attractive. Really looks the part, doesn't she?"

Julia came out of her musings to see Larry leaning over the pit rail.

"She's got to sing, too, you know, Larry," Julia said. "Strauss said she has to look like a sixteen-year-old princess but have the voice of an Isolde."

"I can't wait to see her shed those veils."

"According to what everyone is saying she's one of the few who can cut it both vocally and dance-wise," Julia said. "But I hate to disappoint you, no veils will be shed today. Rumor has it the director and the choreographer haven't been able to agree on the moves yet."

Larry frowned. "Bummer. Guess I'll just have to come to another rehearsal."

"You were lucky to get into this one. I might be able to score you a ticket for the opening, though."

"Good. As long as I can see the important parts. Meaning the *Dance* and John the Baptist's head."

Julia smiled. Larry's preoccupation with sex and violence may have been predictable, but at least he was consistent. She found it alternately endearing and annoying, but mostly the former. "You saw both of those at the Met, remember?"

"I can't get enough," Larry said. "I feel sorry for the tenor, though, incessantly running around the stage and singing at the same time. What is that director thinking?"

"He's French," said Julia.

"That explains everything. Do you have enough break time for coffee?"

Julia checked her Fitbit. "I think so. I'll meet you at the cantina in a few. I just got a text from Molinari that he wanted to go over a few notes with me backstage."

Larry raised his eyebrows. "Hmm. A one-on-one with a hot Italian guy? I'm jealous."

"You've been doing a lot of that lately." This was one of the annoying times. "What's up with that?"

"It must be this mountain air," Larry said, and headed toward the back of the theatre.

Matt stopped practicing and stood up next to Julia. "I could put your violin in the case backstage to save you some time, Julia."

"Thanks, Matt. You're the best."

Julia handed Matt her violin, wound her way through the music stands and out the pit door and headed for the backstage wings. She was beginning to know her way around the theatre. The backstage area felt more crowded than the one at the Met, which was exponentially larger and had more space to accommodate props and scenery flats, but she did enjoy hanging around behind the scenes to watch the stagehands work their magic.

To reach the area where Molinari was waiting, Julia had to squeeze in between backdrops from the four different operas that were in repertoire, which were being stored in between performances: *Lulu, Roméo et Juliette, Lucia,* and *Salome.*

Her mind was intensely preoccupied, divided between her determination to give the best possible rendering of the music she was playing and her bewilderment over the conflicting evidence in the two murders that had occurred at the theatre. At the moment, however, she tried to focus on the matter at hand: whatever Molinari required of her.

Likely he wanted to go over the music with her for the very involved violin solo she was about to play after the rehearsal break. Julia loved the music, how skillfully Strauss wove and dovetailed it in between Salome's vocal lines. She never tired of it. But the passage also represented an example of some of the composer's most difficult violin writing: five sharps in the key signature, terribly exposed in the upper register, some of it in *pianissimo* dynamic, moving into the stratosphere of the instrument's range, then crescendo-ing to *forte.*

*What am I thinking. I should be practicing. After I see Molinari I'll go back to the pit for the rest of the break. I'll text Larry to forget about coffee. He'll understand.*

Spying Giovanni at the rear of the wings, she hurried toward him, while simultaneously initiating a text to Larry. Preoccupied with her screen, she paid little attention to where she was going—until she suddenly found herself face to face with a horrifying, bloody apparition: the severed head of St. John the Baptist, positioned on a table exactly at her eye level, leaking blood onto a silver platter.

Julia was so caught off guard, and the blood and gory features were so lifelike, it took her a moment to realize that the countenance was a mere, if brilliant, imitation of a real human head. Her screams caused alarm among those nearest to her, one of whom was Sandor.

"Julia, what happened?"

Julia tried to take a few deep breaths to quell her hyperventilating, but her sentences still came in short gasps. "I just wasn't expecting to see…It looked so…real!"

"You must still be tense, with the recent goings-on," said Sandor. "It is perfectly understandable."

"That's kind of you to say, Sandor," Julia said breathlessly. "But I'm…I'm so embarrassed. I should have known better."

Giovanni hurried over to Julia and Sandor. "*Che'è successo?*"

"N-nothing has happened, Maestro." Julia frowned apologetically. "After I got your text I was just coming over to find out what you wanted to see me about, when I got a little freaked out by this…this head."

Giovanni looked puzzled. "But I didn't send you a text."

Hearing this, Julia became more unnerved. "You didn't? Then who—"

"Perhaps it was just *scherzo*," Giovanni said. "A joke."

Sandor tightened his grip around Julia's shoulder. "With all respect, Maestro, considering the strain Julia has been under lately, I can't imagine who would consider this funny."

Larry, who had gone searching for Julia when she hadn't shown up at the cantina, became deeply concerned when he found her backstage, in an agitated state.

"Julia, what's wrong?"

"Nothing, nothing, I…" Julia's voice quivered. "I…came backstage to see what the maestro wanted to discuss. It turns out he never texted me at all."

"What?" Now Larry was truly alarmed. "Then who did?"

"No one seems to know," Julia said, shaking her head.

"You look totally freaked out, Julia," Larry said. "Are you going to be okay?"

Sandor put his arm protectively around Julia's shoulder. "She'll be fine. She just had little run-in with very life-like prop."

Larry took one look at the gruesome object in question and grunted. "The same thing happened to her at the Met. You backstage people shouldn't leave these things lying around."

"It's not their fault," Julia said. "There's limited space back here. They have to put things wherever they can. You'd think I'd know better by now."

"You are too hard on yourself, Julia." Sandor attempted a smile. "I think Daniel will be flattered to know you found his work so realistic."

Daniel drummed his fingers on the table in the interrogation room at police headquarters, where he was seated opposite Stella. He represented her first sign of a real lead in either of the murder cases, and she held high hopes that she could be on the verge of a breakthrough. The wig director's access to the sharp implements that might have been the murder weapon pointed to his possible involvement. She just had to make sure she intimidated him enough to make him back down. Unfortunately, he was being stubbornly tight-lipped, and she feared she wouldn't be able to hack through his defenses.

"Do I need a lawyer?" Daniel asked.

"That's up to you," Stella said. She leaned in more closely. She couldn't get a reading on his behavior, whether he was being defensive, evasive, or... "If you cooperate with us, the DA will bear that in mind—should it come to that."

"Need I repeat that I haven't done anything?"

"You tell me."

Daniel did not respond. Stella already could see that her initial hopes were mere wishful thinking. Grimacing, she left the room and faced Constantin, who had been watching through the two-way mirror.

"He had opportunity and access to the type of weapon the CMI thinks caused the fatal trauma," she told Constantin. "But no motive."

"What do you mean, no motive?" said Constantin. "He already told us the first time we questioned him that he virtually wanted to suffocate Emilia."

"So did everyone else."

"Could be that Adam gave him grief, too. Some bad blood between them."

"There's no indication of that," Stella said. "I was hoping he would reveal some info that might lead to the killer, but he's not saying anything. But we have no probable cause to keep him, and he could lawyer up. We'll have to let him go."

"Sonofabitch."

"Well, there is a sonofabitch out there somewhere," Stella said. "But I don't think it's Daniel."

Constantin glared. "Back to square one-and-a-half, then?"

"Not quite. I think it's time we questioned the live guy who's been replacing the expired ones."

## Chapter 38

*Recitar! Mentre preso dal delirio non so più quel che dico e quel che faccio!*
*Eppur...è duopo...sforzati!*
Perform! While I am racked with grief, not knowing what I'm saying or doing!
And yet...I must force myself to do it!
~ Leoncavallo, *Pagliacci*

LARRY REMAINED BACKSTAGE WITH JULIA WHILE SHE TRIED TO REGAIN HER composure. Despite Larry's protests, Julia insisted on continuing to rehearse, though they both felt uneasy about what had just happened.

"Do you think this is a bad omen?" Julia said. "A disaster in the making?"

"You know I don't believe in omens. But I would like to know who summoned you backstage," Larry said. "They clearly wanted you to run across the head at just the right time."

"You mean. . .someone is trying to scare me on purpose?"

"Exactly. The question is, who—and why. At the moment I'm more concerned about you trying to play in your condition. You still look shaken up."

"I'm fine now. Ready to get back to it." She had her doubts, but she didn't want to reveal that to Larry. It would give him an excuse to insist that she take more time to regain her composure, which amounted to her admitting defeat. She was determined to avoid that at all costs.

"Are you sure? Even your solos?"

"Especially those. After what I just encountered, a few solos will seem like nothing in comparison."

"Good. Because you're going to kick ass."

For the first time since her frightening backstage encounter, Julia smiled. She realized how lucky she was to have such a supportive partner. "You've always had such a way with words."

When Stella and Constantin arrived at the theatre late in the rehearsal, Stella told her partner to wait backstage while she watched the stage action from the house.

As Stella unobtrusively slipped into a seat halfway back in the orchestra section, she saw Larry seated across the aisle and nodded to him. He discreetly rose and sat down next to her.

"Something's happened to Julia," he whispered.

Stella's ears perked up. "What was it?"

"A strategically placed prop spooked her backstage."

Stella was wary. A prop just showing up in the right place at the right time couldn't have been a coincidence. "Is she okay?"

"Not really. Frightened her out of her wits."

Stella stood up and motioned to Larry to follow her to the back of the theatre. She listened intently as Larry recounted Julia's alarming experience.

"Sounds like someone's found out she's been poking around," Stella said. "And is not liking it."

"I agree," Larry said. "Question is, what do we do?"

"First, we tell Julia to stop prying. It's too dangerous. Then…" She paused. Clearly she had been mistaken in delegating Julia to investigate. She spent a long moment trying hard to think of a strategy to keep Julia safe. "You try and find out who's trying to send her a warning."

"Me? I thought you swore me off snooping."

"I changed my mind. I need all the help I can get. And you've got expertise."

"I'm out of my jurisdiction."

"I'm aware of that. I'll take full responsibility."

"You're sure?"

Stella knew it was her best choice. She nodded. "You in or not?"

"I never say no to a gal in cowboy boots," said Larry.

Unlike Daniel, Sandor was anything but reticent when Stella sat with him in his dressing room, largely because Stella decided to angle her questioning to show interest in Sandor's personal history. He was talkative, and his responses were given freely—at least initially.

"I'm told you and your sister defected from Hungary."

"Yes. In years after 1956 Revolution, before fall of Communism in 1989, life in Hungary was harsh. Political repression, material deprivation, religious persecution and murder, all rampant. Our parents, who were suspected of being part of Resistance, were illegally deported to Soviet Ukraine, leaving us to fend for ourselves. We later found out they had died in work camps."

Stella had read about this period of history in her student years. It hadn't affected her significantly at the time, but now that it was coming to life through Sandor's personal experience she felt deeply sympathetic. "I'm sorry to hear that. What happened then?"

"Magda and I were worried we might be next. We had to run for our lives. Magda found out where the most hidden alleys were, so we could move about undetected. Under cover of night, we sneaked through streets to American Embassy at Szabadság tér. They took pity on us much as they did Cardinal Mindszenty in 1956, took us in, protected us until they could find us home in U.S. Fortunately, because we both had musical talent, they were able to help arrange scholarships to Manhattan School of Music, and family to live with. So we went to New York."

"What year was that?"

"1985."

"How old were you and Magda when you left?"

"I was fifteen. Magda quite a bit older, thirty or so."

Stella was surprised. Magda could almost have been Sandor's mother. "That's quite a gap."

"Our parents had planned to have only one child."

"I see. And Magda has been protective of you ever since?"

"Always. Once we left school, money was tight. It was long struggle to find first professional singing engagements. Many, many years. Magda gave up her own singing career and took job in costume department of Met Opera. She sacrificed everything for me. There is nothing she would not do for me."

"You must be very grateful to her."

"I am. I will be forever. I owe her everything."

"You're very fortunate to have such a support system." Stella was beginning to wonder how Sandor would have fared without his sister's undying devotion. "How did you two come to Santa Fe?"

"Magda heard about apprentice program here from people at Met. Through her connections she was able to get me audition. When I was accepted, she applied for position in costume department here. Eventually I started singing mainstage roles. We decided to live here all year."

"Is it typical for you to replace multiple singers in quick succession?"

"It is definitely unusual. In fact, it has never happened before. Generally, I have one mainstage role per season and I cover one or two more. But this season is anything but typical, yes?"

"Clearly. It must be exciting for you to step into a role at the last moment, though."

"It can be. But honestly, in the case of Adam, it felt sad, very sad, to have to replace him under such heartbreaking circumstances."

Stella paused for a moment. Sandor's personal history was fascinating, but it was time to find out how he really felt about his chosen career. "Tell me, Sandor, how important is it for you to be able to get up on that stage and perform?"

"There is nothing more important for me. Performing is my life."

"And you would move heaven and earth to make sure that happens?"

Sandor's expression suddenly darkened. "What are you implying?" he said, eyes narrowed.

"Nothing," she said. "I was just wondering. 'One man in his time plays many parts.'"

"And we are 'merely players.'" Sandor rose. "I must get back to rehearsal. Please excuse me."

"Of course. Thank you for your time. We'll be in touch."

"I'm sure you will."

Stella ushered Sandor out of the room. She had made some inroads into the singer's psyche, but nothing earthshattering or, for that matter, conclusive. Constantin was waiting outside.

"What do you think? Do you like him for Adam's murder?"

"As ambitious as Sandor is, he strikes me as too sensitive a soul to be capable of violence."

"You never know. These Hungarians can be pretty feisty. He did escape from the Communists."

"Seems his sister was mostly responsible for that."

"Besides, his middle name is Béla. Magda told me when I questioned her," Constantin said. "She says 'Béla' means 'bold man' in Hungarian. Maybe he's not as fragile as you think."

"I don't put much credence in those things. 'Men at some time are masters of their fates.' At least that's what Shakespeare attributed to Julius Caesar," Stella said. "What counts more is what his colleagues think about him. Have you heard any chitchat from the grapevine?"

"He seems to get along with everyone. His sister...that's another matter."

"By the way," Stella said, "Do you know how to tell when someone's fudging on the truth?"

"How?"

"When they use the word, 'honestly.'"

## Chapter 39

*Il passo è periglioso, può nascer qualche imbroglio*
The step we take is dangerous, I fear for you
~ Mozart, *Don Giovanni,* Act 1

Julia protested when Larry told her she was under orders not to do any more investigating.

"But I was just hitting my stride."

"We want to make sure nothing hits *you,*" Larry said. "Remember what happened with that scenery at the Met?"

Larry's prickly question unnerved her. It brought back an uncomfortable reminder of her investigation into her mentor's murder at the Met, when, as her probe had begun to heat up, both she and Larry could tell she was being threatened in critical ways. Not only had a weighty piece of scenery came loose from the proscenium, crashing down on the stage, narrowly missing her; but ominous written notes had been attached to her sheet music on her stand in the pit.

"That's not likely to happen again," she said.

"Hopefully not, but you must admit that staying on the sidelines would be much safer. You have to give your full attention to *Salome.* Opening night is tomorrow, and you have some very tough solos to play."

Julia realized Larry was right. The solos in *Salome* were tricky: technically difficult, completely exposed and attention-grabbing. Playing them with as much virtuosity as possible was her most important task: her *raison d'être* for being in Santa Fe.

But she still felt a piece of the puzzle was missing. And she was not one to leave the big picture unfinished.

ᘓᘐ

Given Julia's umbrage at having to desist from sleuthing, Larry thought it best not to mention Stella's request that he take over Julia's role. Thus, he didn't tell her about his plan to invade Magda's space.

Since Stella had delegated him to do some poking around, Larry thought picking the costume director's brain would be a good start.

Magda probably had been with the company longer than anyone currently on staff; and as a veteran cop he knew there was no substitute for experience.

Still, he needed a credible excuse to casually drop by. Borrowing some duds for the Santa Fe Opera Guild's *Salome* opening night post-performance costume party seemed the perfect pretext. Invites to swanky company *soirées* were among the perks Julia enjoyed as concertmaster, and Larry was happy to act as her squire.

"I hope I'm not intruding," he told Magda as he followed her from the costume shop into the costume storage area located in a far-off corner of the theatre. "I thought I'd get a head start on the costume search, since Julia is busy practicing her head off for opening night."

Magda smiled her agreement. "It is completely understandable."

Larry stared, wide-eyed, at the high-ceilinged, warehouse-like space and the scores of racks holding a vast assortment of stage clothing draped on padded hangers.

"Julia would be blissed out at all this," Larry said. "But it's pretty intimidating for me. I have no idea where to begin."

"Do not worry." Magda gestured at the sea of racks. "Something romantic for a couple, yes? *Roméo et Juliette* costumes would be ideal, but are still being used at the moment. Perhaps Zerlina and Masetto from *Don Giovanni*. Beautiful production was new in 2016."

She led him through endless rows of female operatic regalia—from Rosalinde in *Die Fledermaus* to Adina in *Elixir of Love* to Violetta in *La Traviata*—flicking one hanger after another, until finally she stopped, pulled out a costume and held it up.

"Is Zerlina's wedding dress from that production," Magda said.

Larry gazed at the confection fashioned of cream-colored silk with brocade bodice and delicate crimson roses cascading from the *décolleté* down to the skirt hem. Judging from the pride in Magda's expression, he could see she was inordinately fond of this particular garment.

"Julia would look like vision in this," she said.

Larry nodded. "And she would flip over it."

"However, I'm afraid Masetto's costume is quite—how do you say—generic by comparison."

"Not a problem. I'll be happy with it. Julia should be getting all the attention anyway."

"Excellent. You can both come by for a fitting at your convenience."

"Thank you, Magda, I really appreciate it." Larry paused. Now was the perfect opportunity to probe into the costume designer's personal life. "You know, I'm so glad Julia met you. She had never told me about her Hungarian aunt. Thanks to you, I have another window into what made Julia the person she is."

"That is very kind of you to say."

"I've never been to Hungary. What's it like?"

"Hungary is very proud country," Magda said, her eyes glistening. "When I live there, it is greatest place on earth. The sun is clear, the air fresh and non-polluted. I don't like air here when I first come. I find fault with almost everything. I am used to it now. I realize I am not in Budapest anymore."

Larry had never been uprooted, but he did feel some sympathy for Magda's situation. "It must have been tough for you at first, starting over."

"I had to give up much. I wanted to be opera singer. But I was blessed with other ability so I could get good job and help my brother."

"I'm sure Sandor is very grateful. They say Santa Fe Opera is a great place to work."

Magda nodded. "Yes. But at first I only find part time work here, and we needed to make ends meet. I had to look for work in other places in Santa Fe. I was lucky they hire me at La Posada."

Larry's eyebrows shot up. He wasn't sure why, but hearing that Magda had worked at La Posada made him uneasy. Certainly it would better not to share that information with Julia. "La Posada? What did you do there?"

"I design room décor."

"How versatile you are. You must have gotten to know every inch of those buildings."

"That is true. You have been there?"

"Yes. Fascinating place. Lots of history." Larry decided against revealing that he and Julia had spent a night there. "I'd better let you get back to it. So kind of you to spend time with me."

"Not at all. I will walk you out."

After Magda had pointed him in the right direction, Larry wandered around the backstage area, pondering his meeting with her. The revelation about Magda's role at La Posada was nagging at him. Undoubtedly, scores of people had passed through those portals en route to jobs in more important places of employment. Still, it was a remarkable coincidence.

Then he remembered: if there was anything life had taught him, it was that there are no coincidences.

## Chapter 40

*La beltà delle cose più mire avrà sol da te voce e colore*
The beauty of all things remarkable from you alone will have their voice and color
~ Puccini, *Tosca,* Act 3

LARRY STROLLED ALONG WEST PALACE AVENUE ON HIS WAY TO RADIANCE Gallery. He had read that the bricks in Santa Fe Plaza had been ripped out and swapped for new ones during a 1974 renovation. He wished he had been there to avail himself of a few when they were being given away. The quantity of history concealed within them must have been astounding.

The gallery was easy for Larry to find. Located just about one block west of Santa Fe Plaza, tucked on a street not far from the Georgia O'Keeffe Museum and the Museum of Contemporary Native Arts, Radiance looked small and unpretentious from the outside, but the interior space was expansive and airy, with hardwood floors polished to a gleam and spotless glass cases of all sizes exhibiting one-of-a-kind pieces.

Spending time with Magda had reminded Larry that Julia had yet to visit the gallery to see the locket matching the one Julia's aunt had bequeathed her. Given the extraordinary difficulties, both personal and artistic, that Julia had suffered since coming to Santa Fe, Larry thought she deserved a nice gift; something refined and attractive, worthy of her sensitive nature. If the locket was for sale and he could afford it, he could show his appreciation and affection by presenting it to her.

Larry didn't consider himself a sentimental person; few people would say he was, least of all Julia. But since coming to Santa Fe, his feelings for her had burgeoned and intensified. Maybe it was the altitude, the romantic sunsets, the transcendent atmosphere of the mountain ranges surrounding them. Or, perhaps it was that, as Shakespeare had said in *The Merchant of Venice,* "the sounds of music…creep in our ears."

Whatever the reasons, Larry lately had felt he wanted to take his relationship with Julia to the next level. He hoped that placing two halves of a heart together would symbolize that desire.

As soon as he entered, the gallery owner greeted Larry with a genial, though somewhat aloof, smile. "Welcome to Radiance. I'm Damian. Are you looking for something in particular?"

"I am. A locket. Or half of one. Half a heart, actually."

"Is it an antique, by any chance?"

"Yes. So I'm told."

"Ah. I think I know the piece you're referring to. Please follow me."

Damian led Larry past showcases of varied shapes and sizes to a wall at the rear of the store, where a brightly lit rectangular case held what looked like a select few vintage pieces. He unlocked the case, removed a small box and carefully placed it on top of a glass countertop. Then he opened the box, revealing a delicate gold half-heart nestled in sapphire-blue velvet.

"We have just a small number of classic items. This one is most unique, waiting for its companion."

"May I?" Larry asked.

Damian nodded, and Larry gently lifted the heart from its velvety cradle. To his untrained eye, it looked like the exact mirror image to Julia's half-heart, identical in every way.

"Exquisite, isn't it?" Damian said.

"It is. In fact, I believe the other half belongs to my…significant other, Julia," Larry said.

"Oh? Are you sure? Chances are very slim of it being the exact match. Is it a period piece?"

"Definitely. Julia inherited it from her late aunt, who brought it from Hungary," Larry said. "Did I mention Julia is the concertmaster of the Santa Fe Opera?"

Damian's expression was no longer standoffish. "No. You didn't." He paused. "We're so proud of our company here. Did you know they've even done an opera about a murderous jeweler?"

Larry, who was taking a long moment to examine the detail on the locket, looked up, intrigued.

"It was called *Cardillac*," Damian said. "Based on a story by E.T.A. Hoffmann about a goldsmith who is so in love with his creations he takes them back by murdering his customers. The work premiered in 1967, the night before the opera house burned down."

"Fascinating." Larry made a mental note to find out more about this murderous opera as he studied the locket's engravings. "That must have been quite a night."

"The air was even drier than usual, bristling with heat. Everyone partied till the wee hours. Then around three-thirty a.m. people heard sounds like firecrackers. When they realized the theatre was on fire...well, let's just say Crosby had nightmares about those sounds for months afterward. You could see flames from miles away. Firefighters used every drop of water they could find. There was nothing anyone could do. It was like one big bonfire. They lost everything. Costumes, sets, pianos. The only thing left of the theatre were two flights of stairs to nowhere. It was like *Götterdämmerung*."

"I hear everyone rallied to rebuild. That says something about the spirit of the company."

"Indeed," Damian said. "People sawed and hammered and sewed day and night. The community spirit was remarkable. Contributions came from around the world from people who cared deeply about opera."

Larry waited a moment out of respect. Then he held up the locket. "What do you know about the engraved inscription on the back?"

"I only know it's in Hungarian," Damian said. "Very difficult to decipher, even if one were familiar with the language."

"I see." Larry's police background kicked in as he inspected the engraving etched into the piece. The letters were too tiny to discern, but a thought occurred to him. "Do you by any chance have some onion skin paper?" he asked.

"Yes, I do. Why?"

"If we do a rubbing of the inscription, we can blow it up and see what the letters are."

"I never thought of that."

"That's what twenty years of NYPD experience can do for you."

"Oh? You're…?"

"A detective with the New York Police Department." Larry waited for his response to sink in. "So, what do you think? About the onion skin?"

"It's worth a try."

Damian reached into a drawer at the back of the case and extracted a small sheet of wafer-thin, almost transparent paper. He rubbed a pencil lead on it over the letters on the back of the locket and handed the sheet to Larry. "Keep in mind, it's still in Hungarian."

"Not a problem. I can blow it up on the hotel printer, and I know someone who can translate it," Larry said, carefully pocketing the paper. "By the way, does the locket open?"

"It does. Please allow me." Damian gently pried open the latch and handed the locket back to Larry. "Just enough room for one cameo-sized portrait. To be paired with the other, of course."

"How much is it?"

Damian turned over the minuscule tag attached to the piece and put on his bifocals to read it. "$9,335, plus tax," he said.

Larry let out a deep breath. "Whew."

"I admit it's a bit pricey, but it is a singular piece," said Damian. "An antique. If you do own the matching half, I would imagine it would be more than worth the price."

Larry was torn. He had no doubt that Julia would be thrilled. He also knew that such a purchase would stretch his resources to the max. But Julia's happiness was worth every dollar to him—and more.

"Do you gift wrap?" he said.

## Chapter 41

*Il mio solo pensiero, Tosca, sei tu!*
My sole thought, Tosca, is of you!
~ Puccini, *Tosca,* Act 1

TO JULIA'S GREAT RELIEF, THE DRESS REHEARSAL FOR *SALOME* WENT OFF without incident: no stabbings, except those programmed into the action onstage; no anguished cries, except the ones specified by the libretto.

Julia had arrived at the pit well before the beginning of the rehearsal to do some last-minute polish on her solos. As she focused on her most difficult passage, out of the corner of her eye she spied Stewart leaning above her on the other side of the pit wall, watching and listening.

She didn't allow Stewart's presence to make her nervous, or to distract her. She kept playing and executed the passage flawlessly. After she had stopped, she saw Stewart's smile of approval and felt gratified.

*Now all I have to do is duplicate that on opening night.*

Once the rehearsal started, Stewart made his presence known: seated in the first row just behind the pit wall, he peeked his head over the railing periodically to nod his head. Giovanni paid little attention to the music director; he had his hands full, keeping control of the massive Strauss orchestration and maintaining synchronicity between pit and stage.

Julia, who made an extra effort to play her solos more superbly than she had in her own practice session, was rewarded with looks of approbation from Giovanni and from Stewart. Having pleased the power duo, she allowed herself a peek at the stage as Salome lay atop a table, her virgin-white dress drenched in Jochanaan's blood, which, to Julia, still looked disturbingly real.

After an hour, Giovanni put down his baton. "Let's take fifteen minutes," he said.

"Great job. Home run. Grand Slam, even."

Julia jumped, startled, and whirled around to see Larry standing right behind her. She glared at him. “Are you trying to give me a heart attack?”

“How about, ‘Gee, I’m so glad you’re here, Larry,’” he said.

Julia turned to Giovanni. “*Mi dispiace, Maestro.*”

“No need to apologize, Julia,” Giovanni said.

Julia suddenly regretted her harsh reaction to Larry’s compliment. She turned back to him. “You’re right. Sorry. Performance anxiety. Solos. You know what I mean.”

“Of course I do. And I wasn’t exaggerating when I said, ‘Grand Slam.’ You knocked them over the right field wall.”

Julia smiled. Only Larry could concoct parallels between opera and baseball. “How did you get in, anyway? I heard rehearsal was closed.”

“What a question. I can get around any barrier.”

“Oh, really? How?”

“How? I’m a cop. Once a cop, always a cop. It’s so predictable,” he said.

First baseball, now policing. She was skeptical but intrigued. “Please enlighten me.”

“As Shakespeare said—”

Julia groaned. Now Shakespeare. What a piece of work he was. “What, you, too? Are you trying to compete with Stella?”

“She’s not the only detective who can quote the classics. May I continue?”

“Please do.”

“As I was saying, ‘Let me count the ways—”

“That’s Elizabeth Barrett Browning, not Shakespeare.”

“Whatever. Do you want to hear this or not?”

“Of course.”

“One, I’m intimately familiar with every nut job who lives in any given location. Two, I can name you every drunk and pross within a ten-mile radius of our Manhattan apartment.”

Julia realized her limited familiarity with police procedurals would not be able to keep up with Larry’s for much longer. “Pross?”

"Prostitute. How can you not know that? You watch *Blue Bloods* devotedly."

"Not lately. It's summer, they're on hiatus. Go on, this is fascinating."

"Three. When people introduce me to their friends, they always add, 'He's a cop.' Four, I look around a room and try to calculate how long it would take me to cuff the heftiest guy there. Shall I continue?"

Julia laughed. "Okay, I get it." She peered at him, eyes narrowed. "You didn't just come here to listen to my solos, did you?"

ഌഌ

Larry smiled. Julia had a look, a certain glow, when she had completed a difficult piece to her own satisfaction. She was glowing that way now. He remembered meeting her, how she wouldn't let anything or anyone touch her but her music, and thought about how far they'd come. "Busted. How did you know?"

"I may not be a cop, but I'm living with one. Some of your so-called 'ways' have rubbed off."

"You're right, God help me. Actually, there's something I wanted to—"

"Julia." Sandor, still in costume, was hovering above her, his hands leaning on the pit rail. "Your solos sounded...*káprázatos.* Magnificent."

Julia looked up at him. "*Köszönöm,* Sandor. You sounded...*káprázatos,* too. That's a new word for me."

Sandor smiled. "Do you have time for coffee?"

Larry placed his hand over Sandor's. "Sorry, pal. I'm higher up on her dance card. Although, maybe you could do me a favor." Larry reached into his pocket and extracted the onion skin parchment with the engraving from the back of the locket rubbed into it. "Could you take a look at this and translate it for me?"

"*Természetesen,* Larry. Of course."

"Thanks." Larry spoke *sotto* into Julia's ear. "As I was saying, there's something I wanted to...ah...share with you. Can we go somewhere more private?"

"I think I can find a place," she said. "Another time, Sandor?"

"*Természetesen,* Julia."

Sandor pocketed the paper and walked off.

"I'm learning some new words from him." Julia said. "Isn't that cool?"

"*Természetesen,* Julia," he said mockingly, only slightly tripping over the syllables.

ꟗ

The musicians all had departed the orchestra lounge when Julia and Larry entered. The atmosphere was quiet and peaceful; just the right setting for Larry to present Julia with his distinctive gift.

He sat her down on a chaise. "I got you something for good luck tomorrow night," he said. "I think you'll like it. At least I hope you will."

"For a supposedly predictable cop, you can be full of surprises." Julia eyed the diminutive velvet box Larry extracted from his pocket. "You really didn't have to get me anything."

He deposited the package in her lap. "Stop protesting and open it," he said.

It took her a moment to comprehend, but once she recognized what she was gazing at, Julia let out a cry of delight. "Is it really…? Oh, Larry, it's…perfect."

Julia lifted the treasure from its velvet nest and stared at it in disbelief.

"Are you just going to gape, or do you maybe want to put it on?" Larry said, grinning.

"Oh, yes. Please."

Larry unfastened the clasp on Julia's necklace, carefully threaded the tiny bale attached to the gold half-heart through the chain that held the other half, and gently pressed the two halves together. They fit seamlessly as one.

Julia, at first speechless in her delight, threw her arms around Larry's neck and squeezed him tight. "I love it," she said finally. "But it must have cost a fortune. You really shouldn't have."

He returned her embrace. "You're worth it," he said.

And he meant every word.

## Chapter 42

*Et le péril, il est en bas, il est en haut, il est partout, qu'importe!*
And peril lies below us, above us, everywhere, but what of it?
~ Bizet, *Carmen*, Act 3

ONCE THE FINAL DRESS REHEARSAL OF *SALOME* HAD FINISHED, JULIA HURried to the costume shop. Despite Larry's queries, she'd insisted on not divulging her plan to go for her fitting by herself. She didn't want to tell him that she thought it bad luck for him to see her in a wedding dress before the opening night extravaganza, even if it wasn't technically a wedding. She knew he would make fun of her superstition.

"I can't tell you where I'm going," she said. "I'm concocting a surprise for you. Just trust me."

"Who am I to argue with the Queen of Hearts of Santa Fe Opera?" Larry quipped.

One thing Julia knew for certain: the now-complete heart locket and her costume would complement each other superbly. After instructing Larry to wait for her at the Inn, she headed off to find Magda. She felt somewhat guilty for not revealing to Larry her principal reason for going alone to Magda's domain, but she didn't want to worry him.

Despite Stella's orders not to investigate, Julia sensed she needed just one more chance to grill Magda. She knew Stella had been working single-mindedly to solve the murders, but no progress had been made in uncovering the identity of either Emilia's or Adam's killer. The investigation had reached an impasse. Something else had to be done. Julia believed if she could subtly manage to slip in a few questions during her fitting with Magda, she might find some clue, some evidence that Stella had overlooked.

When she arrived at the costume shop, Julia was surprised to find Magda in a cordial mood. Perhaps the costume director was not one to stubbornly cling to resentments. Whatever the reason, Julia thought it best not to open up the touchy subject of their recent disastrous encounter.

"You have come for your fitting, Júlia?" Magda said, smiling.

"Yes. Larry tells me you've found something special."

"That is true. I have set it aside for you." Magda gazed at Julia's locket, perfectly positioned in the hollow of Julia's neck. "I see you have now other half of heart."

"Larry got it for me. To make up for all the troubles I've had lately."

"He is very generous. It will go perfectly with costume. Come. I show you."

Magda led Julia along the hallway toward the far-off costume storage area as she had done with Larry. The hallway seemed longer and darker than the others Julia had seen. Uncomfortable, Julia decided to add some small talk to the awkward silence.

"It's been quite a season, hasn't it?" Julia said. "A bit tricky for you, yes?"

Magda quickened her pace. "Tricky?"

"I mean, keeping up with costumes for so many...well, cast changes because of the..."

"Murders?"

"Well...yes."

"I am used to numerous changes, for many reasons," said Magda.

The atmosphere was beginning to feel strained. Julia, sensing increased tension in Magda's disposition, tried to lighten up.

"*Salome* is going well," Julia said. "Despite my little run-in with a severed head."

"Yes. I heard about that."

"Really? News travels fast."

"Sandor told me," Magda said. "He said you were quite shaken. You had him very worried."

"I know. I was touched at his concern."

"He likes you very much."

"Yes. I gathered that. He's very sweet." Julia fingered her locket. "It's amazing, isn't it, that he's been able to sing so many roles in quick succession so early in the season? It's quite a coincidence that he has had such an opportunity to step in for singers who have been…indisposed. I haven't been working here very long, but I know that at the Met it's very unusual for one singer to fill in that much. Not that Sandor doesn't deserve—"

Magda lowered her voice. "He has more talent than all of them."

"Oh, I agree. His artistic and vocal skills are outstanding. He certainly demonstrated that at the *Salome* dress rehearsal. Were you there?"

"I always come to rehearsals. I must be available in case costumes need adjustment."

Julia detected some irritability in Magda's tone. She laughed uncomfortably. "Oh. Of course. Sandor did a fantastic job singing Narraboth, didn't he?"

"Always he does. *Igen*?"

"Yes." Julia paused, trying to get a handle on Magda's inscrutable expression. "You know, Magda, after all the…mishaps, it was such a relief that there were no other incidents in *Salome*. Like the one that happened to me during the *Roméo et Juliette* rehearsal. I wouldn't want to go through that again."

"Opera is sometimes dangerous."

"A little more for me than other people." Julia attempted a lighthearted chuckle. Magda did not respond.

Sensing Magda's increasing touchiness, Julia was relieved to see they finally had arrived at the costume storage area. Magda remained silent as she guided Julia between seas of hanging racks holding the huge collection of stage attire, until they reached the most remote corner of the enormous room. There, on a padded silk hanger separated from the rest, hung the brocaded, rose-embroidered wedding dress that Magda had shown Larry.

Julia gasped. "It's exquisite."

"I think you will find it will fit perfectly. The last soprano to sing Zerlina was petite like you."

"May I try it on?"

"Of course. Screen is over there in corner." Magda removed the garment from the hanger and placed it in Julia's arms.

Julia stepped behind the screen, removed her clothing and slipped the dress over her head. "You're right, Magda. It feels like it was made for me."

"There is mirror here," Magda said as Julia emerged wearing the costume.

Julia positioned herself in front of the floor-length mirror. She felt as regal as a princess.

"Only thing missing is veil," said Magda. When I took it out of storage, I noticed lace needed repair. Do you have time to go back to costume shop and try it?"

## Chapter 43

*Tut chto - to ne ladnoe tvoritsya!*
There's something suspicious about all this!
~ Tchaikovsky, *The Queen of Spades,* Act 2

JULIA FOLLOWED MAGDA BACK TO THE COSTUME SHOP, ALL THE WAY TO the rear wall by the exit door, to a worktable next to a bank of tall picture windows. Julia squinted at the late afternoon sun, gleaming through the glass. It was so bright it almost obliterated the view of the hillside behind the opera house—so bright that Julia couldn't see Magda bolting the exit door or locking the main entrance to the shop.

Magda lifted the costume veil from the worktable and held it up for Julia. It was made of cream-colored organza trimmed at the bottom with white lace; the headpiece was a crown-shaped tiara edged with red rosettes matching the ones embroidered on the costume.

Julia was enchanted. She also was happy to see that Magda's formerly irritable expression had softened.

"Try it on," Magda said. "Do not be afraid."

Slowly, gently, Julia raised the veil, careful not to damage the delicate fabric, and placed the rose-bedecked crown on her head.

The veil reached to Julia's waist. Magda adjusted the fit. "Now effect is complete. With locket, is perfect."

Again, Julia thought Magda's assessment was spot on. The locket was positioned at exactly the right place to set off the sweetheart neckline and décolleté of the dress.

Julia looked around for a mirror; finding none, she stood at a window and admired her reflection.

She expected the costume director to voice her approval, but instead Magda, her back turned away from Julia, opened the door to an adjacent cabinet.

Julia watched as Magda rummaged through the cupboard. "What's in there?"

"Props," said Magda.

"Aren't they usually kept in the prop room, or the dressing rooms?"

"Yes. But when opera is in repertoire, we keep extra props here in shop for singers to try, together with costume. I have access to all props. For instance, this one…"

As she watched Magda reach into the cabinet, Julia narrowed her eyes to get a better look at the contents of the cupboard. Hanging on a hook on the top shelf, she thought she saw something that looked like a straw hat and a pair of men's Bermuda shorts.

*Is that…could it be…?*

She blinked and looked again. This time she was sure. The hat and shorts matched the clothing she had seen…worn by the ghost of John Crosby.

ᘓᘐ

Larry was feeling a combination of impatience and disquiet. He was getting anxious about what might be keeping Julia so long. He wished he had insisted on going with her, or at least her telling him where she was going. Given the near-calamities that had befallen her, he should have known better. He needed to go looking for her, but he had no idea where to start.

He tapped a text into his phone: *"Julia, where are you?"*

There was no response. He tried to think of who might know where Julia was. There was Sandor, but Larry hesitated. He had been feeling pangs of jealousy at the singer's all-too obvious play for Julia's attentions. But he knew that if anyone might have some clue as to Julia's whereabouts, it would be Sandor. Larry swallowed his pride. He looked up Sandor's number and tapped.

To his relief, the singer picked up. "Hello, Larry."

"Hey, Sandor. Where are you?"

"I am in Opera Shop. Maestro told me historic Rysanek *Salome* recording came in. I have just found it."

"Do you know where Julia is?"

"No. Something is wrong?"

"Hope not. Julia said to wait for her here at the Inn, but that was a while ago," Larry said. "It's been a long time and she still hasn't showed up. When did you last see her?"

"At rehearsal. Where did she say she was going?"

"She wouldn't tell me. Do you have any idea where she might be?"

Sandor seemed to consider for a moment. "Perhaps she is going over solos for *Salome* with the maestro."

"Yes, of course. That makes perfect sense."

"Do you know where dressing room is?"

"I was there the first day we were here," Larry said. "I think I can find it. Thanks for the tip."

"Anytime. It is my pleasure. Good luck."

Larry raced out the door and through the hotel lobby, on a mission.

While he waited for the cashier to ring up the CD, Sandor pulled the onion skin parchment from his pocket and studied the writing.

*"Tól Magda, hoz Olga."*

He hurriedly paid for his purchase, squeezed past the cash register and through the back door of the shop. He had his own notion as to where to look for the missing violinist.

## Chapter 44

*Ella mi fu rapita! E quando, o ciel?*
*Possente amor mi chiama, volar io deggio a lei*
She was stolen from me! But when, o Heaven?
Powerful love calls me, and I to her must fly
~ Verdi, *Rigoletto,* Act 2

When Magda turned back to Julia, she was clutching a large sword. Julia instinctively flinched. "Wow, that looks so real."

"That is because it *is* real."

"Of course. *Természetesen,*" Julia said, trying to hide her discomfort. "I should have known."

"I see you are learning new words. From Sandor?"

"Y-yes. He's been quite patient with me."

"Patience is Hungarian trait. Patience…and passion."

As Magda drew nearer, brandishing the sword, Julia began to sweat. "I…I think I'd better change out of this costume. I don't want my perspiration to ruin it," she said, moving away.

With her free hand, Magda grabbed Julia's arm, so tightly that the imprint of her fingers appeared on Julia's flesh. "Is not necessary." Magda dropped Julia's arm, extracted the hat and shorts from the cabinet and held them up. "I see you have recognized my costume."

"Your…costume?"

"I like to wear costumes, too."

Julia's eyes widened.

Magda's mouth curled up. "Do you really think ghost of Crosby is still hanging about?"

"It was you?" Julia shook her head, trying to comprehend. "But I don't understand."

"I want to frighten you away. That is why I fix sword, too."

"You…what?"

Magda dropped the hat and shorts on the floor and pulled on the sword. The hilt separated from the shaft, just as it had during the

*Roméo et Juliette* rehearsal when the blade went flying through the air, striking Julia.

Julia was incredulous. "You did that? But why?"

"I want to frighten you away," Magda repeated. "You are smart. Smarter than detective. After Emilia was killed, I watch you snoop around, ask questions. I could not allow you to solve murder."

The realization streaked through Julia's consciousness like a bolt of dry lightning in a Santa Fe electrical storm. She tried to remain calm. "You killed Emilia! Oh, my God. Why would you do such a thing?"

"Emilia was terrible to me."

"She was terrible to everyone," Julia said.

"True. But more terrible to me. For years she mistreats me. First at Met, then here. Always she complains, makes my life miserable. World is better place without her. After Goran pretend to kill Emilia offstage and show fake knife onstage, I go backstage with real knife."

Julia struggled to comprehend what she was hearing. "And you would implicate Marin, an innocent woman?"

"That is unfortunate. I know she is your friend. But, yes."

Horrified, Julia murmured, "And…Adam?"

"Ah. Also unfortunate. But that was role supposed to be for my brother."

"For…Sandor?"

"I have protected Sandor since he was child. I would do anything to promote his career. Management pass him over for younger singer whose voice does not compare. Sandor's is rich, beautiful. Perfect. He deserved to be on stage."

"You killed Adam…" Julia reeled from the revelation. "How?"

"Everyone was on stage for Mad Scene. When Daniel was placing wigs in dressing rooms, I went to wig shop to get sharp instrument, then to Adam's dressing room." Magda smiled. "It was very quick. He did not suffer. Unlike Emilia. She felt knife. I made sure of that."

"Oh, my God." The weight of Magda's reveal made Julia feel faint. "Does…Sandor know?"

"No. And he must never know. *Érted*? Do you understand?"

Magda's held Julia's gaze. Then, her eyes fixed obsessively on Julia's locket, she said, "Seeing your necklace reminds me of my home. My childhood."

Julia breathed slowly as she tried to ward off her feelings of alarm. "I understand. If it wasn't a family heirloom, I would give it to you."

"*Igazán*?"

"Yes. Really."

"Why?"

"Because," Julia said. "I have great respect for you, Magda. And you remind me of my mother. I miss her so much."

"That is nice to hear," Magda said. "But you will give me necklace. It belongs to me."

༄༅

Once Larry passed through the security gate, he managed to find the conductor's dressing room on his own. Hearing strains of piano music coming from inside, he hesitated to disturb whichever maestro might be practicing within. But his mission was too urgent. He rapped loudly.

Giovanni opened the door and peered at Larry. "*Sì*?"

"I'm sorry to bother you, Maestro. You don't know me. I'm Larry Somers. I'm here with Julia."

"*Piacere*, Larry. What can I do for you?"

Larry peeked inside the room. "Have you seen her? I thought she might be here, working on her *Salome* solos with you."

"Ah, no, her solos were *perfezione* at the dress rehearsal. No further work needed."

"She was supposed to meet me at our hotel, but she never showed. Do you have any idea where she might be?"

"I am sorry. *Mi dispiace*. I do not."

"I see. Thanks anyway, Maestro."

"*Senz'altro*. Of course. I'm sure you will find her."

Giovanni closed the door. Larry remained outside, worried and bewildered. He simply had no idea where to look next. He sent a text: "*Julia, I need to know where you are. ASAP!*"

Then he tried calling her cell. And tried again. There was no response.

*Think, Somers, think.*

He slapped his forehead.

*Of course. What was I thinking?*

Larry wasn't sure if he could remember how to find the costume shop; but if his memory failed him, he could always ask that obnoxious stagehand, Steve. For better or worse, that guy always seemed to be around.

## Chapter 45

*Mille torbidi pensieri mi s'aggiran per la testa:*
*se mi salvo in tal tempesta, È un prodigio in verità!*
A thousand desperate thoughts are whirling in my head:
if I survive such a storm, it'll really be a miracle!
~ Mozart, *Don Giovanni,* Act 2

MAGDA'S DECLARATION LEFT JULIA TOTALLY CONFUSED. SHE GRASPED THE locket protectively. "Excuse me?"

"Locket is mine." Magda carefully laid the sword on the worktable. "You will give to me now."

The menace in Magda's expression was unmistakable. Julia reluctantly unclasped the chain from her neck, removed the locket from it and slowly stretched her hand toward Magda.

Magda held the delicate heart close to her eyes and gazed at it, fingering the zig-zag dividing line between the two halves. "Buda and Pest, now together at last." She turned the heart over and studied the inscription, divided between the two segments. "Do you know what it says?"

"N-no. The writing is too small to read without a magnifying glass. And it's...in Hungarian."

"*Igen.* But I know what it says. I always have." Magda closed her eyes and recited, "'*Tól Magda, hoz Olga. Barátság örökkön örökké.*' 'From Magda, to Olga. Friendship forever and ever.' Do you know who was Olga?"

Julia was mystified. The only Olga she knew was...

*No. It can't be...*

"My mother?"

"*Igen,*" Magda said. "Olga was my best friend in Budapest. We found locket in antique shop when we were girls. We had it engraved, each took one half—she, Buda and I, Pest—and swore eternal friendship. When Olga left for America to live with her sister Zsófia, I gave her my half to take with her so heart would be complete. Olga promised to keep it for me until I came to States. She married your father. Then she died after you were born."

Magda wiped a tear from her eye. One moment of weakness. Then her steeliness returned.

"After your mother died, your father gave necklace to Zsófia. She gave one half to her Mexican husband, but when they divorced he moved to Santa Fe and took it with him. When Zsófia died, her daughter gave her half of heart to you."

The story and its revelations so fascinated Julia that she momentarily forgot her fright. "So that's how the other half ended up in the gallery. From Zsófia's husband."

"Exactly."

"Why didn't you just buy it?"

"*Túl drága.* Too expensive. My salary at Opera is not enough to buy such high-price jewelry. I cannot afford to buy locket even when I work extra hours at La Posada. But I expected your boyfriend Larry would buy it for you."

"You worked at La Posada?" Julia's eyes widened. "Oh, my God, it was you. You were—"

Off Julia's astonished expression, Magda laughed maliciously. "Ghost of Julia Staab."

"The noises, the supernatural activity…my violin strings. That was all you?"

"I tried all I could do to scare you away. At opera house. At La Posada. Nothing worked. You are too stubborn, too determined, too smart. Exceptionally so." Magda paused. "Now you know everything. I have no choice but to kill you."

Julia's terror came crashing back with a vengeance, but she knew she had to quell her panic. Her only recourse was to placate Magda—and buy herself enough time to think of an escape plan.

Larry combed the hallways, ascending and descending staircases, trying to find the costume shop. His pictorial memory, sharpened over nearly two decades of police work, was not serving him in his current state of agitation over Julia's whereabouts and safety. His usual level-headedness evaded him.

*Where could that frigging place be?*

At the bottom of one staircase, he found the stairs to the pit entrance. He leapt up the stairs two at a time and threw open the door. Once inside, he surveyed the rows of empty music stands. It was a dead end.

As Larry had suspected, Steve was indeed around, and much easier to locate than the costume shop. He was not surprised to come across the stagehand outside the pit with a colleague, hauling a very realistic looking black-and-red statue depicting a bloodied tangle of writhing bodies into an out-of-the-way corner near a wall. The two workers grunted from the immense weight and bulk of the piece. Larry could see the statue, which looked like it could have been from post-Vesuvius Pompeii, was just a simulation of the real thing; nonetheless, its gruesomeness made him shudder.

When he and the other stagehand had deposited the statue in its proper place, Steve looked over to see Larry, hovering close by. "Oh, hey. Larry, right? Julia's friend."

Larry thought of correcting Steve's terminology to "significant other," but he had more important things on his mind. "Right."

"What's up?" Steve noticed Larry's look of anxiety. "Where's Julia?"

"Here's the thing," said Larry. "She's missing."

"What?"

"Julia was supposed to meet me over an hour ago at our hotel. She never showed. I've texted and called her. No dice. Seems like she just vanished into thin air." Larry scowled. "So many damn hiding places in this theatre."

Steve frowned. "Did you check the pit?"

"I just did. There's no one there," Larry said. "I even busted in on the maestro in his dressing room. He hasn't seen her since rehearsal ended."

"That's not good. Do you have any idea where else she could be?"

"All I can think of is the costume shop. But I'm damned if I can find it."

Steve wiped his grimy hands on his cargo pants. "Follow me."

Steve strode off. Larry, close behind him, frantically texted as he walked: "*Stella. Julia missing. Meet me backstage at theatre ASAP.*"

## Chapter 46

*Ah...soccorso...son tradito!...L'assassino...m'ha ferito*
Ah...help me...I am undone!...The assassin's blade...has pierced me
~ Mozart, *Don Giovanni,* Act 1

JULIA FRANTICALLY TRIED TO COME UP WITH A WAY TO APPEASE MAGDA. "But, Magda, surely you wouldn't... kill your best friend's daughter?" Julia said. "You're better than that."

"It is true Olga was my best friend. But Olga had everything I did not. A sister to sponsor her in America. Safe passage on a tourist ship. Money to establish herself here. And then a husband...and a daughter," Magda said. "But I...I had to escape through streets of Budapest, with armed soldiers lurking everywhere, and Sandor holding on to me for dear life. We had no money, no jobs, no family to keep us, to take care of us."

Magda placed the locket in her apron pocket, reached over the worktable and grabbed hold of the sword. "First time in rehearsal I only scare you. This time I finish job."

Julia backed away, furtively eyeing the exit door, as Magda inched toward her, the glinting tip of the sword pointed toward Julia's chest. Julia desperately tried to think of a way to impede Magda's momentum.

"Door is locked, Julia," Magda said. "Do not try to escape, you are just delaying the inevitable."

"Larry will be looking for me. He'll find me."

Magda's sword was a mere inch away from Julia's torso. "He will be too late. I will bury your body in desert, in Sangre de Cristo Mountains. Hole is already dug and ready. No one will ever find you."

Julia felt a shiver of dread vibrate through her body, but she spoke calmly. "I think you've lost your mind, Magda."

"*Nem.* No, Julia. You are afraid. I understand fear. We women grow up believing we are defenseless. Do not be afraid. It will be quick, I promise you."

But at that moment a familiar voice resonated next to them.

"No, no, my sister. *Nem, nem, Lánytestvér.*"

ᘓᘐ

The moment Stella got Larry's text, she grabbed Constantin by the arm, raced with him out the door and into their squad car, and sped off to the opera house.

"Text Larry we're on our way," she told Constantin.

Constantin tapped hurriedly into his phone. Larry's response came immediately: "*Headed to costume shop. Meet there.*"

Stella skidded to a stop in front of the security gate, brakes screeching. She and Constantin flashed their badges to the guard and raced inside. When they reached the backstage area, they found Larry and Steve striding toward the back of the theatre.

"Do you know where you're going?" Stella asked Larry.

"No," Larry said, pointing to Steve. "But he does."

They followed Steve's lead, threading their way through dark hallways, dodging countless pieces of equipment, props and segments of scenery, until they reached the entrance to the costume shop.

Steve jerked on the door. "It's locked."

"I'll kick it in," Stella said.

"Not a good idea. It's pure steel," Steve said. "Easier to head around to the emergency exit in the back of the shop. They never lock it."

"I hope you're right," said Larry.

The quartet rushed off, out the loading dock door, toward the back of the theatre, where they could access the back door to the costume shop. On the way, Steve grabbed an axe hanging near a fire alarm.

ᘓᘐ

Magda clutched the sword more tensely. "Sandor, do not interfere."

"I heard everything you said, Magda. About Emilia, and Adam. How could you?"

"Emilia was evil. And Adam...I am sorry, but your career comes first. Nothing is more important, more precious to me than you."

"Nothing is more precious than human life."

"Not all human life is precious, my brother."

Magda inched the sword closer to Julia, aimed at the space between Julia's ribs and her heart. The tip penetrated the bodice of the dress.

A tiny drop of blood seeped through the brocade. Julia winced with pain.

"Magda, no! *Nem*! You must not harm her," Sandor cried. "I love her."

There was a deafening banging noise as the exit door was assaulted.

"Julia! Are you in there? Open the door!"

Julia recognized Larry's voice, but she was too stunned to move and too breathless to shout a reply. Then came an earsplitting crash, as Steve's axe penetrated the exit door, which splintered into jagged metal shards. Steve, Larry, Stella and Constantin burst in and assessed the scene.

"Drop the weapon!" Stella shouted, her Glock pointed at Magda.

Larry started toward Julia. Stella restrained him. "Careful. One more centimeter and she could do serious damage."

"Stay back, or she is dead!" Magda kept the sword trained on Julia. "I am sorry, Sandor. She knows too much. I cannot let her live."

"And I cannot let her die."

With a sudden lurch forward, Sandor grabbed for the sword. Julia drew back, gasping for breath, and watched, horrified, as Sandor and Magda struggled over the weapon. Suddenly Sandor cried out. The sword had penetrated his chest. He doubled over and crumpled to the floor.

"Sandor!" Magda, seething, lunged at Julia. "*Kurva*! Bitch! This is all your fault!"

With Magda charging at her again, Julia panicked, frantically trying to think. Suddenly the swordplay instruction she had gotten from Sam came hurtling into her mind. What was it the fight director had told her?...

*"...Nudge his shoulder with your sword arm. Remember, this is pretend, it's just for show. Be careful not to hit Larry's shoulder too hard, you can jar the nerve and make his arm go numb."*

Using every fragment of her power and energy, Julia thrust her body's full force at Magda's shoulder, just as Sam had warned her not to do with Larry. Magda cried out in pain from the impact. Her arm went numb and the sword tumbled out of her hand, crashing to the floor. Seizing her opportunity, Stella surged forward, throwing Magda down and cuffing her in one swift movement.

Julia rushed to Sandor and knelt by him. "Sandor, you saved my life. I'm so grateful to you," she said. "Sandor, Sandor. Can you hear me?"

Larry darted to her side. He leaned over Sandor, examining the wound and listening to his chest. "He's breathing, but he's losing blood fast."

Stella swiveled her head in Constantin's direction. "Call an ambulance."

Julia lifted her face toward Constantin. "Please, we've got to save him."

"The paramedics are on their way," Constantin said.

"Sandor, can you hear me? Hang on," Julia said. "Please! You've got to hang on!"

## Chapter 47

*Qui sait de quel démon j'allais être la proie!*
Who knows of what demon I was about to become the prey!
~ Bizet, *Carmen,* Act 3

THE OPENING NIGHT OF *SALOME* WAS A GALA AFFAIR. WITH THE PROSPECT of a glittering post-performance party for the patrons and stars, the atmosphere was electrified. Onstage, the wind blowing from the mountains seemed to play with the pleats of the tunic-like costumes, giving the singers an ethereal, sculpture-like eeriness.

Julia decided not to appear at the opening night party wearing the costume Magda had chosen for her. Somehow the associations were more discomfiting than she could handle. And the dress would not have coordinated at all with the swanky cowboy boots Larry had gifted her, the exact ones she had drooled over in the shop window on Santa Fe Plaza, which he insisted she wear for the opening.

But with her locket returned to her, and the loan of a black velvet jacket festooned with sequined bling from Marin, Julia felt as regally operatic as the English Queen in Rossini's *Elisabetta, Regina d'Inghilterra.*

Julia had been thrilled to learn that Marin would be playing the part of the Page of Herodias in *Salome.* It was not as prominent a character as Geschwitz in *Lulu,* but at least Marin would be able to re-establish her worth as an artist with the company.

Now that Magda had been incarcerated and Julia felt safe and secure in her position as leader of the orchestra, she experienced a renewed sense of confidence in her violinistic abilities. Thus, despite the fact that Stewart was watching and listening from the back of the pit, Julia did not waver in her rendition of the violin solos in the opera.

At one point, after she had tossed off a particularly demanding solo passage, Matt leaned over and whispered to her. "Blatchley just gave a nod of approval when you finished your solo."

"How do you know?"

"Just look back there. He's grinning like a Lewis Carroll feline."

Julia fleetingly turned her head and confirmed Matt's assessment. She and Matt bumped fists.

As the drama progressed relentlessly toward its gruesome finale, Julia took a cursory glimpse at the cloak of stars draped above the theatre. She felt part of something that even the majesty of the New Mexico mountains could not transcend: the greatness of the art that was being performed under that twinkling sky.

There was no place like Santa Fe.

ꕥ

Backstage in the wings, Larry watched the action with Sandor. The tenor, his chest taped, wearing a sling and seated in a wheelchair, still had a long way to go on his road to healing. He had confided to Larry that he was content just to be alive.

"Bet you wish you were out there onstage, though," Larry told him.

"Oh, I think I can wait," Sandor said. "In my current condition, I would hardly manage deep enough breath to sing one note."

But Larry had turned his attention to the soprano onstage, ogling her with abandon, as she launched into her sensuous, depraved *Dance of the Seven Veils.*

Sandor took note of Larry's wide-eyed smirk. "Great Austrian soprano Leonie Rysanek once said sopranos who take on this role should be characterized in one of three ways. 'Those who can sing it, those who can dance it, and those who should be shot.'"

"I don't know about the singing with this one, but boy, can she dance."

"I promise not to tell Julia you said so."

"I'm not worried. Julia knows me too well. Besides, I gave her an opportunity to do her rendition for me. For some reason, she declined."

"If it didn't hurt to laugh," Sandor said, "I would find that inordinately amusing."

Unlike the original Met Opera *Salome* premiere in 1907, which was so abhorrent to the sensibilities of wealthy patrons that the rest of the run was canceled, the Santa Fe production was received with wild enthusiasm from its audience.

Giovanni acknowledged Julia with a generous gesture from the stage during his curtain call. Julia felt thoroughly gratified.

"You see? It was worth all your ordeals after all," Matt told her.

"I'm not so sure," Julia said. "What I've been through goes way beyond suffering for one's art."

ꟸ

For the gala celebration, Stieren Hall was transformed into a biblical wonderland, both Old and New Testament. Suspended on golden ropes from the ceiling were seven glowing orbs representing Salome's veils. Realistic-looking palm trees lined the walls. At one end of the room, under a massive, glittering crystal chandelier, the principals of the cast and creative crew sat along a lengthy rectangular table, as if posing for Leonardo's iconic Last Supper. In the middle of the room, A cylindrical cage hovered over a shimmering circle painted on the floor, representing John the Baptist's cistern.

Julia, Larry, Katie and Sandor arrived together to join the revelers. On their way in, they passed Stella and Constantin, who were availing themselves of the luscious fare laid out on a huge table.

Stella winked at Julia. "'Such stuff as dreams are made on.'"

Julia grinned in response but cringed when she saw Lenny hovering by the entrance. She girded herself for one of his usual scowls.

But he surprised her by coming up to her and smiling genuinely. "Great work on the solos, Julia. Congratulations."

Julia had her suspicions as to the motivation for his sudden change of attitude, but she decided to take it at face value. "Thanks, Lenny. That means a lot, coming from you."

Julia leaned over Sandor and whispered, "By the way, did you ever figure out what was written on that scrap of paper I gave you? *Hívja...azonmmal...*"

"'*Hívja azonmmal a rendörséget!*'?" He smiled. "It means 'Call the Police!'"

"What?" Julia was bewildered. "Who could have written that? And why?"

"I think it was Emilia," Sandor said softly. "She was the only other person in the company who knew Hungarian. She might have been worried that Magda would do her harm." His expression saddened. "I thought of giving it to the police. But I think it should remain our secret, yes?"

Julia nodded. They held each other's gaze until Katie and Larry each slipped an arm through one of Julia's. "Forgive us if we kidnap her for a moment," Katie said.

Followed by Sandor, the group moved on, stopping by the cast table to give Marin some hugs. Julia raised her eyebrows when she saw Giovanni's arm draped around Marin. She shot an inquisitive look at the mezzo-soprano, who just smiled slyly and nodded.

"Can we steal you away from your adoring colleagues for a toast at our table?" Julia asked.

"I'll be there in a minute," Marin said.

Julia, her eyes still starry from her success, didn't notice Marin's wink at Larry, which he returned. Instead, she lowered her voice and said to Marin, "Are you and the maestro…?"

Marin shrugged. "What can I say? He's smart, unmarried and Italian-hot. And he really appreciates me."

"Then I'm truly happy for you."

"Thanks." Marin grinned. "I'm happy for me, too."

But when Julia turned away from Marin, she found herself face-to-face with a horrendous sight: Sandor, holding the bloodied head of St. John the Baptist on a platter in his lap.

"Seriously!" Julia shrieked. "Are you guys freaking kidding me?"

The others laughed. "Come on, Jul, can't you appreciate some ghoulish humor?" said Katie.

"Take a closer look, Julia," Larry said. "This one was created especially for you."

Flashing a look of out-and-out menace at Larry, Julia leaned over the contorted lump and realized it was actually a cake in the shape of the prophet's head. Inscribed along the forehead in red frosting were the words, "To Julia, with love, from Jochanaan."

She burst into laughter. "Okay, I give up. This dude is going to haunt me for the rest of my life."

"Lucky him," Sandor said.

"Shall we start with the hair?" Larry said. "I know how much Julia loves licorice ropes."

"I say we eat the lips first," said Katie. "That's what started all of Salome's problems."

"Ugh," Julia said.

The party of five plucked flutes of champagne from a passing caterer, found a table and sat down.

Marin lifted her glass. "I'm back," she said. "And I have you to thank, Julia."

"To Julia, who rocked as usual," said Katie.

"I second that," said Larry.

The group raised their champagne glasses and clinked. Only Katie noticed that Julia did not drink from hers.

## Epilogue

*Gli occhi ti chiuderò con mille baci e mille ti dirò nome d'amor.*
With a thousand kisses I shall seal your eyes, and call you by a thousand names of love.
~ Puccini, *Tosca,* Act 3

THE TRIP THROUGH THE MOUNTAINS BACK TO ALBUQUERQUE AIRPORT took longer than it had when Julia and Larry first arrived in Santa Fe, due to Julia's need to stop periodically and throw up.

"Morning sickness sucks," she said to Larry after one particularly dreadful bout.

"It'll all be worth it in the end," he told her.

"How do you know?"

"That's what my mother told me."

"She might take it back if she could see you now."

Larry laughed. Julia just turned a pallid shade of green and clutched the red stone her Navajo friend Miles had given her after their vision quest high up in the Sangre de Cristo Mountains. Once she had overcome her current wave of nausea, she regarded the mountain views through her window. She was going to miss their stark beauty once she got back to the city's concrete canyons.

"Do you think we'll come back here, Larry?"

"It all depends on what kind of kid Junior turns out to be."

"With any luck, she won't be as much trouble as you are."

"I love you, too."

ꟸ

Julia was not accustomed to being offered a seat on the New York Subway, especially the IRT uptown train, which was always packed. But she figured it was the sight of her burgeoning tummy that elicited sympathy from her fellow passengers. A burly Hispanic guy wearing a Yankees baseball cap and toting a humongous boom box, who seemed eager to share his CD of *Swan Lake* at top volume with the rest of the subway patrons, freely volunteered to vacate his seat for her benefit.

"Even that dude feels sorry for me," Julia said to Larry.

As Larry helped her struggle into the proffered seat, Julia spied a familiar face on the bench opposite her. The man, whose gaze had never left the giant-sized sketchbook balanced on his lap, looked up when Julia shouted his name over the subway car's clacking noise.

"Sam!"

"Julia, Larry! How great to see the two of you." Sam eyed her baby bump. "I see you've been busy."

Julia shrugged. "Must have been all those chile peppers in Santa Fe."

"Red or green?"

"Give *me* a little credit here, will you?" Larry said.

They all shared a laugh, shouting to be heard above the subway clatter, as the car chugged along.

Julia nodded at Sam's sketchbook. "What are you up to there?"

"Next season's Santa Fe Opera plotting," Sam said. "A fight director's work is never done."

"Amen," said Larry.

"Which opera?" Julia asked.

"*Don Giovanni*," Sam said. "That's a huge one for me. I never get tired of it."

Julia shivered slightly as she remembered the fateful Zerlina costume that almost heralded her undoing. "Nor do I."

"How did you feel about your first experience at Santa Fe, Julia?" said Sam. "Offstage violence notwithstanding?"

"Impressive," Julia said. "I'm amazed at what they can achieve there every summer, in just a few months."

"Even as a Met Opera veteran and a native New Yorker?"

"I'm not a veteran just yet. But, yes, seeing what they can do almost makes me feel unsophisticated."

Larry smirked. "Better keep that under your hat when you go back to the Met."

"You never forget Santa Fe. There's no other place like it," Sam said. "When will you be back?"

"It could never be too soon," Julia said.

*Preist mit hoher Freude Glut (ihre) edlen Mut!*

Praise with high blazing joy (her) noble courage

~ Beethoven, *Fidelio,* Act 2

## *About the author*

Former Metropolitan Opera Orchestra violinist **Erica Miner** is an award-winning author, screenwriter, arts writer and lecturer. Her novels and screenplays have won awards in recognized competitions. Her lectures, seminars and workshops on writing and on opera have received kudos on both coasts and on major cruise lines. She is an active contributor to numerous arts websites.

CPSIA information can be obtained
at www.ICGtesting.com
Printed in the USA
LVHW110806051119
636371LV00005B/172/P

9 781606 191309